# LIGHTLY CHILLED

## *25 Original Tales of Horror*

WRITTEN BY JOHN M. LIGHT

# CONTENTS

# THE OLD MAN IN THE CELL

*Three hours now.*

It had been three straight hours, and the old man in the cell hadn't moved a muscle. He simply sat there on the edge of his cot, his skeletal fingers clutching his bony knees, leaving black stains on the green work pants since refusing to clean the ink after his fingerprinting. Almost as if he wanted to be reminded of his crime. Or at least reminded of something.

Sheriff Owen leaned against the gray steel bars and took another drag on his Camel Unfiltered. If it weren't for the quivering of the old man's lips—almost as if he were reciting some monotonous, unheard prayer—he would have thought that the old bastard was dead. He would have preferred it, actually. That way, no one would ever know the real truth. But what interested him and had kept him glued to those bars for the better part of an hour was the old man's grin. Damned if he wasn't sitting there grinning. His lips were curled back—not much, mind you, just a little. Just enough to glimpse those tobacco-stained teeth. Making him look a little like a hungry junkyard dog eyeing a helpless cat. It was that strange, unnerving grin that made even Deputy Foster look away when he took the mug shots, and Owen knew that old man had nothing to smile about.

He had come in just after dark—around seven-thirty this time of year—rapping unceasingly against the front door before one of his deputies—Art Bodine—finally opened it, wondering aloud why anyone would bother to knock on the door to a police station in the first place. And there stood the old man, his hat literally in his hands, and told Bodine—straight out and grim-faced—that he was the one who killed that girl ten days before down at the Old Wash Road.

Well, Owen knew that the old man was innocent, and that's what puzzled him. Any police officer worth his weight in shit knew there were crackpots who would confess to anything for just a little attention. Something that might get their name or picture in the paper. Pathetic, forgotten people who didn't want to be forgotten anymore. And at first, that's what Owen thought he was—until that grin. That bizarre grin of someone who knew a private joke. If it hadn't been for that grin, Owen would have been more than happy to let the wizened old fuck suck cyanide until he dropped dead.

If it wasn't for that damned grin.

No, Sheriff Owen knew—*really* knew—that the old man was innocent.

Because he was the one who actually killed that girl late that night off the Slate River turn-off.

"Sheriff?"

Owen sighed smoke and then turned to little Wiley Carter, who, as usual, hadn't made eye contact since that night ten days ago. Wiley was the mayor's son—Owen's only college-educated deputy—and the only one who guessed what had really happened over at the Old Wash. Although it was Foster who used the grappling hook to pull the body from the water, it was Wiley who examined the corpse. He knew that it was a fresh kill, not the two-day-old murder that

Owen had claimed it to be to the mayor, and Owen figured the little queer would have spilled it right then. After all, Wiley knew that Owen was the only one around who used .45 hot loads, but the kid never said a word. Not a word. He also knew—like Foster and Bodine—that it wasn't exactly an uncommon practice to bring an odd whore or two for a little suck-and-fuck in exchange for a free ride out of town. Still, Wiley wasn't one to partake of such law enforcement perks, and so Owen logically figured it was probably because he really was that low-account faggot with secrets of his own.

**"Yeah, what is it you want?"**

The kid shuffled from foot to foot, unable or unwilling to look him in the eye.

**"I typed up the confession like you told me."**

**"That's good."** He ground out his cigarette and turned to him. **"That's real good."**

Wiley held out the forms.

**"Well, I was just thinking that maybe you should look them over."** He shrugged and looked away.

Owen snorted. **"Why?"**

Wiley shrugged again, a smaller shrug this time.

**"Just to check and see if they were... accurate and all."**

Owen grinned and leaned against the bars.

**"Well, now, what is it you think I should be checking?"**

He still didn't look at him.

**"You tell me."**

3

This time, Owen shrugged.

**"There's nothing to tell. Is there?"**

Wiley continued to avoid his gaze, but even so, Owen smiled and motioned with a thumb over his shoulder.

**"I mean, this old man walks on in here and confesses, right?"**

Wiley still wouldn't meet his eyes.

**"Right..."**

Owen smiled at the young man's discomfort and continued.

**"He done it, he said he done it, and so he oughta know if it's 'accurate' and all. I mean, I wasn't there."** Owen smiled. **"Was I?"**

Wiley paused. His feet shuffled.

**"No sir..."**

Owen cocked his ear toward him.

**"What's that you say? Speak up, son."**

Wiley finally looked at him, his eyes grim, and met Owen's own.

**"No sir. I don't reckon you were there."**

Owen smiled again.

**"Did you call the state boys like I told you?"**

He offered a small nod.

**"They said they'd be here in about an hour. Maybe less."**

Owen patted his shoulder.

**"Well, that's good. So far, you've done real good, Wiley."**

At this, Wiley stiffened. His whole body suddenly became rigid, and then he quickly brought a hand to the back of his head—a move so fast that Owen actually took a step back as if to avoid a punch. He wasn't afraid of this kid—shit, he'd stepped over better men to get to where the fight was—but this sudden, uncharacteristic movement had startled him. It was involuntary—more of a spasm—and Owen watched with some concern as Wiley grimaced and rubbed at the back of his neck.

**"You okay, boy?"**

Wiley didn't immediately answer. Instead, he kept rubbing, even as his confused eyes darted from one side of the room to the other.

**"I said, are you okay, boy?"**

Wiley's eyes finally found Owen's, but the confused look remained.

**"Did you say something, Sheriff...?"**

Now Wiley was never Owen's idea of a man, but he was still one of his deputies, and right now, it looked like he'd contracted something. He looked sick. Very sick.

**"Look, maybe you oughta go and have a sit-down. Maybe even get yourself a shot of something."**

Wiley's eyes seemed to glaze, and his voice was far away as he said,

**"A shot...?"**

Owen nodded but stopped short of actually touching him.

**"We all know everybody in the building has a bottle. Go and find one."**

Wiley continued to massage the back of his neck.

**"A shot... Maybe that's what I need..."**

With an oddly resigned look, he turned and walked away, muttering under his breath,

**"...a shot..."**

Owen shook his head and was about to light another Camel when he glanced over at the old man—and froze.

He was still grinning—only now, he was looking straight at Owen. And that's when Owen realized what had been disturbing him all along as he watched the old man. He finally understood why he'd been so riveted by that grin.

It was because it was the exact same grin Owen himself wore when he knew—*really* knew—that he was going to get away with murder.

* * * *

It was a hot and particularly humid night ten days before as Owen cruised the Old Wash, anticipating a nice, cold beer when he knocked off at two. Duffy's would be closing up about then, but when ol' Duff saw Owen, he'd open her back up for a quick one. It was an understanding they had—that old back-scratching thing. Duffy kept his bar open for him, and Owen made sure that it didn't close despite those *rumors* of underage drinking.

That beer was the only thing he had to look forward to that night, and for the umpteenth time, he shifted in his seat, trying to find a comfortable place for his very angry pecker.

It had been a slow night. All he'd done since he started his shift was roust a couple of horny kids fucking over at Stradler's Creek, and that didn't help any. It had been weeks

6

since he got his pipes cleaned, and seeing those two going at it just reminded him how knotted up he'd become. Shit, he even thought about tossing one off when he got home—and him being thirty-seven years old.

And that's when he saw her—and forgot all about that late-night beer over at Duffy's.

His headlights swung the curve at Slate River and she turned, her cat-like eyes gleaming briefly in the darkness. It was only a quick glance, but enough for Owen to see that she wasn't a local. He knew most of the local girls—and with no false modesty, they knew him too. But this girl—oh, *this* girl—was something.

Her skin was deeply tanned and damned if there wasn't plenty of it to see. Her Daisy Dukes climbed halfway up that perfect ass, and the only thing that held those pendulous breasts in place was a white halter top that seemed to defy gravity. Yeah, she was barefoot, empty-handed, and alone.

He couldn't ask for anything better.

He pulled her over for a "routine check" and was pleasantly surprised when she confessed that she had no identification. Now, he knew she was probably harmless, and there really was no reason to take her in—but he told her they were cracking down on vagrancy, and she'd have to come back with him to the station for a quick run-down. It was an obvious ploy—but then again, this was an obvious game. One that he was sure this girl had played before.

After all, no woman with a body like that was a virgin for long, and she must've known the rules by now. But damned if, when he made his move, she resisted. Hell, she turned into a wildcat. And that's why he had to get a little rough himself.

But as it turned out, this girl was a hell of a lot stronger than she looked, and after a brief but intense struggle, she ended up kicking him in the family jewels and ran for what she must've believed was the relative safety of Slate River.

As any man can tell you, you don't get kicked in the sac without gasping like they were going to outlaw air in the morning. So it took him a moment to recover before he pulled his gun and fired a shot into the darkness.

It was only meant to be a warning shot—just to bring her back to her senses—but instead, it caught her right between the shoulder blades. When that bullet hit, her body arched like a high diver before she pitched forward and splashed into the black of that river—deader than his career would be if the truth were ever uncovered.

It was an unfortunate accident—but one that stubborn girl had contributed to, he thought. All she had to do was give it up, and she'd have been on her way, none the worse for wear.

Now, all he could do was reload the spent cartridge and head over to Duffy's, explaining to Bisby behind the counter that it was so quiet he decided to knock off early. He even shared a laugh with Bis about those horny little fuckers at the creek.

And the next morning, Owen could've won an Oscar for his look of surprise and horror when he was directed to the body of some poor dead girl found tangled in the brush of Slate River.

Despite the unusually heavy press the murder received, Owen managed to stall the investigation, telling the mayor that he was following "very definite leads." But the truth be known, he could feel the walls closing in on him. It was only a matter of time before someone—maybe even one of those asshole reporters covering the case—uncovered the truth.

He needed a way out. And he even had the passing notion of killing Wiley and setting him up as the murderer. It would've been easy enough.

But before he could set any of the wheels into motion, in came that old man.

Bless him.

Yes, sir, bless that old man.

* * * *

Owen retired to his office to await the state police. He even poured himself a healthy, congratulatory shot of Jack Daniels, which he kept in his file cabinet. He preferred his on the rocks, but the damn 7-1 had run out of ice two days ago, and so Elron, the day dispatcher, had brought in a block of his own that could best be described as a glacier. And so Owen set to hacking at it with the ice pick that the former sheriff had kept in his desk.

Shit, he was so determined to get that ice in his drink that he almost didn't hear the shot.

Owen kicked back, and his hand quickly found the gun at his side. He couldn't see through the frosted glass of his closed door, but he knew the shot had come from the outer office, and possible scenarios raced through his mind. Maybe the townspeople, outraged by the brutal, senseless

9

killing, had heard about the Old Man and come to take out some vigilante justice. Or maybe some friends of the Old Man had learned what happened and come to break him out. Hell, it might have even just been an accidental discharge from one of his deputies—probably Wiley.

Whatever it was, Owen wasn't taking any chances. He wasn't leaving this room, and he kept that gun gripped tight as he leaned over and hit the intercom button.

**"Foster? Bodine? What the hell was that shot?"**

There was nothing.

No answer. No sound at all. No movement behind that frosted glass.

Nothing.

Owen remained rooted at his desk. There was something wrong, all right—no doubt about it. But he sure as hell wasn't too keen on going out there. Not yet.

He called out.

**"Foster!"**

No answer.

Louder.

**"Bodine!"**

Still nothing.

**Shit.**

Owen stared, but nothing moved behind that glass—that damned crystal fog he had personally installed for a little privacy. He cut the light, ducked low, and made his way to the door. He let his gun lead, then, as quietly as he could, he turned the doorknob—then flung open the door.

Nothing happened.

In fact, the room was quiet. Peaceful, even. There was the usual snake-like hissing from the police scanner and the soft whirring from the overhead fans, but aside from that, there seemed to be nothing out of the ordinary. Certainly nothing menacing.

And if there had been an actual shot, it didn't wake Wiley.

The night shift was usually the quietest time in the station, and whenever Wiley worked it—which was as seldom as he could manage—he invariably fell asleep at his desk, like he was doing now—

Owen leaned forward. His eyes widened.

Wiley was indeed slumped over his desk in his typical pose—namely, one arm outstretched, the other tucked comfortably under his chin. His eyes were closed, but he wasn't snoring the way he usually did.

No, the bullet he'd put through the roof of his mouth had seen to that.

Blood was splashed across his blotter, and Owen couldn't help but notice—with no small amount of revulsion—that a red clump of hair was now settled like some grotesque toupee atop the police radio.

Owen fell back against the doorframe and expelled, **"...oh shit..."**

The kid had shot himself. He had taken his service revolver, put the barrel in his mouth, and quite literally blown his brains out through the top of his head. The same kid who had only minutes ago told him the state police were on their way.

It must have been the guilt. Wiley had known the truth but didn't have the guts to spill it when the state boys got here. And Owen figured it was probably for the best—because if they discovered the Old Man was innocent, he would have pinned it on the kid anyway. Foster and Bodine would have backed him up, no doubt about it. They never much cared for the kid and—

Owen stiffened.

Foster and Bodine.

**Where the hell were they?** They must have heard the shot, and he'd even called over the intercom for them. Sure, maybe the com was down, the wires chewed through by the mice he knew were in the walls—but then he had called to them afterward. He called loud, too, but not nearly as loud as that gunshot.

**So where the hell were they?**

He raised his gun again and very slowly moved forward.

Even so, it didn't take him long before he found Bodine.

He was in the office supply room, hanging by his own belt from the exposed water pipe overhead. The belt buckle bit deeply into his Adam's apple, forcing his now black tongue to jut between his slightly parted lips, and his eyes were glazed, white, and seemed to shine against the light blue of his face.

Owen could only stand in the doorway, his mouth hanging open, and then urgently looked about the sparse room. But there was no sign of violence, no signs of a struggle. Just the overturned chair in the center of the room.

In the end, there was no denying it.

**Bodine had hanged himself.**

He must have walked in here, positioned the chair under the pipe, calmly undone his belt, and hanged himself. There just wasn't any other explanation.

Owen slumped against the wall and let the gun fall to his side.

**What in the hell was going on here?**

Two officers—two of *his* officers—had just killed themselves. No notes, no explanations, no reason, no words were spoken. One had hung himself, and the other had literally blown his head off. It just didn't make sense. What could have—?

Then it hit him, and Owen's eyes widened.

**Two** of his officers? There were **three** on duty tonight.

**Where was Foster?**

Owen felt grimly resigned, and after an all-too-brief search, he was to find him in the coffee room.

He was still gripping the tin lid from the coffee can he had used to open the veins in his wrists and jugular, and even now, the blood continued to gurgle across the table. Unlike his other deputies, he had managed to hold on until Owen arrived, and his eyes focused on him for a very brief moment before he died—until the blood flow gradually slowed and stopped.

But in those last seconds, Owen saw in his eyes what his sliced throat would not allow him to speak.

**Confusion.** As if he didn't know why he had done what he had just done.

Owen kicked away, skidding slightly on Wiley's still-warm blood, and fell into the wall beside the front door, knocking a Fleishamm's Feed Store calendar to the floor. His eyes were wide, his mind was racing in every direction, his thoughts colliding like Dodge-'Em cars. Without realizing it, his left hand fumbled behind him and locked the door—*even chained it*—before he lurched away.

And before he realized it, Owen found that he had backed into the holding cell, and when he turned, he gasped.

**The Old Man was now standing at the bars**, looking straight at Owen, his smile so wide, his lips so thin, his eyes so sunken that, for a brief moment, Owen thought that by some grotesque transference, the Old Man had left his cell—leaving a grinning skeleton in his place.

**"What is it, Sheriff?"**

Owen briefly felt a strange, unpleasant tug behind his eyes but shook it off and stepped closer, neglecting to holster his gun.

**"What do you know about this, Old Man?"**

**"Know 'bout what?"** That skull grinned wider, and Owen had to remind himself there was still skin over that ghoulish face.

**"You heard the shot?"**

He nodded.

**"Yessir, I did."**

Owen's breath was coming faster, but he didn't notice. The Old Man did.

**"And you know about the others?"**

**"Yessir,"** he nodded again. **"I do."**

"How do you know?" Owen stepped even closer to the bars, so close he could smell the Old Man's putrid breath.

"How? You were locked in this cell, so how do you know what happened out there?"

The Old Man's grin stretched even wider—something Owen hadn't thought possible.

"'Cuz I sees it in yer eyes."

The answer didn't make any sense, and Owen's eyes narrowed.

"What?"

The Old Man pointed at Owen's left eye.

"That one there seen one of them deputies shot in the mouth."

Both of Owen's eyes widened.

The Old Man pointed at the right.

"And that one seen the other two dead. One hung. One bleedin' 'til there weren't nothin' left to bleed."

Owen paused, then rattled the bars—but the gate was secure. It was still locked. And from no angle in that cell could the Old Man see into the outer offices, let alone the store or coffee room.

So how did he know?

Owen puzzled.

"Look, Old Man—"

He broke in.

"—You don't even know my name, do ya?"

Owen paused to think, but the fact was—the old fuck was right. He didn't know his name. When he'd walked in and confessed, Owen had simply passed him over to Foster for pictures and prints, and then he'd called the mayor for the congratulations he had coming.

If the truth be known, he didn't have a clue who the Old Man was.

**None at all.**

The Old Man's grin fell. His eyes hardened, and off that look, Owen couldn't help but fall back a step.

**"Just like you didn't even know the name of the girl you shot in the back."**

Owen stiffened.

**The Old Man knew.** He had confessed to the crime even when he knew the truth. And Owen suddenly understood why. It was suddenly very clear.

He had turned himself in to get closer to his men. To *him*. In some unfathomable way, the Old Man was responsible for what had happened. He had orchestrated the entire event.

**But how? And why?**

Owen looked up and could see that the Old Man—whose name he still didn't even know—had anticipated what he was thinking. *Perhaps even read his mind.*

So he answered.

**"Because she was my daughter."**

Everything seemed to fall into place—along with the pistol that slipped through Owen's fingers and clattered to the cold cement floor, alarmingly loud in the confines of the room.

The Old Man continued, **"You didn't know she was my daughter, did ya?"**

He shook his head.

16

"Hell, boy, I bet you didn't even know her name. No, names don't mean much to men like you. They're just words to be scribbled on a toe tag or carved on a tombstone."

The phrasing disturbed him.

Names were also on birth certificates. Marriage licenses. *Happy* occasions.

And that's what sent a shiver up Owen's spine. Because he hadn't thought of those examples. In fact, the Old Man seemed to have chosen his words with great care.

The Old Man moved even closer to the bars, and for a brief moment, Owen thought he might simply pass through them—like some specter. Some avenging angel.

**"Names has to do with death too, Sheriff."**

That twinge—that *tingle*—was back. It was as if the Old Man wasn't just reading his thoughts but actually *forcing* them into his head. Not just thoughts but *names* of people alive and dead. It was all unfocused, but they kept running, dancing, taunting, and teasing through his mind.

The Old Man grinned again, but this time without humor.

**"That's right. Names. They's important."**

He nodded.

**"So important, they can kill."**

Owen looked up and, upon seeing that expression, again thought of that snarling dog. *Happy to have found his prey but anticipating the kill even more.*

**"Kill like they did tonight."**

Owen swallowed. His throat clicked.

**"What're you talkin' about? Names don't kill."**

"They don't?"

"No..."

He didn't sound convinced.

The Old Man's grin fell. His drawn cheeks settled against his skeletal features, and his eyes turned hardened, dead black.

**"When I heard about my daughter—my baby—how you killed her 'cuz she wouldn't shame herself for ya, I spent the next eight days up to my cabin. Not eatin', not even wantin' no food. Eight days just awaitin' my Juju to come down into me and give ma power."**

He smiled again, but his eyes didn't.

**"I gived myself up to the law. To get my justice, Sheriff."**

Owen winced, though he wasn't sure why. When the Old Man had said *"sheriff,"* he'd felt a tremble inside his head as if some malicious feather was tickling a part of his brain. As absurd as it sounded, it was as if he were afraid the Old Man was going to say his name.

Although he wasn't sure he wanted the answer, Owen asked, **"What are you talking about?"**

**"I done told ya."** Again, that grin. **"Justice."**

**"What happened to my men?"** Another question he wasn't sure he wanted answered.

**"I just gave 'em a notion. Or rather *you* done it. After all, it weren't *me* that called to 'em."**

Owen shook his head. The remark didn't make sense. **"What the hell are you talking about?"**

"I's the one who put the thought in their heads. But it weren't 'til they heard their names that it set a fire." He pointed at him. "And it was *you* that knowed 'em."

Again, Owen felt the touch of phantom fingers gently playing over his brain—like a fine pianist over ivory keys—and didn't even remember asking, "What...?"

The Old Man nodded again and leaned in even closer.

"Like I know *yourn*."

Owen snorted and tried to chuckle, only to fail badly.

"Well, that's no great accomplishment, Mister—"

He realized again that he still didn't know the Old Man's name—something that seemed to profoundly amuse him. Owen pointed.

"It's written right up there on the door. Sheriff Ow—"

He stopped.

That tickling sensation had ceased. And it was almost as if those fingers now hovered over the cerebral keys like Jerry Lee Lewis about to pound out a finale.

The Old Man continued to grin.

"Yeah, yer gettin' it now, ain't ya?"

Owen tried to swallow but couldn't work up any saliva. The knot in his throat wouldn't go down. It was like he'd swallowed a live mouse, and it was trying to claw its way back up. Still, he managed to force out a small chuckle.

"Do you really think anybody is going to believe your Cajun bullshit?"

The Old Man mischievously raised his eyebrows.

"Do *you*?"

Owen found that his mind was racing, but it wasn't getting anywhere.

**What the hell was he thinking?**

Was he himself beginning to fall for this crap? There was no such thing as magic, Cajun or otherwise. Names don't kill people.

**They don't!**

Unable to think of anything else, he blurted, **"You know that the state police—"**

The Old Man finished his sentence.

**"—are on their way. I know."**

Owen was beginning to sweat. His shirt was sticking to his chest, his arms. His collar was moist and suddenly felt like a wet noose being tightened around his neck. He fumbled to loosen it, and the Old Man grinned.

**"And you know what they're gonna do when they gets here, don't ya?"**

The Old Man's face crinkled like old cellophane as he smiled even wider, his bony cheeks pulling back his lips like someone opening drapes.

**"They'll call you by name."**

Owen froze. It was as if all the sweat on his body had turned to ice.

In the outer office, the phone rang, and he was startled. His heart briefly raced and he caught his elusive breath, actually grateful for the distraction, and turned to it.

**"Are ya sure you want to answer that?"** the Old Man asked.

Owen turned back. **"What?"**

"Well, I don't have me no phone, but don't people usually say your name when they say hello?"

Owen cringed when the phone rang again. Louder this time.

"And it ain't just phones now, is it, Sheriff?"

That twinge. That tremor was back—only stronger this time. More intense. Owen tried to catch his stolen breath, but again, he felt his ashen face covered in a sheen of sweat. Still, he managed to gasp out,

"...stop it..."

Another triumphant grin.

"People—that is, friends and family—they'll maybe see you out on the street, smile, call you by name, and wave. Yeah, then maybe yer eyes'll glaze all up, and you'll just step off the curb in front of a truck."

The phone had stopped ringing, but Owen didn't notice. His voice trembled as he rasped out,

"...shut up..."

He didn't.

"And in just a coupla minutes—not long at all now—the state police will be a-knockin' on yer door," he snorted, "and then they'll call ya by your name."

Owen spun to the locked front door, and he *knew* the Old Man spoke the truth.

They would call him by name and then—

**Stop them.**

That was it! He would call them and tell them he had the wrong man. It was all a mistake. The arrest was premature, a case of mistaken identity—and he would tell them not to come. Yeah.

**That was the answer—**

And again, the Old Man knew.

**"If that's what yer wantin', then call 'em. And when ya do, they'll call ya by name."**

Owen wiped the sweat from his face, his neck. The Old Man was right.

No matter what he did, no matter where he went, *someday*, someone would innocently say hello and...

**Run.**

That was it.

That was really the answer.

**Just run.**

Run and hide. Change his identity. Become just another face in the crowd.

Until someone in that crowd recognized him.

**"Oh lord, oh lord, oh lord,"** he heard himself repeat over and over as he roughly massaged his moist face.

From the cell came a humorless chuckle.

**"And you know somethin' else?"**

Owen didn't want to hear anymore.

*Lord, how he didn't want to hear anymore!*

But still, he found himself turning back.

To that hateful grin.

**"Even if them state boys don't call you by name, there's gonna be them, reporters. Can't you see 'em now at one of them press conferences? Callin' yer name over and over and over again."**

Owen slumped and found that he couldn't stop shaking. It was a well-publicized case, and that's exactly what would happen. The reporters would stand, all at once, raise their arms in Hitler-like salutes, and call out, **"Sheriff—"**

Owen covered his ears, terrified to even hear the rest of that phantom question. He could *see* it—*hear* it. Those calls. And what would follow. His eyes would glaze like his deputies must have done. And then he'd pull his pistol.

The reporters would scream and run for cover—never knowing he was simply going to put the barrel in his own mouth and—

Owen's legs gave out. He slid to the floor and, for the first time since he was ten years old—when he was caught skinning the neighbor's dog and was damn near beat to death by his daddy—he caught himself crying uncontrollably.

At this, the Old Man's smile flipped into a frown—though it wasn't out of pity.

No, it wasn't that at all.

It was because he was here for a reason. And he was going to get back to business.

He bent down so that Owen might better hear him.

**"But since I was the one who was wronged, maybe I should be the one to say it."**

Owen urgently looked up, his eyes flying open wide even as he clasped his hands together in prayer.

**"No!"**

**"What's the matter, Sheriff—"**

Owen clamped his hands to the sides of his head, hard enough to box his own ears.

"—NO!"

The Old Man grinned again.

**"There are all kinds of cells, ain't there? I'm in *yers*,"** he pointed,

**"And *yer* in mine."**

Outside, there was a crunching of gravel as the state boys pulled into the lot, and they both turned to the barred window—watching the red and blue lights flutter throughout the cell in a crazy, pixilated dance.

**"Well,"** the Old Man said—

And Owen spun to him, his wide eyes nearly lost in the ghostly white pallor of his face.

**"It looks like they're here, Sheriff—"**

Owen boxed his ears again and screamed,

**"DON'T SAY MY NAME! DON'T SAY MY NAME!"**

The Old Man grinned.

Car doors slammed.

Gravel crunched as they came closer.

Outside, the door rattled, and there were confused voices muffled behind frosted glass.

*Why would the door be locked?*

Tears streamed down Owen's face.

**"I don't want to hear any more..."**

*Where is everybody?*

Owen again cupped his hands over his ears.

**"I don't want to hear any more!"**

*Why wasn't someone waiting? There must be something wrong...*

24

Owen let out an anguished cry—

**"I DON'T WANT TO HEAR ANY MORE!"**

A voice from outside called—

**"Sheriff—"**

Owen screamed.

* * * *

Sergeant Kurtz was the first to take the initiative. He quickly pulled his night stick, knocked out the lower pane, and unlocked the door.

And damned if inside there weren't dead bodies everywhere.

A rookie by the name of Wagner called for backup, riot guns were issued, and the whole station was searched up and down, back to front—but damned if the only living person wasn't some Old Man sitting calmly in a locked cell out back, grinning from ear to ear. He looked harmless enough, but that grin—that secretly satisfied grin—unnerved even the most seasoned of those officers. He must have known what happened here, and so he spent the better part of three days under intense interrogation. But in the end, the facts were undeniable.

All of the officers in the J.C. Police station had killed themselves. Although it didn't make any sense—none at all—there was simply no other explanation.

Wiley had shot himself at his desk, Bodine had hanged himself, and Foster had opened his veins in the coffee room.

But it was Sheriff Owen that puzzled everyone.

They found him barricaded in his office, the windows locked, the shutters closed. His phone cord had been ripped

25

from the wall, and his police scanner had been smashed with a ceramic paperweight—hell, he'd even destroyed his personal C.B., even though there were no batteries in it.

Still, it was the manner in which Owen killed himself that raised eyebrows and accounted for a slew of largely ludicrous assumptions as to why. After all, his deputies had done away with themselves in—sad to say—every day, even commonplace ways. Ways the investigating officers had seen before.

But Owen had been found face down in a pool of his own blood. And for whatever reason, he had bled to death while gouging at his own ears with an ice pick.

# LITTLE PROBLEMS

The key was inserted, and turned, but the door refused to open, and the Landlord apologetically turned to Ed Waters.

"You have to understand that this is an old building and, depending on the weather, the doors may swell."

He offered a small shrug and, with a brief squeaking sound, he forced the door open.

"If you want, I could plane the frame down and—"

Ed stepped past him and waved with one hand while turning on the light with the other.

"—No, I don't think that will be much of a problem."

The Landlord looked relieved and then motioned at the room ahead.

"I think you're going to like this apartment."

Ed eagerly started down the short hall, and the Landlord closely trailed, acting every bit the sniveling, little toady that Ed already believed him to be.

"I'd wager there isn't another like it in all of New York."

"Well, we'll see, won't we?"

The Landlord grinned, his head bobbed.

"Yes. We will."

Ed stepped inside, and his jaw dropped open in astonishment. The apartment came furnished—that had been a prerequisite before he'd even agreed to view the place— but these furnishings looked as if they'd been taken straight from a museum.

Sure, there were a myriad of styles, everything from Louis the XVI to art deco, but this confusion of influences seemed to work. Overhead, as if the centerpiece, the radiant crystal chandelier served as central lighting, gently illuminating the oak-beam ceilings and stained-glass windows that lined the wall leading to the terrace.

This room, this striking, breathtaking room, was something lifted straight out of that old show *Lifestyles of the Rich and Famous*, and he was standing smack dab in the middle of it.

"Wow…"

The Landlord's head continued to bob, his uneven teeth exposed in a victorious grin.

"I told you. I knew you'd like it."

"Like it?" He spun in a circle. "I love it!"

The Landlord continued to grin—until Ed turned to him and said, "That's why I'm so sorry I can't take it."

"Why not?" was the question, spoken in a tone St. Peter might have used if a man declined an invitation through the Pearly Gates.

Ed sighed.

"I'm afraid your secretary misquoted the price on the phone."

"What did she tell you was the rental?"

He chuckled.

"She told me it was six-fifty a month." He sadly looked around at the apartment of his and everyone else's dreams. "I mean, I'm only a legal assistant—"

"—But it is six-fifty a month."

Although his hearing was perfect, Ed still cocked his head to one side and leaned closer.

"What?"

The Landlord nodded.

"Utilities included."

Ed's head swam, and he found himself repeating, "What?"

The Landlord offered a sideways nod.

"You have to pay the phone, of course, but—"

Ed took a step closer.

"—How can you do that?"

He smiled again, showing those teeth, and stepped around him.

"Well, like I told you, it's an old building, and frankly, we don't have all that many tenants."

The statement didn't make any sense.

"Why?"

The Landlord shrugged, tucking his hands in his back pockets.

"You know, I couldn't tell you. We're equipped with all of the conveniences, old and new."

He strolled easily into the room, and Ed followed on his heels.

"You've got your microwave, dishwasher, cable television, and, of course, every apartment comes with a full complement of elves."

Ed couldn't believe his luck. His last apartment had run six hundred, and that place was a dump. He was ashamed to bring a woman home to it. You know, the dates that never bothered to return once they saw how he lived. Apparently, they saw no future with him, and so when he got his long-overdue raise, he thought he could afford to upgrade a little and—

He stopped and turned to the Landlord.

"Excuse me?"

He also turned. "Yes, sir? What is it?"

Ed shook his head. He had to have heard him wrong.

"Did you say *elves*?"

He nodded.

"Yes, sir. A full complement, as I stated."

He turned and headed toward the bedroom.

"Now I have to tell you that the air-conditioning isn't working at the moment, but this being February, it shouldn't be a problem until I get a chance to—"

Ed gently took him by the arm and turned him around again.

"—Wait a minute, just give me a minute here."

He rubbed at his forehead and said again, "*Elves?*"

The Landlord looked uncomprehending.

"Yes, sir. Is there a problem?"

Ed chuckled. This guy didn't have all of the old dogs a' barkin'.

"What do you mean by *elves*?"

The Landlord shrugged.

"Well, it's what I call them. Some people call them gnomes, leprechauns." He rolled a hand. "I guess it depends on where you're from."

Again, he headed for the bedroom.

30

"Now, like I was saying, the air-conditioning isn't working, but just as soon as I can get away, I'll fix it right up for you."

Ed didn't move.

"Elves?"

He turned back but didn't stop walking.

"I'm sorry. Did you say something?"

"I have *elves*?"

He nodded.

"Very attentive ones, yes, sir."

He motioned toward the bathroom.

"Now, in here, you have your bathroom, complete with sunken tub and—"

Ed crossed his arms and smirked. He was beginning to realize why there were so few tenants.

The Landlord was nuts.

"So where are these elves?"

In an off-hand backward wave, he said, "In the baseboards, I expect. It's a little bright for them right now."

Ed snorted.

"And you believe this?"

The Landlord turned back.

"Believe what, sir?"

The question was absurd, and so he made his own sound equally ludicrous.

"That you have elves?"

"No sir, they're not mine. If you take the apartment, they'll be yours."

Ed loved the apartment, and that was true, but this guy was looking at a room in the Rubber Hilton.

"Is that right?"

"Yes, sir."

The old man paused, curiously looked at Ed, and then asked, "You *have* had elves before, haven't you?"

Ed crossed his arms and shook his head.

"Not to my knowledge, no."

The Landlord's eyes widened, and he urgently stepped toward him.

"Then I have to warn you."

Ed tried not to smile but did anyway.

"About what?"

The Landlord looked at him with dead-set eyes and said, "Be very careful what you ask them to do."

He couldn't stop smiling. He knew it was rude, perhaps even dangerous, but he couldn't help himself.

"Why is that?"

The Landlord leaned uncomfortably close and said in a hushed whisper, "They take things literally."

Suddenly, the circumstance had lost its appeal, and Ed leaned away from him.

"Is that right?"

He grimly nodded.

"Yes. Be very careful what you say to them."

He looked around the apartment, apparently searching for unseen eyes, and added, "Whatever you ask, they do."

What a fucking whacko.

"Okay. I'll be careful."

That seemed to appease him, and once again, the Landlord grinned.

"So you'll be taking the apartment then?"

Ed put his hands on his hips and said, "I'd be crazy not to."

* * * *

Ed didn't have many friends—by actual count, none—and so it took him three days to get his things moved in, even with a furnished apartment. Long Island traffic is a bitch, and he had been working overtime researching the Overton case. Still, come Monday, he was settled in, and a little past midnight, he finally managed to drift off.

And that night, he dreamed of elves.

In point of fact, he dreamed of one standing on his chest. This funny little apparition was six inches high, with a long white beard, who good-naturedly removed his pointed green hat and smiled.

"And how are you this fine evening, sir?"

"I'm okay."

The little man's grin was infectious. "How are you?"

"Oh, I'm as right as rain, sir, right as rain," he said and squatted down, crossing his legs as he did. "Aren't you the fine gentleman for asking me so."

Ed chuckled. "What can I do for you?"

The little old elf tucked his hat neatly in his lap and said, "Oh, I'm afraid you have it wrong, kind sir. It is what *I* can do for *you*."

"And what is it you can do for me?"

He raised his hands—the answer was obvious. "Why, anything. Anything at all."

"Anything, huh?"

"All you have to do is ask."

Ed crossed his arms and briefly considered. "Okay… How about breakfast?"

"And what would it be that you'd be wanting?"

He chuckled again. "Well, I like scrambled eggs, some crisp bacon, and lightly buttered toast."

"Would you be wanting coffee with that?"

This was too much. He had his own little, bearded waiter sitting on his chest, taking his breakfast order.

"No. No, thank you. I don't like coffee. But orange juice would be nice."

The elf nodded, stood, and replaced his cap. "It'll be waiting for you."

He began to hop down from the bed when he stopped and turned.

"Oh. And what time would you be thinking about waking up?"

Ed smiled and shook his head. This was great.

"I get up every morning at six o'clock," he pointed, "sharp."

The elf nodded and said, "Then six o'clock it is. And I'll be apologizing for waking you at this late hour."

As the little man crawled to the edge of the bed, Ed sat up and asked, "If I'm not being too forward, what's your name?"

He turned, removed his cap again, and in an apologetic tone said, "I'm begging your forgiveness for my lack of manners, sir."

Ed smiled and waved a hand to show that it wasn't necessary. "It's okay."

The elf vehemently shook his head. "No sir, it's not. A terrible breach of etiquette, I'm afraid."

"No, really. It's all right."

"I'll be thanking you." He bowed. "My name is Beemshoo."

Ed extended a hand. "Mister Beemshoo, it's a pleasure to meet you."

Instead of taking it, Beemshoo merely looked at the hand with something like contempt, and Ed withdrew it.

"It's simply *Beemshoo*, sir."

The look fell like a penny from a high-rise, and he smiled again. "Just Beemshoo."

And with that, he was gone.

\* \* \*

At six, the alarm went off, and at two-after, Ed was on the phone with the Landlord.

"You want to tell me what's going on here!"

On the other end of the line, the Landlord yawned and asked, "What are you talking about...?"

Wearing only his boxers and a snarl, Ed replied, "You assured me that I would have the only key to this apartment!"

He yawned again. "What time is it...?"

"Answer me! Do I have the only key to this apartment?"

He sleepily answered, "Why, yes, sir. The locks are changed with each new tenant…"

Ed growled. "Is that right?"

"Yes sir," yet another yawn, "Is there a problem?"

If that old man had been standing in front of him instead of the relative safety of Ma Bell, Ed thought he might be bitch-slapping him at this very moment.

"Then do you want to explain how I've got a table set for breakfast?"

"Excuse me?"

He turned to the table—the one that had been lovingly set and provided him with scrambled eggs, bacon, and lightly buttered toast, not to mention the fresh-squeezed orange juice.

"Someone was in my apartment and fixed me breakfast!"

There was a pause on the other end—the kind people often have when presented with a nonsensical statement.

"I don't understand the problem."

Ed's mind reeled.

"How can you *not* understand the problem? Someone broke into my apartment!"

The Landlord sniffed and said in a tired voice, "I thought I explained this to you."

Utterly flabbergasted, Ed yelled, "*Explained what*?!"

There was a loud sigh, the kind only those rudely awakened from a peaceful slumber can muster, and then:

"Did Beemshoo visit you last night?"

Ed's eyes widened.

There was no way the old man could have known about his dream-time encounter, and he gripped the phone tighter.

"Beemshoo...?"

"Yes, Beemshoo." He quickly added, "You didn't call him *Mister* Beemshoo, did you? He hates that."

*(How could he know that? How could he possibly know that?)*

Breathlessly, Ed answered, "Yeah... he was here..."

The Landlord let out a groan and said, "Did he ask you what you wanted for breakfast?"

*(It was a dream. It had to be a dream. Elves don't exist. They just don't.)*

He looked back at the steaming plates on his dinner table. He couldn't believe his response even while he spoke it.

"...yes..."

"Is it there? Just the way you wanted it?"

This wasn't possible—it just wasn't.

Still, he answered, "Yes..."

On the other end of the line, the Landlord sighed, coughed, and said, "Then I'm going back to bed."

He hung up.

Ed looked at the phone.

"You little bastard."

He slammed it down and turned to the table.

True, the spread looked delicious, and he was starving, but he'd be damned if he was going to eat it.

Who knew what that elf-loving fuck had put in it?

*(That's what happened to the previous tenants. He had poisoned them. That would also account for the differing*

37

*styles in the apartment. He murdered them and didn't even bother to remove their belongings.)*

But that didn't make sense.

The old man couldn't have possibly known about the previous night's exchange.

*The dream encounter.*

Still…

He poured the breakfast down the disposal and called for a locksmith.

\* \* \* \*

It took the locksmith, some kid by the name of Buzz—an annoyingly appropriate name—over an hour to finish the job, and Ed was late for work, something his boss, Mister Lazenby, made a point of telling everyone in the office.

He was forced to work overtime—damn those Overtons anyway—and it was well after midnight before he got home. He didn't bother to undress, opting instead to simply fall into bed, where he immediately drifted off.

"Was there something wrong with the eggs?"

Ed woke with a start.

"What?"

Beemshoo was again sitting on his chest, his legs crossed, his pointed cap in his lap.

"I say, was there something wrong with the eggs?"

Ed cried out and kicked back to the headboard, the sudden move causing Beemshoo to nearly tumble off the bed.

"What the hell?"

Beemshoo collected himself and dusted off his short pants with his cap, looking at Ed with a truly annoyed expression.

"Would you be a-minding how you move? I may be small, but I have my feeling."

Ed blinked, but when he opened his eyes, Beemshoo was still there.

"You can't be real."

The elf replaced his hat.

"Is that what you'd be thinking?"

With a small amount of difficulty, he pulled himself back up onto Ed's chest, straddled his neck, and with both hands, tweaked Ed's nose.

"Ow!"

"Am I real enough for you now?"

He grinned.

Ed grabbed his nose and wriggled it back and forth, making sure this bizarre little troll hadn't broken it.

(*Strong hands for someone so short.*)

"What do you want?"

Again, Beemshoo sat and said, "Bless the beasts, the children, and the slow of mind."

He slapped his hat against Ed's chin.

"I've been a-telling you that it's not what *we* want; it's what *you* want."

This couldn't be happening. Elves just don't exist. A plain and simple fact.

Still…

Without taking his eyes from the little apparition, he said, "Okay… How about a million dollars?"

He was quick to add, "And I want it all in single bills."

Beemshoo rolled his tiny eyes.

"It is always the same with you. You could have anything the good world provides, but it always comes down to the coin."

Ed nodded.

"That's right. If I'm not dreaming, there will be a million dollars in the living room come morning."

Beemshoo sighed, slapped his knees, and stood.

"If that's what you'll be a-wanting, sir."

Ed nodded.

"That's what I want."

Beemshoo tipped his hat and said, "Then it'll be waiting for you."

\* \* \* \*

Come morning, Ed untangled himself from the sheets and stumbled into the bathroom. He undressed, showered, shaved, and upon entering the living room, damn near fainted.

Because piled on top of the coffee table were stacks and stacks of fresh dollar bills, arranged in a pyramid that reached to the chandelier and beyond. Unable to contain himself, he stumbled into the room, stark naked, and rolled in the money.

He tossed it in the air.

He smelled its fragrance.

He ran it over his face, over his entire body.

And then he called the office and quit. Let some other overworked, underpaid asshole handle the Overton divorce case.

It was party time.

* * * *

Ed bought himself a bottle of Napoleon brandy and with snifter in hand, waited for midnight. He wasn't an unkind man, and so he had placed a stepladder beside the bed so that Beemshoo wouldn't have to claw his way up the covers.

Beemshoo did arrive, as expected, and said, "What else can we do for you, sir?"

He wasn't smiling.

Ed didn't notice. Instead, he smoked his cigar and sipped his brandy.

"Oh, I have plans for you, my friend."

Beemshoo didn't bother to remove his hat.

"You don't already have enough."

Ed shook his head and grinned.

"Not nearly enough."

"Then what is it you'll be a-wanting," he appeared to scowl, "*this time*?"

Ed tapped off his ashes.

"A woman."

Beemshoo's fuzzy white eyebrows raised.

"Oh, so it's a woman you'll be having now?"

Ed nodded.

"That's right."

He smoked his cigar.

This time, Beemshoo did remove his hat.

"And what kind of a woman will she be?"

He mused, and then said,

"Blonde. Leggy."

And very quick to add:

"One that keeps her mouth shut."

Beemshoo nodded. His eyes gleamed.

"So that's what you'd be wanting then?"

"You got it, old elf friend of mine."

Beemshoo stood.

"Then that's what you'll be a-having come morning."

And with that, he scurried down the ladder and scampered into the living room.

Ed smiled.

\* \* \* \*

The following day, right around noon, Ed was led from his apartment, and the attendants made sure that the straitjacket was securely tied before locking him in the wagon.

The guy had snapped—overwork, stress, or whatever psychobabble you chose for breakfast that morning—and had left enough evidence behind to cause even the most jaded of D.A.s to salivate.

Stacked neatly in the closet was the money he had undoubtedly embezzled from the law firm's accounts—a million or so—which he must have thought would somehow buy the affections of Louise Overton, the woman the police psychiatrist said he must have developed a fixation on over the past few months, and who now lay splayed across the blood-splattered bed.

Whether this assessment was true or not, they would never know. No one could really understand him. He was quite obviously—as one very astute patrolman philosophized—

*the guy was fucking nuts.*

After all, the guy was babbling something about elves.

Be that as it may, the coroner zipped the late Ms. Overton into an oversized body bag, and as he watched the pale-looking attendants wheel the corpse from the apartment, he puzzled on why any man, insane or otherwise, would have sewn her mouth shut before murdering her.

And how—and why—*why-oh-why*—he would have surgically attached six more legs to the body.

# CIGARS ALL AROUND

**"What's the gun for, Nate?"**

Of all the words I have ever uttered in my life, those will stay with me to the grave. After I tell you my story, I'm sure you'll understand why. Provided you believe me. I hope that you will—but whether you do or not, I'll—as they say—start at the beginning.

Yes, I think that would be best.

My name is Aaron Sturgis, and I work here at Providence Community Hospital. Just for the record, I'm a surgeon—forty-three years old, never married—and two years ago, I caused something of a stir in the medical community when I became the youngest doctor ever to turn down the post of Head of Thoracic Surgery at Boston Memorial in order to retire here in Tyler, South Carolina.

Well, I should say *semi-retired*. I like to keep my hand in—albeit a poor choice of words—and sometimes, during the night shift, I come in and see if I can be any kind of assistance.

Then again, if I were to be completely honest, I'm something of an insomniac, and I also enjoyed keeping Karen company here at the nurses' station.

She's dead now, of course, and so I'm sitting here alone.

It was yet another sleepless night for me, but instead of taking one of the pills I had prescribed for myself, I decided to head over to the hospital, arriving just after ten. Normally,

Karen's old Tempest was the only car in the lot. She worked the graveyard shift—

*How ugly that sounds now.*

—alone, manning the phones that seldom rang while she played Candy Crush on a second-hand tablet. It wasn't the most exciting job by any means, but Karen seemed content with her life, and that's quite possibly the reason I moved to Tyler. That sense of inner peace the townspeople seemed to radiate.

As I was saying, she was usually alone at this time of night, but as I pulled into the lot, I noticed that Nate's car was parked beside hers—the driver's side door was wide open, and the engine was still running.

If the car had belonged to anyone else, I might have been curious, even alarmed, but you see, Nate was an obstetrician, and the old story about babies only being born in the middle of the night is more often true than you might think.

I pulled into one of the two remaining staff parking spaces, crossed to Nate's car, cut the engine, and pocketed the keys. I remember smiling at the prospect of seeing Nate again—it had been over a month—and at possibly assisting in the delivery.

I'm afraid that, being a surgeon, I've spent too much time dealing with death and not nearly enough witnessing the miracle of birth. At that moment, I envied Nate.

I don't anymore.

I can't.

The electric hum of the doors announced my arrival, and as I removed my coat and started down the hall to the nurses' station, I couldn't help but notice the almost—I don't know—*sinister* quiet.

At this hour, the hospital is more or less shut down, but even so, there is a... feel to the place that was no longer there.

Instead, there was a stillness in the air I'd never noticed before—one that nearly made it difficult to breathe. My footsteps seemed to echo, and I found myself acutely aware of the buzzing sound coming from the fluorescent lights overhead.

I should have realized there was something wrong.

Looking back, I should have known it.

But I didn't—and continued on.

As I walked closer to the station, I became aware of another sound. A *beep-beep-beep* sound that was oddly familiar but still curiously out of place.

I rounded the corner and tossed my coat onto one of the empty chairs in the waiting room.

"Karen?"

There was no one there.

This confused me.

You see, you never knew Karen, but if you had, you'd know that she never left her post—as she called it. Even if there was an emergency—the only time she ever left it unattended—she made sure that all her calls were forwarded to the Tyler police.

And that's when I realized what that sound was—that monotonous beeping.

It was the phone that had been left off the hook. And as I replaced it, I again had the feeling that something was wrong.

Maybe *very* wrong.

I turned back, and that's when I noticed the smell.

And the blood on the floor—sporadic drops that led from the station directly to the delivery room.

The first thing that came to mind was that a mother-to-be had arrived, possibly in the throes of a painful and potentially dangerous birth, and the two had been forced to act immediately.

That would explain Nate's car and the abandoned station. And it occurred to me that this birth could possibly be even fatal to the mother. The thought alarmed me, and so, as I ran to the delivery room, I rolled up my sleeves, forgoing any opportunity I might have to scrub up, and pushed open the doors.

Even though I was a surgeon and had seen virtually all manner of physical trauma and human suffering, *nothing* prepared me for what was in that room.

In fact, I actually turned and vomited.

I had never seen anything like that in my life.

And I pray that I never do again.

Lying on the delivery table was Donna Meyer.

She was Tyler's only known prostitute, who worked out of Rory's Pool Hall on Bedford Street and had presumably gotten pregnant by one of the many johns who frequented that dive.

Before the age of political correctness, I guess she would have been called *retarded*—her I.Q. hovering somewhere around sixty—and had apparently learned her trade from her father, who was now serving a richly deserved life sentence in the Georgia State Penitentiary.

Well, Donna had never learned to—or chose not to—use condoms, and since, as those bastards down at Rory's often said, *she was the only game in town*, it was only a matter of time before she became pregnant.

I never learned who the father was (although I suspect that Nate did), but Donna had become pregnant a scant six months ago, complaining to Nate that she was gaining weight and her bleeding had stopped.

Something I couldn't conceive of now.

At first glance, it looked as if she had been cut in half at the midsection, just below the rib cage. But upon closer examination, it appeared as if she had actually exploded from the inside out.

Entrails spilled from what was left of her abdomen, looking not unlike tentacles, searching out the many spent pieces of tissue surrounding the table. Blood literally covered the floor of the small room, and her eyes were still open—seemingly staring in horror at the angled mirror overhead.

But perhaps what was most horrible of all was that her feet were still in the stirrups, although her legs were no longer attached to her body.

Instead, they were crooked at grotesque angles and dangled from either side of the table.

Nate and Karen weren't in the room.

I staggered outside, managing to keep from vomiting again, and braced myself against the wall to catch the breath I had been holding. I couldn't conceive of what had happened in that room, but there was one thing that I knew:

Despite the amazing amount of trauma poor Donna had suffered, I couldn't account for much of the tissue. Much of it was simply missing.

Just... gone.

Where was the child?

Well, I wasn't about to try and figure it out by myself. I wanted police—a lot of them—and I quickly started back toward the nurses' station, following the droplets of blood on the floor as if it were a terrible trail of breadcrumbs until I reached the phone.

Karen had the police on speed dial, but before my trembling finger even found the button, I heard it.

A low and melodic humming.

And I froze.

I mean, I was suddenly very cold and could feel—*actually feel*—the hairs on the back of my neck stand up.

Because there was someone in the lounge behind me.

Someone who—although they must assuredly be aware of what had transpired here—was in there, calmly humming to themselves.

I'm not sure how long I stood there. Looking back, it seemed like it must have been a long time before I finally found the courage to turn.

49

The door itself was closed, and it struck me then how frightening something as simple as a closed door could be.

You never really know what's on the other side of a closed door.

Especially now.

My voice trembled, and I wasn't even sure I'd said it aloud.

"Nate...?"

The humming stopped, and again, I could feel my body stiffen.

After what I had just seen, I couldn't be sure that the person on the other side of the door was Nate. I mean, I *know*—I really *know*—that Nate could never have been responsible for that horror.

It had to be some maniac. Some monster.

Still...

I turned back to the welcome comfort of the phone.

"Aaron...?"

I spun back to that closed door again. That *damn* closed door.

"Nate?"

I couldn't look away, even as I backed away from it.

"Is that you, Nate?"

There was nothing for a moment. Such a long moment. And then:

"Yeah. It's me."

Though my mind raced, I couldn't move.

The truth was, all I really had to do was get my ass out of the building. I didn't even have to make that call.

After all, my car was unlocked. The police station wasn't far. I could be there in a matter of minutes.

But I knew Nate.

I liked him.

I trusted him.

At least, the Nate I thought I knew.

Then, from the other side of that damn door came two words that truly chilled my blood. Two everyday words:

**"Come in."**

I didn't want to go into that room. More than anything else in the world, I didn't want to go into that room.

But I guess I had to.

And so I did.

There was Nate, seated at his usual table, his back to the coffee machine.

He seemed calm—even tranquil—the way I always pictured him.

Except now he was covered head to toe in blood.

And was pointing a gun at me.

"Coffee?"

He motioned over his shoulder at the vending machine. There were three bullet holes above the change dispenser, and the door now hung open, exposing the contents inside.

"It's free."

I don't think I even heard the offer. I was too busy making sure the door didn't swing closed behind me.

**"What's the gun for, Nate?"**

He briefly looked confused, as if the question itself didn't make sense. Then he squinted at the gun, turned it over in his hand, examining it from several angles before he answered.

"Oh. This."

He shrugged.

"I'm just waiting."

My foot was firmly at the base of the door. I wanted it open.

"Waiting for what, Nate?"

He didn't seem to hear me.

"Did I ever tell you why I bought this gun?"

I didn't repeat my question. I decided it was best to let him lead—at least for now.

"No. No, you didn't."

"No?"

He rolled it over in his hand again.

"It was just before you moved down here. I was working late one night, and this guy came in—an out-of-towner—complaining of chest pains. Well, I took him into the back examination room, turned my back, and BAM!"

I jumped.

Who wouldn't?

Nate briefly looked amused, as if he'd been intentionally provocative, then continued:

"Hit me right here."

He pointed at a spot at the base of his neck.

"Clubbed me a good one and made off with all the morphine in the storage room. Dumb, huh? Turning your back on a stranger like that?"

I didn't answer. I just waited for him to make some kind of sense and watched with some small revulsion as he ran a hand through his blood-matted hair.

"So I decided to buy a gun. So I wouldn't be caught off guard again. Not me. No sir."

He looked close to tears.

"Not me..."

I hesitated. I wasn't sure if I should ask the next question. But again, I had to.

"Where's Karen, Nate?"

He paused, then cocked his head and looked at me as if the answer should be obvious.

"She's dead."

I reacted—who wouldn't?—and took a numb step toward him, finally allowing the door to swing closed behind me.

"Dead...?"

He nodded without emotion.

"Down in the boiler room."

"...How...?" was all I could muster.

He looked at the calendar on the wall—the one that depicted a Norman Rockwell Christmas scene—and sounded far away as he answered.

"I didn't have the gun..."

He paused again and then looked at me. Or at least in my direction.

"Do you think I should get a holster? You know?"

He pointed under his arm.

"One that hangs under here?"

"How did she die, Nate?" I said and took another step closer.

He looked at me as if I should already know the answer.

"She was helping me."

I don't remember if I was more frightened or curious as I pulled out the chair across from him.

"Can I sit?"

"I don't know," he chuckled, "*Can* you?"

I sat down—but I kept my eyes on the gun that was still aimed at me. And I was careful how I framed my words as I asked him:

"Helped you with what?"

"The delivery."

He shrugged.

"I guess that's what you'd call it."

I have to admit that I was baffled. He was still making no sense, and so I pressed on.

"But how could that—?"

His eyes hardened, and for a moment—another terribly long moment—I honestly believed my friend was going to pull that trigger.

That I had said something wrong, crossed some line without knowing it, and by doing so, had made him lose the grip on that slender thread of sanity he had been holding on to.

He seemed to smile, revealing teeth that had turned slightly pink, and said:

"And then she helped me get rid of it!"

My initial fear momentarily disappeared and was instead replaced with a morbid curiosity.

"Get rid of the child? Is that what you're saying?"

He adamantly shook his head.

"No. That was no child, Aaron. That *thing* was no child."

*Thing?*

I took a deep breath and could smell the stench of death even from across the table.

"Then what was it?"

His eyes met mine, and I felt as if I were looking into my own grave. I had never seen eyes so... empty.

Being a surgeon, I had heard from patients who had clinically died on the operating table, only to be resuscitated and claim to have seen Heaven. There was a look of rapture in their eyes—the kind of look that made even a cynic like myself believe they had actually been there. Had actually *seen* Heaven.

And now, looking into Nate's eyes, I honestly believed that he had a 20/20 glimpse into *Hell*.

For a moment, it looked as if he didn't have an answer to my question. Only now do I understand that his hesitation was because he *didn't want* to answer me. I could hear that in his voice when he finally said:

**"It was the Nightman's kid."**

I shook my head, uncomprehending.

"Nightman?"

He grimly nodded.

"That's what Donna called him. The Nightman."

He again motioned over his shoulder.

"Are you sure you don't want any coffee?"

It was now obvious to me that Nate was in some form of shock and was possibly experiencing a psychotic break.

I shook my head.

"No, thank you."

He shrugged and then cocked and released the pistol's hammer several times. In the quiet of the room, those clicks were *very* loud.

"Anyway, that's what she called the father."

He looked up at the lights overhead as if to assure himself they were still on.

"I didn't believe her when she told me about him. I mean, who would? And then Donna wasn't exactly the brightest girl in the world, right?"

I didn't answer.

Nate cocked the hammer again, his bloodstained teeth slipping into a snarl.

"I *said*, am I right?"

I fell back, my eyes widening, and I could feel the sweat spill down my face.

I wanted to say something—*anything*—that might calm him, but all I could think about was how far away the door seemed to be from me now. Still, I managed a weak response.

"Yes..."

He sighed, carefully released the hammer, and settled back in his seat.

"I'd like another cup of coffee, but I'm probably wound a little too tight as it is right now. What do you think?"

"Nate?"

He didn't look at me.

"Tell me about the Nightman."

He paused, sighed, and then—with a terribly resigned look—he slowly leaned over the table as if to tell me a secret. A secret he was afraid would be overheard despite the fact that we were alone.

"She told me that he lives in the swamp off the Old Wash Road and that he only comes out at night."

He leaned closer and whispered:

**"He has horns."**

I felt my eyes widen again.

It was now clear that Nate was not simply in shock—no. He had lost his mind.

Whatever he had seen, whatever had happened in that operating room, had driven him insane.

At least, that's what I *wanted* to believe. That it had been someone else. And witnessing that horror had driven him over the edge.

I *hoped* that, anyway.

I didn't want to believe that Nate could be responsible.

Just the thought—the *possibility*...

Nate glanced over both shoulders as if to assure himself we were still alone, then leaned even closer.

"Well, you know people told her not to walk that road alone. There's been more than a few who didn't come back from there. I always figured it was moonshiners protecting their interests, but now..."

He shook his head.

"Well, either she didn't listen to the warnings or couldn't remember them..."

He swallowed hard.

"Anyway, walking home from the pool hall, on one of her *bleeding days*—that's what she called her menstrual cycle, her bleeding days—he was there. The Nightman."

He shuddered, and I could see that he was rapidly losing whatever control he had managed to retain.

"She said he just *rose up* out of the swamp, just rose up, and grabbed her and then..."

Suddenly, he stopped. Like someone had thrown a switch and simply turned him off.

I even thought about reaching across the table to shake him—

And then he looked up and laughed.

A disturbing chortle without humor, and he continued even as he spoke:

**"I guess Donna didn't get her ten bucks, huh!"**

"Look, Nate—"

Just as abruptly, he stopped laughing and looked close to tears.

"I saw the scars on her arms. And on her thighs. But I still didn't believe her!"

There was no way around it now.

He was obviously slipping away, and it was time to call the police.

So, as quietly and carefully as I could, I began to push away from the table.

"I'm just going down to the nurse's station, okay?"

I raised one hand and tried to sound as comforting as possible.

"But I'll be right back."

Again, Nate raised the gun.

"I'd really prefer if you stay, Aaron," he said. "I really would."

I stared down the barrel.

"Why, Nate?"

His eyes looked haunted.

"Because before she died, Donna told me the father would be here at midnight."

I actually stiffened and watched as he gripped the gun with both hands—hands covered in drying blood.

"What...?"

His voice sounded thick and far away.

"And so I'm sitting here. Waiting for him."

I paused a long moment. Nate was the first friend I'd made after moving to Tyler, and he had always proven to be a rational and highly intelligent man.

But as I looked across the table, all I saw was a madman with a gun, looking as if he had been dipped in a vat of red paint.

I had to know exactly what had driven him to this—and there was really only one question that could explain it all. The one question that I had perhaps been afraid to ask.

I should have been.

**"What happened in the delivery room, Nate?"**

He paused, then shrugged—suddenly and surprisingly, becoming the Nate I remembered.

His tone was calm and measured, almost as if he were one of my early college professors explaining a routine procedure. In fact, we'd had similar discussions in this very room, over this very table.

"I guess it was around nine when Karen called. I had my first real date in six months—Colleen Quist. Do you know her? She works down at the courthouse?"

He was beginning to frighten me again. Because now he sounded *lucid*.

"No, I'm afraid I don't."

He offered a small smile.

"Isn't that always the way? No action for months, and right when I get cooking—boom."

Again, I looked at the gun, still clasped in both hands.

He sighed.

"Well, like I said, Karen called. I came in and found Donna in the waiting room. She was having severe abdominal cramps, and at the time, I didn't think anything of it. Labor's no picnic."

"No, it isn't," I said, feeling I should offer something to the conversation.

"So anyway, I helped her to the delivery room, got her into the stirrups—"

He shuddered at the memory. We both did.

"—and then she began to scream. Now, I'm used to screaming. But not like this. She hadn't fully dilated, but she was already bleeding. Bleeding badly. So I asked Karen to call you. I guess she was on the phone when..."

He swallowed hard.

"It began.

...And I asked Karen to assist me."

He frowned.

"I guess I shouldn't have done that..."

He stopped again. The faraway look returned.

And I found myself looking at the door again. But I didn't leave. I didn't take that chance.

Because I had to know. Heaven forgive me; I *had* to know.

"Nate? What happened then...?"

He looked up and smiled.

I can't describe that smile, so I won't try. But it made a shiver race gleefully up my spine—even before he said:

**"Have you ever seen a baby born with a full set of teeth, Aaron?"**

"No, I—"

Froze.

At that moment, I realized what had happened in that room. And I finally understood what people meant when they said their blood ran cold.

He nodded and continued with that awful smile.

"That's right. It *chewed* its way out."

I suddenly found that I couldn't form words. It was as if I'd simply forgotten how. My mouth just gobbled open and closed, and even when I managed to regain my composure—however tenuous—I still struggled with my next question.

"How does a—?"

He spared me, finishing the sentence.

"—It delivered itself."

61

He briefly laughed again.

"I guess you could say it *de-livered* her too!"

His laughter turned to tears, moistening the blood on his face—tears that streaked red down his cheeks.

**"And it just kept eating and eating and eating..."**

The story was impossible—it *had* to be.

But still, I pressed on.

I wish I hadn't.

I truly do.

**"What happened to the... baby?"**

He sniffed and cleared his throat.

"We wrestled it out."

He motioned at the blood on his clothes.

"Then Karen managed to wrap it in her lab coat."

**"And then?"**

He choked back more sobs.

**"And then she began to scream!"**

He looked up at me, the tearing blood making it look like his face was melting.

"I once had a patient wake during a cesarean when I worked at County General. I guess the anesthesiologist was asleep at the wheel."

He shook his head.

"But even those screams were nothing like that. Her screams were nothing like..."

His tears fell to the tabletop, leaving small red drops against its surface.

I can't tell you how terrible that sight was, and I could only imagine what Nate had been through.

Or more importantly—what Karen had endured.

**"And then, Nate? I have to know what happened th—**
**"**

He screamed:

**"It was eating her too!"**

I couldn't move. I couldn't think. And Heaven knows, I didn't want to hear anymore.

Nate continued to cry.

Continued to melt.

"Still, she didn't let go of it. She just ran out of the delivery room, that thing clutched to her breast."

He ran a hand through his hair and didn't seem to notice as he pulled a matted clump from his own scalp.

"I followed. I swear I did. But those screams..."

Again, he began to sob uncontrollably, and for a moment, I wasn't sure he could continue.

Unfortunately, he did.

"I found her in the boiler room.

What was left of her..."

He was sprawled face-down, halfway down the stairs.

He massaged the pistol between his blood-moistened hands.

"You know? The metal stairs with all those holes poked in them?

The kind that makes your footsteps sound so loud?"

I was still walking on eggshells.

"Of course..."

"So loud..."

He briefly removed one hand from the gun and rubbed at the blood that had congealed at the bridge of his nose.

"Even though the door was closed, I could hear her blood. *I could hear it!* Running through those holes, splattering onto the floor, and I swear it sounded like rain! Just like rain..."

He was exhausted. I could tell.

By relating this story, it had proven to have some kind of cathartic effect. His words were now dull and forced, but he continued on.

"Seeing her there, like that... I never would have known that her coat was once white. That *thing* had chewed right through to her spine."

I could feel my stomach roll over, even more so when he looked at me with an almost childlike curiosity and asked:

**"How do you figure something that small could eat so much? How do you figure that, Aaron?"**

I couldn't answer.

I didn't have one.

I couldn't conceive of such a thing.

All I could do was ask him the obvious question.

**"Where is it, Nate?"**

He snorted—as if the question had been uttered by an imbecile—and said:

**"I threw it in the furnace."**

I don't remember standing, but I was on my feet.

I was stunned, shocked, and again found myself wondering if maybe he had just *snapped* and done all of these things himself. He had invented this nighttime boogeyman and the delivery room horror to cover his own murderous carnage.

I didn't want to believe it was possible—

But he himself had just admitted to cremating a newborn child.

**"You threw it in the furnace...?"**

Even after I said it aloud, it was still incomprehensible to me, and I shook my head as if it would somehow make the answer easier to understand.

**"You burned that baby alive?"**

He waved a hand at me as if to say the question was absurd.

**"Of course not. I wouldn't do that. You know me. This is Nate. *Nate!*"**

I admit I felt a small sense of relief—

And he must have felt it, too.

Because he offered a reassuring nod—

Just before he leaned forward and added:

**"First, I crushed its skull with a hammer."**

He smiled—

And then put the pistol in his mouth.

\*\*\*\*

I didn't call the police. I probably should have, but I didn't.

Instead, I went downstairs to the boiler room.

Karen was there, just as Nate said—but I didn't examine the body. I couldn't.

Instead, I stepped over her, my footsteps loud against the metal steps, and yet I could still hear the furnace.

65

I could hear the fires raging inside, devouring what it held. I could feel the heat even though the grate was closed.

And as I stepped over the bloodstained hammer beside the overturned handyman's toolbox, I thought more than once about opening that grate.

Inside that makeshift crematorium were the answers to what happened here tonight.

Either Nate had truly gone insane—

Butchered two women and burned an innocent child alive—

Or...

I opened it.

Immediately, I fell back from the intense heat, and shielding my eyes, I looked inside.

Barely glimpsed through the dancing flames, I could see something indistinguishable—but what could possibly be the charred skeletal remains of a newborn child.

It only took a brief search to find a mop against the wall, and using it as a crude form of rake, I managed to pull the remains from the flames.

They tumbled to the concrete floor, shattering like black glass—

But I could still see that the child's skull had been crushed.

Apparently, with a hammer.

The child's skull sported a full set of razor-sharp teeth.

The skull that sprouted *horns*.

Well, it's midnight now, straight up.

And so I sit here at the nurses' station, Nate's gun resting comfortably in my lap.

Around the corner, I can hear the electric hum of the door as it swings open—

And closed again.

I can hear footsteps coming down the hall. Low and oddly hollow sounding. But I guess that isn't unusual in an empty hospital in the middle of the night.

Still, I cocked the hammer.

Soon, whoever—

*Whatever*—

Will round that corner.

And so I'm sitting here.

Waiting for him.

# THE GIRL IN THE CORNER CAFE

It was 2:02 AM when the damn reception finally broke up, just long enough to miss the last call at O'Shaley's Pub. Maria had probably planned it that way, and so Paul was glad that he'd had the foresight to bring his own bottle to the wedding. He knew that it was going to be a dry affair—a *very* dry affair—and so to get through it, he was going to need a little fortification, which he certainly did. Being the best man, he knew that he was going to have to stay until even the busboys went home, but he'd only brought along a half-pint, and that was long gone.

Unfortunately, he also knew that he didn't have anything back at his place, and with the liquor stores closed—

(*Damn that bitch anyway*)

—he was straight on dry until ten the next morning.

Which is why he was now in a booth at Kelly's Cafe, still wearing his one-hundred-and-thirty-dollar rented tuxedo and staring at a piece of apple pie that he didn't really want. His coffee cup was empty, and he would have preferred that it stayed that way when the platinum-blonde waitress appeared and, with a nails-on-a-blackboard voice, asked, "Any more *cof-fee*?"

Paul's eyes widened. If you've never had a buzz wear off, you can never understand the kind of pain a voice like that can induce. It is like having a finishing nail driven straight into your brain.

Paul raised a hand in what he hoped would be the universal signal to stop talking.

"Half cup. Just a half cup…"

Apparently, she was from a different universe, and she loudly exclaimed as she poured a full cup and pounded that nail into his head, "Oh-kay!"

He waved the same hand. "That's good. That's just fine. Thank you…"

She smiled, showing way too many teeth. "Oh, you're welcome!"

(*pound, pound, pound*)

Then she turned and sashayed away, her high heels clicking so loud you would have thought that Sammy Davis Jr. was tap-dancing on his grey matter until she disappeared back into the kitchen.

He closed his eyes and covered his face.

It had been one long fucking day. One long fucking week, if the truth be known. Paul had never known what Tommy saw in that bitch Maria. The guy was the fucking Warren Beatty of the blue-collar set, and why he had decided to marry her—well, shit—it didn't make any fucking sense. She was a major religious nut, and Tommy—well, he would never be confused with a choirboy. Still, there was some inexplicable attraction between the two—the *key word here, inexplicable*—and when Tommy asked him to be his best man, he couldn't figure out a way to say no, no matter how desperately he tried, and so he had said yes.

He comforted himself by falling back on that old adage that *opposites attract*, but before the ceremony, he performed the true best man's duty—namely, telling the groom, that poor sap, to run like the wind.

But at this, Tommy merely shook his head and grinned. He said that she was *the one*—even though he admitted he'd never even fucked her! It didn't make a damn bit of sense to Paul, and now that the whole obnoxious farce was over, he didn't want to think about it anymore. His head hurt enough as it was.

Outside, a fire truck raced past, the sirens wailing, and he realized those weren't finishing nails. They were railroad spikes.

It took a moment for the throbbing to subside, and only then did he hear the voice, "Paul…?"

He gripped the sides of his head and said, "I don't need any more *cof-fee*, thank you…"

There was a tap on his shoulder. "Paul?"

It wasn't the waitress's voice, and he looked up, his blurry eyes taking a moment to focus. When they finally did, he found Maria standing over him. She was still wearing her pure-as-the-driven-snow wedding dress—only now, her dirty blonde hair clung in tangled strands to her face like seaweed. He hadn't noticed earlier, but sometime between entering the cafe and now, it had begun to rain.

This didn't make sense. "Maria?"

She nodded. "Yes. It's me."

He briefly shook his head, but it didn't rattle anything back into place. "What the hell are you doing here?"

She slowly shook her head—the way an old-west schoolmarm, like he always pictured her to be, would do to one of her unruly students. "Don't curse."

In the months that he'd known her—those increasingly painful months—he had learned to watch his language and his other annoying little bachelor *picadillos*, and so he rolled his eyes and briefly waved a hand. "Yeah, right. Sorry."

He patted himself down, but to his annoyance, he couldn't find a smoke.

"I do so apologize—"

And then he realized.

His hangover was kicking into third gear, but even a low-grade moron would notice that Tommy wasn't with her.

Shit, Tommy had never managed to save a penny in his life, and *that's* the reason Paul was sitting in this booth in the first damn place. He had given up his own apartment so these two could have a place to *honeymoon*.

So where the fuck was he?

Paul looked over his shoulder, but the café was empty. Shit, even that waitress with the annoying voice was nowhere in sight. He turned back. "Where's Tommy?"

Maria brought a hand to her heart and offered an exaggerated gasp that even Scarlett O'Hara couldn't pull off, then slid into the booth across from him. Paul stiffened and caught himself looking over his shoulder to make sure no one would see them together. He *did* have a reputation to uphold, and even at this hour, he was afraid someone might see them. I mean, for cryin' out loud, he was sitting in a booth with this bizarre-looking woman in a wedding dress,

71

and him still wearing his tuxedo. Even among the dumbest chicks he dated, one and one still added up to two, and all he needed was to try explaining to one of them about the flake queen at the café.

Since she seemed intent on just staring at her clasped hands, Paul thought he should repeat the obvious. "Maria? Where's Tommy?"

She pulled a napkin from the dispenser and dabbed at her tearing eyes. "I've left him..."

He couldn't have heard that right and leaned closer. "You've *left* him?" She nodded, and Paul looked at his watch, but he couldn't read the time. "You just married him a couple hours ago."

She sniffed. "Yes, but I didn't know what kind of man he was."

He managed to find a single crumpled cigarette in his vest pocket and put it to his lips. "Is that right?"

She nodded—a slow, affirmative nod. "Yes."

He sighed. Sadly, it looked like this might take some time. "So, what kind of man *is* he?"

Paul again patted himself down until he found the cigarette lighter in his pants. It had been a gift from the happy couple for being the best man and bore the inscription: *Take Care, Old Buddy, Love Maria and Tommy*. He snapped it several times but was only greeted with ineffective sparks. Apparently, they had neglected to fill it. Typical of the duo. He tucked it back in his pocket and began another jailhouse pat-down to find a match.

Maria's eyes darted like a thief scanning for potential witnesses to a crime she was intent on committing. Paul was puzzled by the furtive glances but was even more confused when she crooked a finger and wagged it at him. *Come here.*

With a resigned sigh, he leaned closer, and she whispered, "He was a sinner."

And with that, she quickly leaned away and clutched at the front of her dress as if she were ashamed of the admission.

Now, Paul had known Tommy since the third grade. They'd grown up two doors down from each other over on 5th Street, so this particular bit of information wasn't exactly a shock. Hell, in the past, when they *did* go to church, it was only to knock over the poor box.

He leaned back in his seat and said, "You don't say?"

Another firm nod. "Yes."

"Well, I always thought the two of you were..." He rolled a hand as he searched for the right words, "Different types."

Maria sat straight up, clasped her hands in prayer, and Paul was amused to find that the decorative lamp hanging behind her offered a 100-watt halo.

"Yes. When I met him, he was unrepentant. A lost soul."

Paul rolled his eyes. The sermon had begun, and so he resumed his search for his elusive matches.

Maria continued, her eyes glazed over and far away, "But with the grateful help of the Lord, I helped put his feet back on the path of righteousness!"

Paul finally found a pack of matches in his back pocket. "Righteousness, gotcha." He snapped one alight. "So tell me—what was it that knocked that old sinner off the path anyway?"

With surprising speed, Maria leapt forward, her claw hands leading, and clutched him by the lapels, pulling his wide eyes closer to her own as she snarled, "It's not funny, Paul! It's not funny! IT'S NOT FUNNY!"

Paul stared into those wild eyes, and as carefully as he could manage, he tried to loosen her grip. "Okay... I'm sorry."

But for someone so small, she was unusually strong, and it wasn't until one of his tuxedo buttons actually popped off that he was finally able to free himself.

"Hey, come on! Calm down. I didn't mean anything by it. Just relax."

A brief moment passed. Then her eyes cleared, her clenched teeth slipped back into an angelic smile, and she settled back into her seat.

"It's okay, Paul," she smiled wider. "We're friends."

*This chick is out of her fucking mind,* he thought. He had long suspected it, but now she had removed all doubt. She was fucking nuts. And as placating as he could manage, he said, "Yeah. That's right. We're friends."

She offered a sideways nod as if to say *of course we are,* then said, "It's just that I'm married now, Paul."

Paul had dropped his matches during her impromptu attack but luckily found them beside his plate.

"Yeah, I know. I was there. Remember?"

He peeked over his shoulder but found that the café was still empty. Shit, even the waitress wasn't there. He turned back.

Maria sadly shook her head. "I can't divorce."

(*Poor Tommy...*)

Paul replaced the fallen cigarette to his lips and pulled another match free. "That sin thing, right?"

She nodded again. "That's right."

He was careful to choose his next words. "Well, getting back to that"—he quickly raised a hand—"and believe me, you don't have to tell me if you don't want to, but…"

He was walking on eggshells. "What was it that Tommy did? Exactly?"

She gasped and again clasped her hand to her chest. And again, he raised that hand.

"Remember, we want to be calm here."

She timidly shook her head. "I don't… I don't know if I can tell you."

He again offered a hopeful glance over his shoulder, but damned if the café wasn't still empty.

"Well, take your time." He turned back and let out a resigned sigh. "I'm in no hurry..."

She shifted in her seat but couldn't meet his eyes. "He… he wanted me to…"

He shrugged. "He wanted you to *what*?"

She shook her head. Whatever this was, it seemed intensely painful for her.

"It's hard, Paul…"

He pulled yet another match from his book. "Just spit it out. It's not like we're in church or anything."

Immediately, her face contorted into an expression of unconcealed rage, and he dropped the match again, raising his hands in the same move.

"Whoa. Sorry. My mistake."

Almost miraculously, her smile returned. "It's okay. It's just that I'm so tired."

*Fuck-ing nuts.*

"It's okay. Just go on and tell me."

She wrung her hands but still wouldn't meet his eyes. "You promise you won't tell a soul?"

Paul sighed again and held up a hand in his best Boy Scout salute. "Promise."

She still appeared unsure and looked at everything but him.

"He wanted me to…"

She hemmed and hawed, struggling with what she had to say, until she finally managed to again force out:

"He wanted me to…"

She shook her head, but in the end, she just couldn't continue.

Paul thought this was getting old. After all, he had a smoke to light.

"He wanted you to *what*?"

She closed her eyes, took a deep breath, then leaned over the table. And with another sigh and a weary expression, he did the same.

Again, her eyes darted—apparently making sure no one would hear such a horrible admission—then she whispered:

"He wanted me to go to bed with him."

And with that, she quickly leaned back, clutching both hands to her chest as she attempted to catch her breath.

On the other hand, Paul remained frozen. There are times in your life when some things are so absurd it takes them a moment to sink in.

And this sure as hell was one of them.

After a long pause, he managed, "Uh-huh…"

He gradually allowed himself to settle back in the booth, shook his head, and then, in a quizzical tone, offered,

"Well, you *do* know you are man and wife—"

He only had time for a startled look before she dove over the table again. Her expression was even more crazed, and this time, her powerful hands were around his throat like some hydraulic press.

"Sex is for sinners!" she hissed. "AND ALL SINNERS WILL BURN IN HELL!"

Paul again tried to pry her fingers free, only this time, he failed. She furiously held on, and all he could do was croak out, "…oh yeah… I forgot…"

At this, her eyes cleared, her grip loosened, and her smile immediately returned. She let out a small, contented sigh and reclined back.

"Oh, that's okay," she said.

She picked up the matchbook and absently played with it. "We're friends."

He cleared his throat. "That's right. You got it."

He looked over his shoulder. The café was still empty, and he thought he had never wanted to be anywhere else more in his life. He reluctantly turned back.

"Do you know what I think?"

"No, Paul," she said, pulling a match free. "Tell me."

He loosened his tie, which had somehow become a noose.

"I think that maybe if you went back to Tommy, well… you two might be able to work something out." He motioned between the two of them. "I mean, just the two of you."

She shrugged and said simply, "I can't."

Even though Paul found himself perspiring, he also thought that the room was unusually cold. "Why not?"

She struck the match. "I told you."

Paul glanced at the match, then back to her. "Told me what?"

She looked up as if the answer were obvious.

"He was a sinner."

She smiled wider, the flame dancing in her wide, vacant eyes, and said:

**"And now he's burning."**

# HEART OF THE WEST

Oogie Stimple weren't never book-read, but even he could read the letter from the El Vero Bank. It was the fifth such letter he'd received in as many months. The numbers were still the same, with the only difference being that this one had stamped across it: **FINAL NOTICE**. He owed the bank six hundred and eleven dollars, and if he didn't come up with it in two days—two lousy days—he was going to lose his business.

He was going to lose his home.

He was going to lose his life.

It had been five years since he completed his first and only business transaction, namely the purchase of the old Harley Cribbons' service station, *Heart of the West*. It was the only gas for damn near ninety miles (although up the road some ten miles, there was a bar, restaurant, motel, and assayer's office that used to offer frequent referral business), and when the cattlemen were still running beef through the county, he'd had one hell of a time keeping up with the trade. For the first year, he was actually in the six figures and had even considered hiring one of them big-city accountants to handle all that money—so much that he couldn't even count it all.

That's what—at the time—didn't make sense to Oogie. The place was a friggin' gold mine, and so he couldn't understand why Harley would sell the place to him for a measly ninety-five hundred dollars—his entire life savings.

Sure, he told him the workload was getting to be too much, and he wanted to retire to his brother's ranch over in Arizona, but with the freeway coming through, he could have hired additional help. Shit, Oogie himself would have hired on for minimum wage and a cot in the back. But Harley was adamant. He just wanted out. And so, Oogie had bought the place, bid Harley a fond farewell, and watched him head on down the dirt road toward Vegas way—laughing as he did.

He should have known then. But Oogie wasn't the brightest star in the sky, and so he waved until the truck disappeared, then set about making repairs. The first order of business was to refurbish the towering, heart-shaped sign that not only bore the lyrical name of the place but also the logo:

**No Gas For Ninety Miles! Besides, If We Ain't Got It, Y'all Don't Need It!**

Now, nobody would ever mistake him for an artist, but he was a proudful owner, and he spent many an hour climbing up the ladder to care for that sign—and just as many climbing back down to take care of the truckers who'd blare their horns when their beasts demanded to get fed.

That is when the truckers still came.

Before they moved on.

Before the freeway passed him by.

That was two years ago. He had never contacted those accountants, instead putting all his money into his slowly dying business, assuring himself that things would improve. They had to. Old Harley had assured him that things could only get better, and Oogie had gambled his life savings on that dream.

He was going to be a millionaire.

But all he saw now when he closed his eyes, was Harley laughing up his sleeve. He must've seen it coming—or going, as the case may be—and so he'd pocketed a few more dollars before heading off to a safe haven, leaving Oogie to die with his dream.

Leaving him alone in a cluttered office with an empty garage.

"Damn you, Harley," he said to no one. "Damn, you straight to hell…"

He closed his eyes.

And *that's* when he heard the crunching.

At one time, it had been a familiar, welcome sound—back when the trucks still came—but he hadn't heard it for weeks. He leaned forward, wiping away the smoke that had collected on the glass over the years to see outside.

Now, Oogie didn't smoke, but Harley did, and since he'd spent so much time repainting his sign, he'd never bothered to clean the office, let alone the windows. After all, this was his private domain, and he could live like he wanted.

He leaned forward, his stool squeaking under him, and squinted through the tobacco-stained glass to see a Porsche parked at the pumps outside.

It had been so long since he had any trade that he momentarily thought it must be a mirage—

That is until whoever was inside sounded the horn.

"Your lights are on!" came the glass-muted yell. "But does anybody *work* here?"

Oogie chuckled. "I'll be damned…"

The horn sounded twice more. A sweet sound.

Another call: "Yo! Clem! I can see you sitting there! How about some gas?"

A woman's voice chimed in—a chastising voice.

"Would you shut the fuck up!"

Oogie sprang from his chair—fast enough to cause it to roll into an unused file cabinet—and ran outside. The thought of a cash sale had him damn near salivating, and he slid through the loose gravel, nearly skidding past the car before coming to a stop beside the passenger window.

Inside was a married couple—or at least, by their demeanor, he assumed they were married—both dressed in what appeared to be their best clothes, slightly rumpled from what was certainly a long trip.

The window electrically lowered, and with a wide smile, Oogie said, "Howdy folks, and how we doin' tonight?"

The man smirked and turned to his wife. "*Howdy?*"

The woman looked embarrassed and turned away. "Carl, don't…"

Unaware of the affront, Oogie leaned even closer to study the dashboard. Damned if it didn't look like the cockpit of one of them airplanes he saw on television.

"Hope yer all right."

The man turned back, eyed him with obvious distaste, and adopted a taunting southern accent despite the fact they were deep in the heart of Utah. "Yep. We're just *dandy*. How's by you, Clem?"

Another chastising: "Carl!"

The man waved her off as Oogie said, "No, the name's Oogie." He extended a hand. "Oogie Stimple."

The man ignored it. "Now there's a surprise." He motioned over his shoulder. "How about filling it?"

Oogie glanced to where the man pointed, then back. "The tank?"

The man sighed. "No, I mean, how about filling the Grand Canyon with your drool, you banjo-playing bag of—"

The wife cut in. "Carl!"

He waved her off again. "Just fill it up," and, as if he had to be told, "with gas."

"Yessir, right away."

Oogie shuffled over to the pumps he'd installed during the high times (after he'd stored the old hand pumps in the service bay) and removed the nozzle.

"Yessir, I sure am glad to see you folks. Ever since the cattle people done moved on, there ain't been much traffic through here."

The man patted himself down, apparently searching for a cigarette. "Do tell?"

He glanced in his rearview mirror and urgently leaned out the window. "Hey! You! Gomer!"

Oogie looked over his shoulder—believing there must be someone else behind him—then pointed at his chest. "Me?"

The man slumped. "No, the other five Gomers out there!"

"Carl!"

Again, Oogie looked over his shoulder.

This time, the man ignored her. "You want to tell me what you're doing?"

Oogie looked confused. "Well, I'm just puttin' the gas in yer car like you told me."

The man vigorously waved a hand. "Wait a minute, just a damn minute! You're not going to put *that* gas in my car."

Oogie looked even more confused. "You told me to."

"What? Are you trying to fuck up my engine?"

Oogie straightened and took a step back to avoid the verbal punch. "No, sir! I would never—"

"Yeah? Then give me the *super* unleaded, you low-grade moron!"

Oogie looked at the pumps, uncomprehending, and the man slumped. "What's the problem now?"

He offered an apologetic shrug. "Well, see, I'm sorry—"

The man nodded. "You are that."

"Carl!"

Another wave.

"But see, all I gots is the regular and the unleaded. I have been meanin' to get—"

The man turned to his wife and threw up his hands. "This is just fucking great. Isn't this just the fucking *best*?"

The wife shook her head. "You're being an asshole again. Or should I say—*still*?"

Oogie shut the pump down and sheepishly put his hands in his pockets. "I don't figure this gas will hurt your engine none—"

The man interrupted again and pointed at the heart-shaped sign overhead. "Is that sign still right? There's no other gas for ninety miles?"

"No, sir. I mean, yes, sir. Not in either direction."

The man slapped the wheel. "Great! This is just fucking great."

The wife rubbed at her forehead. "Carl…"

Oogie felt that he should say something, and so he stepped forward and pointed. "There's a town about ten miles up the road, but they don't got no gas." He shrugged.

The man sighed again. "Then how is that supposed to help, Clem?"

The wife finally exploded. "*JUST GET THE FUCKING GAS!*"

Oogie took a step back. He needed the business—weren't no doubt about that—but right at this minute, he wanted to be back in his office and away from these folks.

The man looked at his wife. "Yeah! This is a fine-tuned machine! You put the wrong stuff in this car; we're gonna chug all the way home!"

She leaned closer and snarled, "*Get the fucking gas so we can get out of here. NOW!*"

Now, Oogie didn't exactly have virgin ears, but he'd never heard folks talk to each other like that. His mama and papa—rest their souls—would *never* talk to each other like that. Not even the cattlemen did. They showed respect. They was gentlemen.

Not like these two.

They was trash.

Just trash.

The man threw up his hands and said, "All right! I'll get the fucking gas!" He turned to Oogie and offered a patently false smile.

"You heard the lady, Gomer. Fill it."

Oogie sneered. "Right away…"

He did.

"That'll be twenty-seven-fifty."

The man extended a credit card. "You take MasterCard, right?"

"No sir, 'fraid I don't."

"Shit." He fished through his wallet and produced another. "How about Visa? You *do* take Visa, don't you?"

Oogie offered an apologetic shrug. "Sorry. Strictly a cash business."

The man slumped and turned to his wife. "Do you believe this?"

She rubbed at her temples. "Just pay the man."

"Oh, *just pay the man*?" He opened his wallet to expose ten new one-hundred-dollar bills. "And you think the banjo-player can break one of these?"

The wife hissed, "Ask him!"

The man waved her off yet again and turned to Oogie. "So how about it, Gomer? Can you break a hundred?" He held out a bill.

But Oogie didn't immediately answer. Instead, he stared at the open wallet, looking close to salivating.

The man didn't seem to notice and instead snapped his fingers. "Yo! Hayseed?"

Oogie shook his head, as if coming out of a trance. "What's say?"

Speaking very slowly, as if to a retarded child, the man repeated, "I said, can you break one of these? It's a one-hundred-dollar bill, in case you've never seen one. Can you get me change?"

He held it out.

Oogie paused. He found that he couldn't take his eyes off the wallet's contents.

"I'll have to check…"

"Yeah? Well, why don't you do that? I don't have any intention of growing old here, know what I mean?"

Oogie's voice sounded far away. "Yes sir…" He wiped his hands on his pants and hesitantly took the bill. "I think I do…"

As he started toward the station, Oogie heard—or thought he heard—the couple's conversation:

"I bet he can't. He'll probably try to pay us off in old tires or dead batteries."

"Can't you just shut up? Ever since we left Vegas, it's been bitch, bitch, bitch!"

The man motioned, "Look at this. Twenty-seven bucks and he doesn't even clean the windows."

"Would you *shut the fuck up!*"

Oogie closed the door, neatly cutting off their voices, and fell against it. He realized that he was sweating.

It wasn't the heat—in fact, it was a pleasantly cool night.

No, he was sweating because of what he planned to do.

**No one'll miss 'em.**

They're two ugly people with too much money.

And no one'll ever miss 'em. No one.

He opened the register and took out Harley's old pistol. It felt cold.

Oogie stepped back up to the driver's side window.

The man wearily glanced at him. "So, have you got my change?"

Oogie clutched the gun to his side. His hand was trembling.

The man glanced at his wife, then back. "You can't do it, can you?"

Oogie didn't remember doing it, but he heard the click as he pulled the hammer back.

The man let out a loud sigh and turned to his wife again. "I told you he couldn't do it—"

Oogie raised the pistol and fired a shot through the back of the man's head.

Even before he heard the wife's scream, he put another bullet in her open mouth.

The whole event had taken only a second or two, and when he finally stopped vomiting up his frozen dinner, he realized how easy it had been.

It wasn't like hunting with his daddy back in the old days—you know, lying in wait, killing something that had no real business dying.

This wasn't a sport.

These folks—these victims—had something he needed. Something they had too much of, even if they didn't know it.

What that man had in his wallet was food on his table.

**They were just meat.**

Still...

He carried them to the back of the station, finally understanding the true meaning of the term *dead weight*. They were indeed heavy, but he had time.

There were no headlights coming down the road—the very reason for killing them in the first place—and so he laid them against the north wall, beside the water heater, and well out of sight.

Even though there was no one around to see them.

Oogie wiped his mouth on his sleeve and turned to the corpses, grimacing at the blood that had pooled in the wife's mouth.

"I'm sorry, folks. I truly am. But you gots to understand something."

He turned in a slow circle.

"This is all I got."

Their glassy eyes stared at him as if to say that his explanation wasn't good enough, and, unable to witness those accusing eyes, he tossed an old tarp over them.

"I'll bury you come mornin', I promise."

He took a step back.

"I promise ya that…"

Despite the fact that he had been around cars all of his life, he was still unaccustomed to a stick shift, and so it took him some twenty minutes to get the car into the back lot, loosely covering it with sage grass and tumbleweeds before retreating back to his office—

—where he now sat, staring at the ten bills spread over the desktop.

It was more money than he needed.

More than most decent folks *ever* needed.

But the fact was, that green paper was going to get him out of a heap of trouble.

At least, that's what he thought—until he looked out through the smoked windows and saw the flashing red-and-blue lights of what was certainly Sheriff Andy's car, even though he hadn't heard the crunching from the gravel lot.

Oogie covered his mouth and spun out of sight.

He didn't know those poor, murdered folks.

Didn't even know their names.

But it was damn sure that someone did.

Maybe they'd stopped along the way to call their loved ones, perhaps telling them they'd be late but were on their way home. Telling them to keep a light burning.

And when they didn't arrive on time, said loved ones called the police.

Oh yeah.

Oogie was up the creek named *Shit*.

And he hastily scooped up the money, tucking it into the bottom drawer.

"Oh lordy. Oh lordy, lordy, lordy…"

He caught his breath and his eyes widened at the sound of approaching footsteps. Two fellas, by the sound.

He had to get his story straight. Had to think.

*They never come through here. I ain't seen 'em.*

But maybe somebody else did. A nice car like theirs was not a common sight in these parts, and if Sheriff Andy suspected anything, he'd certainly take a look around the place. And that'd be the end of it.

Oogie rubbed at his forehead and then seemed to massage the sweat over the rest of his face.

"Oh, lordy… what have I gone and done…"

The footsteps were closer now. Soon they'd be at the door.

He thought maybe he could hide in the garage. They might not find him there. But when they didn't find him, they'd search the station.

And then they'd find…

"Oh, lordy…"

He thought hard, but he didn't have no options.

They had him.

"All right…" he said, tears spilling down his cheeks. "I'm comin'…"

With a resigned sigh, he stood and looked through the clear spot he'd rubbed in the glass. And his eyes damn near sprung out of his head.

91

Because those flashing lights *weren't* coming from Sheriff Andy's car.

No.

They was coming from some kind of saucer-shaped thing that was silently hovering over the gas pumps outside.

Now, he'd *heard* about flying saucers—some even claimed that was what run off the cattlemen, something about cattle turning up dead—but he had never *seen* one.

That is, until now.

There was a knock on the door. Actually, three loud knocks.

Oogie jumped.

Through the crack in the rotted baseboard, glimpsed through the flickering, multi-colored lights, he could see four thin shadows. Two sets of legs belonging to whatever was standing there.

The door rattled with three more knocks.

"We're closed!" he ludicrously called out, his voice cracking for the first time since he was a boy.

Three more knocks. Louder.

His knees gave out and he fell to the floor.

"...please... just—just go away... please..."

There was a bright flash of light. So bright that he had to clamp his eyes shut.

When he finally opened them, his face feeling flush and sunburned-hot, he found two small beings standing in front of him.

They were just like them little aliens he saw in a movie years ago—*Close... something*, he couldn't remember—all skinny-boned with big black eyes.

They didn't bother to open the door. They just sort of stepped through the wood.

The big one—the one with the bigger head—was carrying what looked like a weird kind of gas can and said, without moving his lips:

"We saw your sign."

Oogie didn't know what to do. He had never seen anything like these little fellas, and he sure didn't know what they were doing here.

"What was that you said...?" he asked—or *thought* he asked.

The one with the smaller head took a step closer and Oogie kicked away from him.

"We need fuel," it said.

The request didn't make sense, and Oogie felt his brow burrow, the skin again feeling hot and tight.

"What? What's that yer sayin'?"

Big-Head held up the little jug in his four-fingered hand. "You have fuel."

Again, the request didn't make sense.

"Wait a minute here." He leaned closer to make sure he'd heard these little fellas right. "Are you sayin' you want some gas?"

"We need fuel," it repeated.

Oogie chuckled.

They weren't here to eat him or stick one of those spider-looking things on his face like he thought.

They was just customers.

Funny-lookin' customers, sure—but if they'd come all this way just for some gas, well *shit*, he could oblige them. *Shit yes!*

He pushed himself to his feet and extended a welcoming hand.

"I can fix you up! Damn straight! I got all the gas you need right outside here."

The doll-like being merely glanced at his hand and said in an even voice, "You do not understand."

The second alien added, "We need fuel."

Oogie lowered his hand, glanced at the craft hovering outside, and then back.

"Yeah, well, I heard ya—but I don't get what kinda fuel y'all are talkin' about." He motioned at the pumps. "I mean, I got regular and unleaded but—"

Big-Head interrupted. "Our vessel is very much like your own."

Oogie looked uncomprehending. "Mine?"

The second alien chimed in. "It works on the same propellant."

He shook his head. Once, he tried to learn Spanish but couldn't figure it out. But these—whatever they were—was speakin' English. Still, he didn't understand none of it.

"Look, see, I don't know what kind of vessel, you know, yer talkin' about." He motioned out the window at the saucer. "See, I ain't got no vessel."

94

"Yes. You do."

Oogie looked from one to the other.

"You are covered in it now," the second said.

Oogie looked down, but all he saw was grease-covered overalls.

"You mean—"

Big-Head stepped forward, raising the container higher.

"We believe you call it your body."

Oogie's eyes narrowed—then widened again.

"My...?"

"Our vessel is also organic."

His eyes darted between the two. "What...?"

The canister was pressed against his chest.

He looked down at it—then back to them.

"If you would please fill this with your fuel."

Oogie tried to swallow but found he couldn't.

"Fuel? What fuel—?"

"We believe you call it *blood*."

He looked at the canister—and, more importantly, to the syringe attached to it.

These fellas—whatever they were—couldn't be serious.

"You expect me to—?"

Again, the alien interrupted. "We are in—" It seemed to puzzle a moment.

"A hurry," the other answered.

Oogie stepped back, away from the canister.

"No, y'all don't get it. I can't be doin' that."

He finally managed to swallow the lump in his throat. "I just *can't*."

95

The second alien seemed genuinely confused by the word. *"Can't?"*

Oogie backed away as far as he was able and pointed at his chest.

"See, *I* need my blood."

"As we do," Big-Head said as he moved toward him again.

"Fill the container, please."

"I *can't!*" Oogie insisted.

The second alien stepped up beside his comrade.

"Your sign tells us that if you do not have it, we do not need it."

"And we do need it—so you must have it."

Oogie glanced at the sign, then back as they stepped closer.

"Fill the container."

His head worked wildly, but his earlier thoughts had been right. There were no options.

They had him.

And then... his eyes narrowed.

"Wait!"

They stopped.

He looked toward the back lot—or at least, in its direction.

"Maybe I can help you out."

* * * *

It took less than a minute to drain the blood from the couple out back, and Oogie found he had to turn away as the corpses shriveled into withered husks. The skin drew tight and wrinkled, embracing the bone as all their bodily fluids were literally sucked from them. Even the blood in the woman's mouth disappeared.

And then, with their container filled, the beings turned to him and said,

**"Thank you for your kind and courteous service."**

Oogie's stomach rumbled. He cupped a hand over his mouth, barely croaking out a,

"...yer welcome…"

The second alien raised a hand and Oogie recoiled. But instead of a death ray—or whatever he'd expected—there was simply a leather pouch that sagged under the weight of what was inside.

**"We hope the amount is adequate."**

This time, Oogie blinked.

"...amount...?"

The alien didn't lower the pouch. Apparently he—or at least Oogie assumed it was a he—was a patient alien.

**"What is that?"**

Big-Head said simply,

**"Gold."**

Oogie's eyes widened.

**"Gold?"**

**"You still use it for currency?"** the second asked.

Forgetting the night's horrific and certainly unusual events, he sprang forward and snatched the bag away— nearly dropping it as he did. It was heavy. Damn heavy. As he furiously grappled at the cat-gut string holding the satchel closed, he wondered how those puny little alien arms had managed to hold it out.

Inside were ten gold, faceless coins, each the size of a silver dollar. That bag had to be worth thousands. Maybe more.

**"Is the amount adequate?"** Big-Head asked.

He looked up.

"Huh? Oh!"

He clutched the bag to his chest.

**"Oh yeah, the amount's adequate. It's just fine. Thank you."**

They turned.

**"Then we will leave you now."**

Oogie stood and offered the same ingratiating wave he gave to all his customers.

**"Y'all have a nice night."**

They didn't turn but seemed to glide away.

**"We will tell our friends about your station."**

Oogie's smile fell—as did the coins that spilled at his feet.

**"What's say...?"**

As their voices receded, he heard the second say,

**"We believe that you will become a very wealthy man."**

And with that, they were gone.

Oogie remained on his feet as long as his knees would hold him, and then he collapsed, hands over his face. Alone in the darkness, he slowly rocked back and forth, sobbing,

**"Oh lordy, oh lordy, what have I gone and done..."**

But there wasn't anybody around to hear him.

\* \* \* \*

The car radio, as usual, was little more than static.

**"Police still have no firm leads concerning the mysterious disappearances that have plagued Southern Nevada, but there are those who are still claiming that the increased UFO activity in the area could be in some way responsible. Chief Warren Saunders of the Nevada State Highway Patrol referred to such claims—and these are his words, folks—as 'monkey dung' and likened them to similar stories of cattle mutilations we had a few years back. In the weather…"**

Sheriff Andy turned to Ed, his deputy, and sighed.

**"Turn that damn thing off."**

Ed did just that.

**"I still don't get the reason for this trip."**

Andy didn't look at him.

**"Nobody's seen or heard from Oogie for two weeks. He hasn't been answering his phone either."**

Ed snorted.

**"Hell, knowing Oogie, he just forgot to pay his bill again."**

**"Yeah, well, that's the pure hell of it. If he couldn't afford to pay his bill, then how could he afford that freezer unit he just picked up over Silver City way?"**

**"Freezer unit?"**

Andy nodded.

**"One of those industrial-size ones."**

"What the hell would he need with something like that?"

He shrugged.

"That's what I figured on asking him."

They rolled into the gas station lot, pulled past the pumps, and right up to the front door. Andy put the car in park.

"Why don't you go see if his truck's around back?"

Ed pointed at the station.

"He's got the open sign in the window. I figure he's got to be here."

"That doesn't mean he's all right. Something could've happened to him."

He opened his door.

"Go check around back."

"Will do."

As Ed circled to the rear of the station, Andy hitched up his belt and rapped on the door. Three times.

There was a brief shuffling from inside…

…and then Oogie opened the door.

The sudden move made Andy leap back, his fingers tickling the butt of his revolver—

Because although Oogie stood in the doorway, it wasn't the Oogie Andy knew.

This wasn't the good-natured, if somewhat mentally-impaired, gas station attendant.

No, this was a **wizened** old man whose hair had turned bone white.

A man who, although he was looking right at Andy, didn't appear to *see* him.

**"You need some fuel…?"**

Andy shook his head, but when he looked back up, he was greeted with the same sight.

"Oogie…?" he said breathlessly. "Oogie, you all right, son?"

His glassy eyes stared back—the kind of stare that sends a shiver gleefully up your spine.

**"I gots fuel…"**

"What? No. I don't need no gas."

He reached out, took Oogie's arm, and immediately pulled his hand back. Oogie was ice cold.

**"What the hell has happened to you…?"**

The question seemed somehow absurd to Oogie, who smiled.

**"Got plenty of fuel now, you betcha."**

The smile fell.

**"Got plenty of fuel…"**

Andy didn't want to touch him again, but he did, and gently led him inside.

**"Let's get on in here and sit you down."**

He looked up—

—and his eyes widened again.

Because the office was *literally filled* with gold. Coins, bars, dust—you name it. It was piled in every corner, stacked on shelves, covering the desk. Shit, you couldn't swing a dead cat in this office without hitting a fortune.

**"Holy…"**

Oogie grinned again. A faraway grin.

**"You need a fill-up…?"**

Ed stepped inside, shaking his head.

**"Sheriff, you ain't gonna believe this, but there's gotta be fifty cars parked out back—"**

He looked up, and his hat flew right off his head.

**"Well, *shit!*"**

Andy ignored him and settled Oogie into his chair.

**"You're gonna be okay now. You just relax."**

Ed couldn't take his eyes off the impromptu Fort Knox.

**"What in the high-flying fuck is goin' on here?"**

Andy shook his head and leaned away from Oogie, who still appeared unaware of their presence.

**"I don't know. But it looks like he hasn't eaten in a good week."**

Ed motioned toward him.

**"What's with the hair?"**

**"Don't know that either, but I figure we better be getting us an ambulance out here."**

He glanced around.

**"Where's the phone?"**

Without looking away from Oogie's serene—yet unsettling—expression, Ed pointed.

**"On the wall there…"**

Andy turned to the pay phone—the one stacked with gold coins, like it had been used by a very wealthy Good Samaritan. He lifted the receiver, and just as he began to fish for a coin of his own, he noticed the frost spilling out from under the door to the garage.

**"Now what have we got here?"**

He hung up the phone and opened the door.

As Andy pulled his gun, his eyes wide in horror, Oogie grinned wider and said to no one in particular:

**"Got plenty of fuel now, yessir... Plenty of fuel now..."**

\* \* \* \*

Forrest Kroger and Wilfrid Evans were playing checkers out in front of the hotel like they did every Saturday afternoon.

**"Well, what did Andy see in that garage?"**

Forrest didn't look up from the board. His voice never changed tone. If you didn't know better, you'd think they were just talking about a community dance.

**"Them people that been disappearing."**

**"Is that right?"**

He pushed a checker forward.

Forrest nodded.

**"That's right. He had one of them big old air-conditioners keepin' 'em cooled off so they wouldn't turn. And do you know what else?"**

Wilfrid shook his head.

**"Nope."**

**"He had them folks rigged up to his old hand pumps."**

**"Now why would he go and do a thing like that?"**

Forrest studied the board.

**"He was drawin' the blood outta 'em and storin' it in old gas cans and oil drums."**

For the first time, Wilfrid looked up.

"I wonder what for."

Forrest looked over the top of his wire rims and shrugged.

"Couldn't tell ya."

They played in silence a moment.

"You know that sign out in front of his station?"

Wilfrid nodded.

"*Heart of the West.* Sure do."

"Was a time when folks would've said that was true of Oogie hisself."

Again, Forrest nodded.

"They'd be sayin' he had the biggest heart around these parts."

* * * *

It was the bright flash that awoke Oogie from his sound sleep, and he blinked away the tears in his eyes, the straitjacket not allowing him the option of wiping them away. When they finally cleared, he found the two aliens at the foot of his cot.

Oogie grinned.

"I knowed it. I knowed it! I told 'em you'd be comin' back, but they didn't believe me!"

He struggled to sit up.

"Figured I was crazy and locked me up, but I *knowed* it!"

They didn't move.

"We stopped by the station, but you were not there."

"Well, like I told ya—" He stopped short.

Dangling in one of their hands was a clear, crystal container. The other held what could best be described as a post-hole drill.

Oogie nodded at it.

**"What've you got there…?"**

The first said simply:

**"We need a fuel pump."**

The room was suddenly without air.

**"You need a *what*…?"**

**"Our senior vessel is badly in need,"** said the first.

**"You seem the logical choice,"** the second added.

Oogie's eyes widened. He looked down at his chest.

**"…you don't mean that yer gonna…?"**

**"The sign told us where to find what we need."**

They approached. Oogie screamed.

\* \* \* \*

Folks still report seeing UFOs in the night sky.

Greta Scruggs even says she saw a cigar-shaped one that she swore up and down was damn near a mile long. She'd been sleeping when the racket woke her up and watched as it passed over her small ranch house.

Most people don't believe her, though. Everybody knows that flying saucers don't make no noise.

But still, she claimed it made a loud

**chug-chug-chug** sound.

You know—

The kind of sound it makes when you put the wrong stuff in a well-tuned car.

# BE CAREFUL WHAT YOU WISH FOR

Arnie Bullock was a rapist and a murderer. There was simply no other way to describe him. Now, he sat on death row, the chair anxiously awaiting him come morning.

All of his appeals had been denied—rightfully so—and, with his options now decidedly limited, he opted to spend his last night on Earth comfortably finishing off his pack of Kools before his 8 AM call, when he would fry for the vicious killing of a little nobody by the name of Karla Dillon.

Even so, he smiled.

Like the others, that little bitch had been asking for it since she moved to the big, bad city two weeks earlier. He'd been watching her, of course—he noticed every leggy blonde—and the fact that she was dumb enough to cut through the 7th Street alley after her midnight shift at Denny's? Well, come on.

Yeah, he'd waited for her in that alley just minutes after she'd served and dismissed him with a polite smile and a tepid "Have a nice day," knowing full well that was exactly what he intended to do. Still, it had taken her longer than he'd anticipated, and he was just about to light up a third cigarette when he heard the click-click-click of her high heels as she rounded the corner and started down the alley. The one with the busted light.

*Just asking for it.*

At first, he crouched behind the restaurant dumpster, watching with wide, watering eyes and a growing hard-on as she briefly stopped beside a broken window to adjust her stockings—the same stockings he would soon rip off and stuff in her mouth when she tried to scream. When she began to plead for her stupid, miserable, and ultimately disposable life.

Then he raped her.

Hard and dry.

Grinning like he was now, remembering how the black mascara teared down her cheeks.

And then, oh—the knife.

To Arnie, *that* was the best part. Even better than the sex.

The slicing. The whimpering. The pleading eyes. The blood.

The glorious blood.

Oh yeah, that was the fun part, all right, and he still felt a swell of pride recalling how he broke his own record: two hundred and thirty-one cuts before she finally bled to death. Even when they fried him, he figured that record would stand for quite some time.

**"If you were that good, then how did they catch you?"**

Arnie turned, surprised to find a man casually leaning against the sink. Though he didn't have a cigarette, every time he spoke, smoke spilled from his lips.

Arnie stood.

**"Who the hell are you?"**

He briefly tried the bars, but they were still locked tight.

**"How'd you get in here?"**

The man smiled. His teeth were very white.

"Oh, I pretty much come and go as I please. The real question is: do you want out of here?"

He stepped closer, and Arnie could see he wasn't a guard—not one he'd come to know anyway. But there was something about him. He thought he'd seen him before. There was something familiar. And as the man stepped into the light from the hall, Arnie noticed the red T-shirt he wore.

It read:

**"If You Can Read This, You're Going to Hell."**

**"Well? Do you?"**

This didn't make any sense. Arnie shook his head. But when he opened his eyes and looked up again, the man was still there.

**"I asked you—"**

The man waved a hand and sat down on the toilet.

**"—And I heard you. Did *you* hear *me*?"**

**"Hear what?"**

He sighed.

**"I'm going to make you this offer just one more time, so try and pay attention."**

The man leaned forward, speaking slowly and evenly.

**"Do you want out of this prison?"**

Arnie looked around the cell.

**"Well, now, what do you think?"**

**"It's a yes or no question, Arnie. So what's your answer? Yes or no?"**

He paused, then nodded.

**"Yeah. I mean—yes. Yes, I want out of here."**

The man smiled.

"Good. That's good. But you forgot the one little word that makes it all possible."

Arnie frowned.

"What little word, you miserable grinning fuck?"

The man didn't seem insulted. In fact, he looked amused.

"What did Karla say when she first saw you in that alley and knew what you were going to do?"

Arnie thought back. He never really paid attention to his victims—not before the fun anyway—but he did remember her. When he'd stepped from behind the dumpster, her doe-eyes had widened and she'd gasped out a single word. A word that meant nothing to him... but one the man clearly expected to hear.

He obliged.

"Please."

The man stood and patted him on the shoulder. Even through his prison grays, Arnie could feel the cold.

"See? Now that wasn't so hard, was it?"

Arnie pushed the hand away and rubbed at the shoulder, now aching.

"No. That wasn't so hard."

"So let's cut to the chase."

The Man turned away and hopped onto the bunk, resting his hands behind his head.

"What will you give me to get out of here?"

Arnie looked around the small cell and said,

"Well, I've got half a pack of smokes, a bar of soap, and some toilet paper. Help yourself."

"Not interested."

**"Then what are you interested in?"**

The answer was obvious, and the Man shrugged.

**"Your soul."**

He grinned.

Arnie smirked and nodded.

**"Oh, I get it. You're the devil, right?"**

A sideways nod.

**"Basically."**

Arnie had anticipated seeing the devil sometime in his future—say, eight the next morning, and probably since the day he'd strangled his first cat—but he didn't expect to see him *before* he died.

**"And you want my soul?"**

**"Well, the truth is, I already have it."**

The conversation was absurd—he was probably just asleep—but Arnie figured, under the present circumstances, what the hell?

He smiled.

**"Then why the offer?"**

The Man sat up.

**"The fact is, you're a nasty motherfucker."**

He chuckled.

**"That's the rumor."**

**"But I can still use you."**

**"Use me how?"**

The Man patted his hands as if he'd soiled them just by being in the cell.

**"I'll give you a second life."**

Arnie leaned closer.

"What's say?"

The Man nodded.

"That's right. I'll put you in another body and you'll be on your merry way."

Arnie paused, then sat down beside him.

"A second life?"

The Man nodded, and Arnie rolled a hand.

"And all I have to do is give you my soul? Something you've already got?"

Another nod.

"That's right."

"Yeah?" Arnie kept the hand rolling. "So what's the catch?"

The Man tried to look innocently confused.

And oddly enough, he did.

"The catch?"

This time, Arnie nodded.

"Yeah. The catch. What is it?"

The Man shifted on the cot to face him, and for the first time, Arnie noticed his eyes.

They were yellow. *Pus* yellow.

"I exist through suffering. Human, animal, it doesn't matter."

He placed a hand on Arnie's shoulder and this time Arnie grimaced.

The ache was sharper now.

"And I must say—you have been a truly sensational contributor."

He removed the hand, and Arnie noticed the smile was gone.

**"So what's it going to be? A second life... or the chair?"**

It felt like a nail had been driven through his arm, but Arnie met his eyes anyway.

Those yellow, lifeless eyes.

He said simply,

**"Deal."**

The Man smiled and shook his hand.

**"Oh, you are going to make me *so* happy."**

And with that, they were both gone.

* * * *

**Click-click-click.**

Arnie stopped in front of a broken mirror to adjust his stockings.

*(His stockings?)*

*(What the fuck?)*

He looked up, surprised to find himself—*(Herself.)*—still dressed in the Denny's uniform.

Staring at the smiling man coming toward him. A man by the name of Arnie Bullock.

He thrust out a hand and offered a plea that wasn't heard.

**"Please..."**

# GOBLINS

"You called about an intruder, sir?"

The old man wheeled himself back beside the alcove window and urgently waved a hand at the two patrolmen.

"Close the door! Close the door!"

Officer Curtis looked at his partner, who shrugged.

"Okay."

He did, and the old man let out a ragged sigh of relief.

"Thank you. Oh, thank you..."

Curtis looked into the nearest bedroom, then briefly shined his flashlight into the dark kitchen. Nothing.

"Are you alone in the house, sir?"

"Ever since my wife Eileen passed. Six months now."

The old man pulled the shade aside, barely an inch, and peeked outside.

"I called forty minutes ago. What took you so long?"

Patrolman Massey leaned into the bathroom and flipped on the light. Small and empty.

"It's Halloween," he said, shutting it off.

"The streets are filled with little trick-or-treaters."

The old man stiffened. A brief, uncomfortable silence followed. Then he whispered:

"Are you sure?"

Curtis opened a closet door and gave a cursory look inside.

"Yes, sir, there must be a hundred of them out there."

"No."

The old man swallowed, the sound clicking in his throat.

"I mean... are you sure they're trick-or-treaters?"

The two men exchanged a glance. Massey chuckled.

"Yes, sir. They come out every year about this time."

The old man again stole a glance into the darkness outside. His eyes were haunted.

"I know they do..."

Curtis looked behind the curtains and then behind the couch before turning back.

"Look, Mister—"

The old man didn't hear him at first.

"What? Oh. Crawford. Owen Crawford."

Curtis offered a curt nod of acknowledgment, then replaced his flashlight in his belt.

"Mister Crawford, why exactly did you call 911? I don't see any evidence of an intruder—"

"Oh, but there will be!" the old man exclaimed.

"It's just a matter of time now."

Curtis glanced at his partner, then back.

"You mean, you're expecting an intruder later on?"

Massey tried to stifle a small chuckle.

He didn't try hard enough.

The old man didn't notice.

"If I'm left alone, yes. That's why I had to call you. Before it's too late."

Curtis sighed.

"And what makes you think someone is coming to get you, sir?"

"Because of what I know."

"What you know?"

The old man grimly nodded.

Massey chimed in.

"And just what is it you know that's so important?"

The old man unconsciously squeezed the blanket tighter in his lap.

"I know who killed that man across the street exactly one year ago today."

"Across the—?" Curtis looked over his shoulder, then back.

"Are you talking about—?"

The old man finished the sentence for him, his nose wrinkling as if he'd caught a foul smell.

"Warren Baxter."

Massey looked intrigued.

"Right. The Baxter murder."

He pulled up one of the kitchen chairs and positioned it in front of the old man.

"You say you know who killed him last Halloween?"

He sat down.

The old man nodded.

"I not only know... I saw who did it."

Curtis looked at Massey and took a step closer.

"You *saw* the murderer?"

Again, he nodded.

"I got a good look at them."

Curtis' eyes brightened, and he pulled up a chair of his own.

"Them? Did you say *them*?"

The old man nodded but didn't meet their eyes.

"The rules are that trick-or-treating ends at eight or eight-thirty, but there are always stragglers. The odd few who want to see if they can get that last piece of candy folks are hoping to save for themselves. I usually don't pack it in myself until I can see up and down the street that no more of 'em are coming. Until the porch lights start going off and people are taking their lawn chairs back inside the house. I wait until then... and just as I was taking in my own bowl, I seen them. Four of them."

Massey's brow creased.

"Four?"

This time, the old man didn't seem to hear him but instead continued.

"I don't know what it was, but I just couldn't stop looking at them. Maybe it was because they didn't look like the other trick-or-treaters."

Curtis shook his head and waved a hand.

"Wait. Are you talking about four little kids?"

Again, he didn't hear him. Instead, he scrunched up his face as if trying to squeeze the memory out.

"They didn't go from house to house. And even though they all carried paper sacks, they didn't seem interested in candy at all. No. They were just walking down the middle of the street with a..."

He paused, searching for the right word.

"Single-mindedness to them. Like they was focused on something else. Something they were about to do."

Curtis basically repeated his question.

"Wait... you're talking about four *children*?"

The old man paused. Still, without looking at them, he shook his head.

"No. See, that's what I'm saying. I don't think that's what they were at all."

Curtis also shook his head.

"You don't?"

The old man continued.

"They just kept walking. Eyes front. Straight down the street and right up to Baxter's front door. For a long time— at least it seems like a long time when I think back on it— they just stood there. Like horrible little lawn ornaments. And then the one on the end reached out and pressed the doorbell."

He hesitated.

"For a while, I didn't think he was going to answer. Baxter was a weird one."

He gave each officer a knowing look.

"If you know what I mean."

Massey waved a hand.

"Why don't you explain it to us."

The old man shifted in his seat.

"Well, Baxter..."

He cleared his throat.

"He liked children. In fact, this was his favorite time of year. When they would actually come up to his house and he wouldn't have to go out looking for them."

His voice tightened.

"And when he answered that door, he stretched the biggest smile I've ever seen. He was like those kids begging for candy—and he was savoring the treats that were right in front of him. I watched him open the door wider to let them in. And after he did, he looked both ways... making sure no one had witnessed their arrival. And then he closed the door, still with that same smile."

Again, the old man shifted in his seat. It was clear he was in real discomfort the longer he told his tale.

"They were in there a long time. I even thought about calling the police."

"Why didn't you?"

"I was about to!" he blurted.

"I really was. But then they come out. All four of them. Baxter—he wasn't with them. No, they were alone. Just stepped outside, closed the door behind them, and started back down the street, their paper bags sagging under the weight of the treats they'd collected from him. I only found out later what they were."

He grimaced and shuddered.

"Baxter's eyes. His fingers. His tongue... and his privates."

"Okay, so why didn't you tell the investigating officers at the time?"

The old man looked down at his knotted hands and wrung his fingers.

"Because they wouldn't have believed me."

"They wouldn't have believed you because you say it was kids that killed Baxter?"

The old man slapped a fist against his thigh.

"No! I told you—they weren't kids!"

Massey raised his hands in a placating manner.

"Okay. Okay. Then tell us why they wouldn't have believed you."

Again, the old man stiffened and summoned his courage before answering.

"Because I saw them—the real them—when they passed by my porch."

"The real them?"

He grimly nodded.

"Even though I was hid back in the shadows, they must've known I was there. Maybe they could smell me, I don't know. But when they passed, they raised their masks and stared right at me."

He looked at them helplessly.

"You see, that's why I couldn't tell the police. They would've asked me to describe them... and I couldn't do that. Even though I remember them clearly. I mean—who could forget those faces?"

Curtis leaned forward and, in as soothing a voice as he could manage, asked,

"Will you describe them for us now?"

The old man swallowed again—that dry, clicking sound.

"They were all rotted flesh and exposed bone. And they didn't have eyes. Just sunken, empty sockets. Even so, they stared at me. Like they were committing me to memory. Memorizing my face so when they came back... they could find me."

"And then?" Massey asked softly.

"Then they put their masks back on... and continued down the street."

Curtis and Massey looked at each other. Then back to him.

They said nothing.

The old man deflated—like someone had simply let the air out of him.

"You see? I knew you wouldn't believe me..."

"Well, for the sake of argument," Curtis said, "if there *were* such things, why do you think they'd come back for you?"

"I told you. Because I've seen them. And whatever they are, I think this is the one night they can walk among us. Hiding behind those masks. Disguising what they *really* are."

He looked up now, and there was urgency in his eyes.

"We *think* they're children because they're *supposed* to be children. But they're not. They're *not.*"

Curtis tipped back his cap and rubbed at his forehead.

"You know, it seems to me that you see these—"

He rolled a hand, searching for the right word,

"—creatures as some form of avenging angels."

"Devils," Massey corrected.

Curtis offered a smile and a conceding nod.

"Devils."

He looked back at the old man.

"But is that the real reason they'd come back for you?"

The old man stiffened.

It was a question he *should* have anticipated—

But it was clear he hadn't.

And now, he didn't know what to say.

Massey leaned forward and looked into the old man's darting eyes.

"Could it be there's something you're not telling us?"

Before he could find an answer, the doorbell rang—surprisingly loud in the quiet of the small house.

Outside came a chorus of

"Trick or treat!"

And the temperature in the room dropped twenty degrees.

The old man gasped, and Curtis pushed to his feet.

"Just let me get the door."

Alarmed, the old man lurched forward.

"No! Don't open it! Don't you see? That's how they get you!"

Curtis chuckled and continued to the door.

"That's not the *only* way they get you. But you are right... you *do* have to invite goblins in."

The old man squinted, uncomprehending.

"Goblins?"

Massey leaned his chair back on its two rear legs and nodded.

"They come out every Halloween. All sizes and shapes."

He chortled—a sound that didn't belong in a human throat.

"But they weren't coming for you because you saw them."

With one finger, he reached back and playfully turned off the porch light.

From outside came a collective groan of disappointment and the shuffling of small feet as the children headed away.

Only now the old man didn't even notice.

He looked from one patrolman to the other.

"What are you saying...?"

Curtis pulled down the shade.

"You were at Baxter's house when the children arrived, weren't you?"

"What? That's absurd!"

His voice was loud—but unconvincing.

Massey settled the chair back on all four legs and leaned closer.

There was a smell coming off the young man now.

A terrible smell.

Like rancid pumpkin.

"But he sent you away," Massey said.

"He would share the pictures on his computer, but not the children themselves."

Curtis added,

"Your wife found out too, didn't she?"

He turned the deadbolt.

It clicked.

The old man found himself ping-ponging between them as Massey rose from his chair. Together, they inched closer.

"And one night, six months ago, she said she was going to leave you."

"She was going to go to the police."

"So you killed her."

"And buried her under the tiles in the basement."

The stench coming from the men was overpowering now, and the old man covered his nose with the blanket.

"You're not the police! Who are you?"

Curtis looked at Massey, but neither stopped advancing.

"I told you he would never let us in if we used the other masks."

The old man felt his heart seize.

His eyes widened.

"Other masks...?"

Massey peeled off his face.

The old man screamed.

"You didn't really think we'd try the same thing twice?"

The *Curtis mask* hit the floor beside Massey's own—

And the goblin's corpse-cold grin gleamed in the darkness.

"Did you?"

# AN INNOCENT WAGER

Ed Meyer was a gambler, not by trade, but by nature.

Good ol' Ed would gamble on anything, and more often than not, he'd come up with the shit end of the stick, as his empty bank account and his many returned checks would attest.

Now, don't misunderstand here—Ed was no welsher. No, sir, no way, not at any time. He didn't even have a nodding acquaintance with luck—*not* good luck anyway— but whenever he did come up short on a bet, you know, a few bucks light on a gentleman's wager, he'd always find some way to pay off the debt. A barter of some kind. There was even a time, after betting on a kid's boxcar race and not having the ten bucks, he made good by streaking through the crowd.

No, you could say a lot of things about Ed Meyer, but you'd never say he didn't pay his debts.

And that's exactly why he was where he was—

Buried up to his neck in a swamp in the middle of the night.

But let's take a step back...

See, Ed knew there was always a game at Finney's—you know, the place off the Old Wash Road? Yeah, every Friday night, they cracked a new deck, but someone had to *die* before you could even hope to get a seat there.

Well, that's just what happened to Cranston Spokes the night before. Just keeled over, leaving The Red Light

Massage. Dropped dead right there in the parking lot. Something even his brother-in-law, Sheriff Smatt, couldn't keep out of the *J.C. Newsletter*.

Anyway, Ed had had his eye on that seat for coming on two years. But he needed a nod from the fella who ran the game—

And damn near everything else in J.C., if the truth be known.

A bear of a man by the name of Burton Croade.

You'd probably have to see this guy to believe him. Then again, maybe you *have*. If you've ever seen any movie with a fat, ill-tempered, cigar-smoking redneck tyrant—

Well, that's him. Big as life and twice as ugly.

Although Ed didn't know it, Croade had had *his* eye on *him* for that seat.

After all, there wasn't a gamester in the world who didn't appreciate an eager sucker—

And Ed was, well... shit.

The next night, Ed was in that seat, staring at a two-hundred-dollar pot, a pair of aces...

And exactly two one-dollar chips.

Croade sighed an enormous cloud of smoke and gripped the stub of his cigar.

Although he had most of the money in the county, no one had ever seen Croade with more than a stub of a cigar.

"I said, I raise you ten, boy."

Two chips. Two aces.

Ed caught his foot tapping—a nervous habit gamblers can't afford—and reached toward the pot.

"I'm light ten—"

Without two shits or a hot damn, Croade tapped his ash to the back of Ed's hand.

Ed jerked it back, the *sizzle* still ringing in the room.

The scent of burnt flesh hung heavy.

Croade puffed on the stub until the embers flared again.

"This is a money game, son. We don't go 'light' here. That's how faggots play poker."

He gestured to the smiling faces of the other players— three men who not only approved of what they'd just seen but looked like they wanted to see it again.

"You see any faggots here?"

Ed rubbed at the rising blister on the back of his hand.

"No..."

He glanced at the others, who nodded in agreement.

"No. No faggots here."

"Then you'd better show me some cash or show me them cards."

Two aces.

His best hand all night.

He couldn't let it go.

Not over eight lousy bucks. He just *couldn't*.

Ed looked up.

"What if I work it off?"

The men reacted—two with raspberries, the other two with furrowed brows and *incredulous* stares.

"If I lose, I mean."

Croade leaned forward.

"Work it off?"

126

Ed nodded.

"Yeah."

"I done told you—there ain't no faggots in this room."

A man to Ed's left laughed.

Ed glanced at him, then back to Croade.

"I'm on the up-and-up on this. No bullshit."

Croade looked him up and down. Paused.

Then something strange happened.

He chuckled.

"Okay, son. We might just have ourselves a deal."

Ed smiled.

Croade waved a hand.

"Now, don't be gettin' too happy on me just yet. You haven't heard the deal."

Ed could hardly wait to lay those cards down and rake in that pot.

His foot was tapping again.

Tap-tap-tap.

"Just tell me."

Tap-tap-tap.

"I'll let you slide on the eight bucks. But if you lose, you gotta do somethin'."

He grinned, revealing those tobacco-stained teeth.

Tap-tap-tap.

Ed's palms were sweating.

"What?"

"Oh, just a little something. Nothing major."

Tap-tap-tap-tap-tap.

"Just tell me what it is!"

Ed was apparently the only man at the table who didn't know what this "nothing major" was—because the rest of the men were grinning from ear to ear.

Croade kept smiling and raised a placating hand.

"Now don't go gettin' your panties in a bunch. I told you—it's just a little thing."

The cards felt slippery in Ed's moist hands, and he became aware—too aware—that he was actually snarling.

"What *is* it?"

Taptaptaptaptaptaptaptap.

"Why, all you'd have to do for them eight bucks is spend the night out there in the bog."

Now, Ed had been raised right down here in Georgia, and bogs didn't scare him none. Hell, when he was a kid, he and Jimmy Briggs used to sneak out at night and go hunting for bullfrogs not a mile from this very tavern. There wasn't anything out in the bog of any real menace—mostly bugs and a few snakes. It wouldn't be a problem to spend a night out there. No problem at all.

Besides, he wouldn't *have* to.

He had two natural aces in a draw poker game where nothing was wild.

Ed smiled again.

"You're on."

Croade smiled even wider.

"Buried up to your neck."

The other men laughed.

Ed didn't.

"What...?"

Croade nodded.

"You heard me."

He pointed that soggy cigar butt at him and added,

"You don't have the cards, and me and the boys go out there and bury you up to your neck in the bog. See you in the mornin'."

Ed offered an unbelieving smile.

"You've got to be kidding."

He looked around at the other men at the table—but none of them were smiling. Not unbelieving. Not amused. Just still. Waiting. Staring at him with quiet expectation.

Ed turned back to Croade.

"You're serious? I mean... you're *really* serious about this?"

Croade looked serious.

"It's your call, boy. What's it gonna be?"

Ed looked at his cards, then back at the man.

"You'd really bury me up to my neck in the bog and leave me there by myself overnight?"

Croade gave a flat reply.

"Call or fold."

Still, to Ed's mind, it wasn't just a simple statement.

Nothing is *ever* simple to a gambler.

What Croade said was a challenge—

And holding two natural aces, well, that was more than Ed could resist.

So, with the flourish managed only by a very confident man, Ed laid his cards down.

"Two aces. Jack high."

The other men turned to look at Croade.

* * * *

Croade had a large wooden crate in his storeroom—and oddly enough, three shovels, one for each player, which were gleefully accepted.

Ed had allowed himself to be led—

(As already stated, Ed was no welsher)—

To a small, seemingly clear area that smelled faintly of Spanish moss with just a hint of kudzu.

All in all, not an unpleasant place.

Unless you were going to be buried there.

Ed turned back and looked at the tavern.

"At least I can still see the place."

One of the men—his name was Dick or Bill or something like that—drove his shovel into the moist ground with a small, yet somehow unnerving, *sloshing* sound.

"Well, hell, boy," he smiled at the others, "we're gonna want to keep an eye on ya after all."

"That's good to know."

One of the others—an ugly little man with bad dentures—nudged the fat man beside him.

"That's good to know, he says..."

They both laughed.

Croade didn't.

"Come on, fellas, let's dig us a hole."

He glanced at his watch.

"We ain't got all night."

Dick-or-Bill—or whoever he was—looked annoyed and pointed at Ed.

"Why don't *he* dig it?"

There was general agreement—except from Croade, who shook his head as he re-lit his cigar.

"Weren't part of the deal."

He motioned at Ed.

"He's keepin' up his end. So will we."

There was the usual grumbling, then the men dug in—pushing aside the syrupy black earth until they were content the crate would fit in the hole.

It did.

Croade motioned at it.

"Well, get in, boy."

Ed hesitated. The players bristled.

He turned to Croade.

"Should I take my clothes off first?"

They all laughed then—including Croade, who finally managed to say:

"We don't wanna see you naked. We just want you in the box."

Ed looked into the crate—already filling with black water—and then back.

"But see, I—"

Croade made a slashing motion, neatly cutting him off.

"We'll wash 'em up come mornin'."

Ed looked again at the crate and sighed.

"Eight stinkin' bucks..."

Croade shrugged.

"You called. And last I heard, three queens beats a lousy pair."

Ed snorted and shook his head.

"A lousy pair is right."

He sighed again and hopped into the crate, the black water sloshing beneath him and immediately soaking his shoes. Still, it was a shallow crate, and as he straightened, he found that he was only going to be waist-deep in the muck.

Or so he thought.

"Squat," Croade said.

Ed looked at him.

"What did you say?"

The fat man raised his shovel like a rifle and said in a low, threatening voice:

"He told you to *squat*, boy. You best get to it."

Ed did.

They filled the crate, lovingly smoothing the oily mud around his neck, chuckling as they did. He found he couldn't move his arms—

Shit—

He couldn't move *anything* but his head.

He was caught *tight*—

Like they'd dropped him into a vat of wet cement. A cement that was sealing, settling, *hardening* around his entire body.

He was completely paralyzed.

And damned if that didn't strike Croade as funny— maybe as funny as anything he'd ever seen.

"You comfortable, boy?" he laughed.

"I mean, we all know you ain't too bright, but are you comfortable?"

Being the lapdogs they were, the other men chimed in with laughter—

But the truth was, the mud was *tightening*. Constricting.

Ed found it hard to breathe.

Croade didn't notice.

He turned to his cronies with a wide, yellow grin.

"What's say, boys?"

He raised one booted foot.

"Anybody for a game of soccer?"

For the first time, Ed began to realize how helpless he really was.

How vulnerable he'd made himself.

It was obvious now—his life, never mind his *comfort*, meant nothing to these men.

If they chose to, they could use his head for a soccer ball.

Hell, they could use his head for a toilet if they wanted to.

He tried again to move his arms but only succeeded in working his head wildly from side to side—

Which, naturally, prompted another eruption of laughter from the players.

Croade went into a brief coughing jag, then crouched beside Ed, even offering him a small pat on the head.

"Don't worry, son. I wouldn't do nothin' like that. We're just havin' a little fun with ya, s'all."

Ed tried to look back at him but couldn't.

"Yeah, I know. Y'all are just good ol' boys, and this is just clean fun."

Croade shrugged.

133

"Come on—it don't look *all that* clean."

The lap dogs chuckled.

"Asides," he glanced at his watch, "it's already three-thirty in the A.M. I don't know about you, but I consider morning to be six sharp. You're only lookin' at two-and-a-half hours. You could do that standin' on your head."

He grinned.

"I mean, if you *could* stand on your head."

"Two-and-a-half hours? That's all?"

Croade nodded.

"Back to dig you up at first light."

Ed found himself smiling.

He could do two and a half hours—he really could.

All he had to do was relax. Squat in that box until sun-up, and his reputation would be secure.

He wouldn't be considered a welsher—

And that meant he could get into the game.

Maybe even get a shot at that pot again.

Even these guys would have to respect him after this.

They'd *have* to.

His reputation would be solid gold.

He kept smiling even as he heard the men heading away, back to the tavern.

Back to their game.

Just two-and-a-half hours.

\* \* \* \*

Of course, there was no way Ed could have foreseen the fire.

See, as you might've guessed by now, Croade was not a nice man—

And over the years, he'd acquired a significant number of enemies.

Sadly—

At least for Ed—

Several of them decided to pay a little visit to Finney's in the wee hours.

They pumped a few rounds into Croade and his lap dogs and set the place on fire to cover their tracks.

Ed, of course, could smell the smoke—

Even though he couldn't turn his head to actually *see* the fire.

Or the fire department.

And because of that damn constrictive mud, he couldn't even manage a call for help.

It's been two days now—

And still, he squats in that crate.

But it's not completely hopeless.

Somebody *might* find him.

Maybe a couple kids sneakin' out of the house to hunt for bullfrogs.

It's possible.

But I wouldn't bet on it.

# SAY CHEESE

My radio tells me that I've got another perfect day outside. The sun high, the humidity low—but hey, what's that to me, right? Hell, I can't even remember the last time I saw the light of day, and according to my calendar, I wouldn't be out of the darkroom until sometime in May.

Still, I've got no one to blame but myself. I mean, *I* was the one who accepted the job. It was my fault, no one else's. Just me.

You'll have to forgive me. Sometimes I forget my manners. I guess the long and the short of it is that I'm not very cultured, refined—your choice. Anyway, my name is Elliot Collier—hi—and for the past six years, I've made my living as a—well, for lack of a better term—commercial photographer. Most of the people I know call me Eddie. I don't know why, so I guess you can too.

It was September 4th, my birthday—the big 3-0.

As you might have guessed, I wasn't in the best of moods and had cracked a bottle of J.D. well before noon. I mean, I had just turned thirty, I was alone, and, let's face it, I hadn't exactly set the world on fire. And right then, looking into that shot glass, I figured I never would.

As it was—*still is*—I ran a small shop in Soho, had no regular customers (at least none I'd care to talk about), and my last referral was ten days ago.

In short, I was feeling sorry for myself.

Yeah. Poor, poor pitiful me. The big 3-0 and going nowhere at light speed.

**Congratulations, buddy.**

I poured myself another shot and toasted myself.

**"Happy birthday, Eddie. And many more."**

I tossed it back—this one tasting oddly bitter—and began to pour another when the bell over the door rang, announcing the arrival of a potential customer.

That in itself surprised me. But looking back, I wonder if maybe that's why he showed up then. Sensing my mood, my guard down—I don't know. I guess it's as good an answer as any.

The man smiled.

**"Mister Collier? Eddie Collier?"**

My eyesight was fuzzy. My mind, clouded—I admit that—and so maybe my memory isn't as good as it could be. As clear.

Still, there isn't a person on this planet who wouldn't remember *this* guy.

He wore a striking red sports coat, green pants, and wing-tips. You know—a *cheesy* look.

In my profession, I'd met this kind of guy a thousand times. The kind you see at the track tearing up a ticket before turning to buy another he couldn't afford.

Yeah, he was the type I was accustomed to—and probably the reason I was drinking alone on my birthday.

I wearily pushed myself up, set the glass aside, and sighed at the prospect of yet another "referral."

**"That'd be me."**

He crossed the room, extending a hand, his easy smile never faltering.

**"My name is Stark. It's a pleasure to finally meet you."**

I looked at his hand for what I thought was an inordinate amount of time, but still, he didn't retract it. I wasn't usually rude—bad business—but it was my birthday, the big 3-0 (didn't I already say that?), and I preferred to be alone. Suffer in silence, all that shit. But I needed the money.

**Boy, did I need the money.**

I offered my hand.

**"Mister Stark."**

He took it, and I damn near jumped back.

His grip—to use an age-old-yet-relevant metaphor—was like a vice, but that wasn't the reason. In my business, my *sideline*, I'd grown accustomed to that kind of posturing. You know, the power plays these types enjoy.

But this guy's hand was cold—

And I mean *ice* cold.

Like I think I already said, it was September, and we'd been having a record hot spell. Still, it felt like that grinning son of a bitch had ice cubes in his pockets.

He released his grip and I unconsciously wiped my hand on my leg.

**"What can I do for you?"**

He kept smiling. He had perfect teeth. *Model's* teeth.

**"Well, to get right to the point, I understand that you take pictures."**

I looked at the many framed photos on the wall and then back at him.

**"What was your first clue, Mister Holmes?"**

He kept smiling, seemingly amused by my drunken sarcasm.

**"I meant your own pictures."**

I didn't know how he knew that. I'd never told anyone—not even the preferred customers—but somehow, *he* knew.

The displayed pictures weren't mine. What I'd done—and I'm sure I wasn't the first—was take photos from the more prestigious magazines, re-shoot and develop them, and hang them on the wall claiming them as my own. I figured in this part of town, no one would know. It was a harmless ruse.

Still... somehow, he *knew*.

**"What do you mean?"** I asked, the question sounding as lame as it actually was.

He smiled even wider and lazily strolled over to the framed photos, studying them with those frigid hands clasped behind his back.

**"What I'm interested in is..."**

He glanced over his shoulder at me, still smiling.

**"Discreet pictures."**

I knew what he meant.

But I asked anyway.

**"Who sent you?"**

He didn't answer.

Instead, he kept studying the bogus photos, his smile never wavering. I remember sighing and pouring another shot, not bothering to offer him one.

**"I'm not in that line of work anymore."**

He didn't look at me, apparently satisfied just to study the photos—pausing even to straighten one.

**"What line of work would that be?"**

I was about to drink, but stopped short.

He could've been a cop. And I figured I'd better keep my head clear.

**"I do portraits now. Just portraits."**

He turned to me, looking genuinely surprised.

**"Really?"**

I nodded—then noticed he no longer looked amused.

Instead, he shrugged, pulled a cigarette case from his inside pocket, and sat down.

**"There really isn't any reason to be concerned, Eddie,"** he said, easily striking a match with one hand. I could smell the sulfur even from across the room.

**"I'm not a cop."**

He lit what looked like a home-rolled cigarette and exhaled.

A surprising amount of smoke, I thought.

Then he dropped the match to the floor.

**"Besides, I'm not interested in kiddie porn."**

I remember bristling at that.

Yeah, those were lean years. And yes, I *do* apologize. But business is business.

No need to bring it up—and certainly not from someone who just walked in off the street.

He raised a hand as if sensing the offense he'd caused.

**"Now don't go getting yourself in a lather,"** he said, flicking his ashes beside the spent match.

**"I didn't mean anything by it. Like I said, I'm not interested in that."**

He took a long drag on his cigarette. The smoke swirled—filling the room more than it should have.

**"Not anymore,"** he added.

"What are you interested in, Mister Stark?"

He looked at me as if the answer were obvious.

"Passport photos."

I have to admit—that answer threw me for a loop.

Sure, I'd done some bullshit I.D. in the past—

Okay, if the truth be known, it was *half* my trade—

But this guy, the one with the easy smile and the casual attitude, didn't fit the profile.

And once again, I figured something was up.

It had to be some kind of sting. A set-up.

Well, shit—

If he was gonna play, then so was I.

"Passport photos?"

He nodded.

"Yes. Passport photos."

"Why?"

He looked confused.

"Why what?"

"Why me?" I answered.

"You can just hop on down to the post office for that."

I tossed back the shot—finally feeling comfortable enough to do so.

It tasted even more bitter than the last.

He looked amused.

"Well, my clientele—"

"Clientele?"

He suddenly stopped smiling—

Apparently angered by what he perceived to be a rude interruption.

Smoke drifted from his slightly parted lips—

Only now, somehow, it appeared as if it were coming from somewhere *beside* his lungs.

Someplace *hotter*.

And even from across the room, I noticed an acrid smell.

Like burning leaves.

(*Or flesh.*)

And then, all at once, his smile reappeared—

As if he'd heard and appreciated my thoughts.

Maybe even *enjoyed* them.

"Let's just say that I..."

He searched for the right word.

"Represent them."

Business was lousy—

(I think I said that before too)—

Otherwise, I wouldn't have indulged his bullshit song-and-dance routine.

I mean, it was obvious he knew my reputation. Knew how I sometimes made a living.

Hell, he even knew my *nickname*. So I couldn't figure out why he wanted to play this game.

Maybe he enjoyed it.

Maybe he'd grown *used* to it.

I didn't know.

What I *did* know—from too many years of experience—was that I'd have to play too.

"You're an agent, then?"

He stopped in mid-drag, and this time, his smile appeared genuine.

"Exactly."

I sighed and sat back down.

"You said 'clientele.'"

He nodded.

"Yes."

"That implies more than one."

He chuckled.

"A lot more, yes."

He hadn't put away his cigarette case and now extended it to me.

Even though I hadn't smoked in two years, I accepted.

*Playing the game.*

"Thank you."

He snapped the case closed without offering me a light I didn't have.

"Most welcome."

I supposed this was his way of getting even for me not offering him a drink.

But like I said—it wasn't anything I was going to let get to me.

I'd kicked that filthy habit, and so I merely dropped the cigarette into the wastebasket beside my desk.

"So how hot are these people of yours?"

At this, he laughed out loud and didn't stop until a coughing jag kicked in,

Forcing him to drop the cigarette.

At the time, I didn't know what prompted such a reaction.

Unfortunately...

I do now.

"Hot," he said, catching his breath and wiping a tear from one eye,

"Very, *very* hot."

\* \* \* \*

My usual price (yes, I had done this before—many times. *Hard times*) was a hundred, but I told Stark it would run him five hundred a session. To my surprise, he eagerly agreed— apparently expecting a much higher price.

And I could still kick myself for that.

Stark explained that I could expect my first appointment, as he put it, at eight the following morning.

**Eight sharp.**

He further informed me that she was in her mid-twenties and that I was to ask her **no questions**.

No questions—and I agreed.

After all, that was pretty much standard procedure. And even if it weren't, I doubted she could tell me anything I wanted to hear—or hadn't heard already.

Stark nodded, handed me an envelope (good faith money, as he called it), and again extended a hand, flashing those perfect teeth.

I have to admit, I was wary of shaking that freon-cold hand again—and sensing this, I think he even smiled wider.

Still, the game was afoot. And according to the rules, you don't refuse a challenge.

You don't back down. You don't look away.

And you *don't* end a business transaction without shaking hands.

No.

That would be a breach of etiquette.

I took it.

His eyes met mine. His smile froze.

And he squeezed my hand until I grimaced.

Until I thought he was actually going to *break* it.

He pulled me closer, leaned to my ear, and said quietly—*evenly*:

**"No questions."**

\* \* \*

I usually open at nine—give or take, depending on the amount of booze the night before.

But that morning, I opened at seven.

Now, I'd had more than my share of dealings with underworld figures—*sorry to say*—but this guy Stark made me nervous.

145

There was something about him. I didn't know what.

But I *knew* that my ass had better be there come eight.

It was the kind of deal where you made sure the I's were dotted and the T's crossed—if you know what I mean.

I figured I'd play solitaire to pass the time—no cards.

I figured I'd read the paper—not here yet.

I figured I'd listen to the radio—batteries were dead.

Another great start to what was sure to be another *great* day.

There was nothing left to do but watch the clock and twiddle my thumbs—both of which I actually caught myself doing.

Well, at eight o'clock—**sharp**—there was a gentle knock on the window.

So soft I wasn't even sure I'd heard it until I glanced over.

Behind the backward lettering on the door, a plain-looking woman offered a small wave.

But unlike Stark, she didn't smile.

I waved her in and she stepped inside, seeming to take a momentary interest in the doorknob—as if the design confused her.

I didn't really notice it at first, but she looked... *out of place.*

I mean, she was wearing an out-of-date dress—like something out of the 1900s—that failed to hide what used to be called a *sturdy build.*

And in my professional opinion, could've greatly benefited from a liberal amount of makeup.

Like I said—she looked out of place.

**Out of time**, really.

And without a word, she walked over to the counter and stopped—

Merely staring at me with a vacant expression.

A look that, I don't know...

Made you feel somehow uneasy.

**"Can I help you, Miss...?"**

She offered no response, and I nodded.

We were still playing games.

I wearily picked up a notepad and a pencil.

**"Okay. So what do you want to be called?"**

No answer.

A vacant stare.

I slumped.

I was getting too old and tired for this shit.

**"Did Mister Stark send you?"**

Again, I was greeted with that look.

A cat eyeing a mouse.

Now, I know it's not what you'd call gallant these days, but this chick's attitude had really gotten on my nerves.

And frankly, if she'd woken up that morning craving an ass-kicking, she'd come to the right place.

**"Look, lady—if you plan on doing business, start talking. If not, the door's right behind you."**

She stared.

I waited.

Finally, she reached into her purse—an antique, I thought absently—and held out a business card.

I took it.

It read:

**MISTER STARK PROUDLY INTRODUCES CLARA BEACHUM**

*1981 Stewert Street*

*New York City, New York*

**Born: 6–14–98**

**Brown Hair, Brown Eyes**

**Sex: Female**

**Height: 5'4"**

**Weight: 110 pounds**

**Destination: Florence, Italy**

**No Corrective Lenses Needed**

I held it up.

**"So this is you?"**

She said nothing—and I figured it was pointless.

I pushed away from the counter.

**"Okay. Let's do it."**

She followed.

\* \* \* \*

The photo shoot took only a minute or two.

After all, you just sit them down with the appropriate background color and click.

Done and over.

You don't pose them, don't light them—none of that shit.

The fact is, you want it to look as amateurish as possible.

Still—

As any good photographer will tell you—things look different through the lens.

People.

Places.

Things.

They all seem to acquire a new perspective.

And depending on the photographer, that perspective can range from the mundane to the abstract.

As I looked through my own lens,

**Clara Beachum**—or whatever her real name was—

**Took on a new look.**

A familiar look.

Years ago, I'd shelled out two hundred and forty bucks on a memory course

(*In my business, having a good memory can come in handy—especially should a plea bargain become necessary*)—

and one of the tricks I learned was to associate a face with a song.

And when I looked through that lens, a song immediately sprang to mind.

Well, not really a song—a jingle, I guess you'd call it.

One of those irritating commercial jingles that sticks in your head and stubbornly refuses to leave.

**Something about Florsheim Wax**, I thought.

Anyway, like I said, the session didn't take long.

I told her that developing—and let's face it, doctoring up—her phony passport would take at least twenty-four hours.

At this, she merely maintained that weird, vacant, yet-somehow-unnerving stare,

passed me an envelope,

then turned, walked across the room, and out the door without looking back.

And without ever saying a word.

**"That is one strange broad..."**

I stuffed the envelope into my back pocket.

* * * *

Completing the passport took much longer than I had anticipated.

Sure, I had the equipment—this wasn't exactly my first foray into this kind of thing—

but the developing turned out to be a royal pain in the ass.

For whatever reason, the prints came out with a yellowish cast that I couldn't explain.

I mean, the developer and fixer were new—I'd just cracked the seals—

and the plates and paper were fresh out of the box.

Before I'd started, I made sure the lenses on the camera and printer were clean.

And that's what pissed me off.

Everything should've been perfect.

But every damn print looked washed out.

**Like they were a hundred years old.**

Well, I'm a professional, and since I'd already *accepted* the money, I kept at it.

Finally—using overexposure and a couple of drops of bleach—I managed to get a manageable print.

Good enough, anyway.

*(Florsheim Wax?)*

I found the blank passport folders where I'd left them—behind the bogus driver's licenses

(not much call for those anymore—used to be pretty damn lucrative)—

and set about the tedious task of reducing the shot, slicing and pasting,

before I began the ridiculously long search for the counterfeit stamps

that eventually turned up in a bottom drawer marked *Address Labels.*

*(Florsheim Wax?)*

Like it always did, piecing together a passport took time,

even though customs agents and members of their ilk usually give them only a cursory glance.

Still—if you wanted to stay in my line of work, or *alive* for that matter—

you'd better make sure they're as legit-looking as possible.

So I tried to focus.

Tried to concentrate on what I was doing.

But that damn jingle kept running through my head.

Something I just couldn't shake.

**(Florsheim Wax.)**

**(Florsheim Wax.)**

**(Florsheim Wax.)**

I picked up the final stamp, plopped it into the ink pad beside me,

and wondered what in the hell—

And then I froze.

I still remember my eyes widening

and the stamp slipping through my fingers,

leaving a messy stain on my pants before clattering to the floor.

At that moment, I couldn't move.

I couldn't even catch my breath.

I could see her face

—even though I was no longer looking at the photo.

I didn't need it now.

Because I had seen that face before.

While I was studying photography in junior college,

Professor Madsen had presented a photo to the class—

a photo *of her*—to remind us just how far photography had come in the last hundred years.

It was an example, he said, of poor lighting, poor staging—

in fact, everything I had done earlier that day.

The photo was passed around like countless others in his monotonous class—

until it came to me.

As I looked at it—not particularly interested in whatever newspaper Madsen said it first appeared in—

the guy beside me

(I think his name was Wyatt, I don't know, something like that) leaned over and recited a rhyme to me in a sing-song manner.

As I told you before,

**associating a memory with a specific song can greatly enhance an opportunity for recall.**

Only it wasn't a song.

It wasn't a jingle.

It wasn't Florsheim Wax.

**(Took an axe...)**

I fell back in my seat.

Even though I could feel my lips working, I don't remember hearing the words.

All I remember is staring at the picture.

**Her picture.**

**Her eyes.**

"Lizzie Borden... took an axe...

And gave her mother... forty whacks...

And when she saw... what she had done...

She gave her father... forty... one..."

\* \* \* \*

**"Is there a problem?"**

Stark smiled, smoke rolling from his lips as he crossed his legs.

**"Yeah,"** I said, my voice barely audible.

I felt both hot and cold, clutching at myself even as sweat poured down my face and soaked through my shirt.

**"I know who she is..."**

**"And?"** was all he said, casually flicking ashes to the floor.

I shook my head. Or maybe I was trembling.

**"How…?"**

**"You ever heard of prison overcrowding, Mister Collier?"**

**"Prison overcrowding?"** I echoed, uncomprehending.

He stood.

Even though he didn't make a move toward me, I took a step back.

**"It's the same where—"**

He paused. Smiled wider.

**"—I come from."**

I suddenly felt weak.

And even though I already suspected the answer—and didn't want to hear it—I asked:

**"Where you come from?"**

He strolled easily to the window and closed the Venetian blinds.

Then he pulled the shade over the door.

I stiffened when I heard him lock the deadbolt.

Then he turned to face me.

**"It's not like the old days,"** he said, his teeth gleaming in the dim light.

**"Back then, you didn't need I.D. You could pretty much come and go as you pleased."**

He took a long drag from his cigarette. His eyes never left mine.

**"Isn't that right, Eddie?"**

I shuddered.

Said nothing.

He continued.

**"But times change. Nowadays, you need a driver's license. A Social Security card. And..."**

He looked at me then.

The kind of look that makes you *see* blood.

**"Passports."**

I couldn't breathe.

That acrid smoke seared my lungs and made my eyes water.

He looked amused.

**"Which brings us back to prison overcrowding."**

He took one last puff and tossed the butt to the floor, grinding it out beneath one well-polished wingtip.

**"I mean... there's only so much room in hell."**

My legs gave out.

My head swam.

And just before I fainted, I heard him say,

**"Isn't that right, Eddie?"**

* * * *

It's been over a month now, and business has never been better.

You figure—one a day at five hundred a pop—and it won't be long before I can think about expanding.

I've already got my eye on a shop over on King Street.

Still... I can't help but feel a little guilty.

I mean, it *is* partially my fault they're back on the streets again.

But I can't really be to blame, right?

A guy has to make a living—

155

(or a killing)—

Doesn't he?

If I hadn't done it, somebody else would've.

Right?

Am I right?

Well anyway—

From what I understand, **Jack the Ripper** will be in at three o'clock tomorrow.

At least that's what I've got penciled in here.

So I guess come three o'clock—*sharp*—

I'll finally know what he looks like.

And from the itinerary Stark provided...

**Heaven help me...**

**So will a great many women in Japan.**

# JUST FOLLOW THE DIRECTIONS

Even though his friends called him Charlie (as in *Good-time Charlie*), his name was actually **John Jackson**, and he was on his way to L.A., cutting a nice swath across the country in his '77 Delta 88.

He had gotten the job out of the blue—if you could consider twelve years plugging away at it "out of the blue"—and was now finally headed to Hollywood to work with his director-slash-hero, **Wes Pollock**. All those years of bullshit film school, all those years of bullshit spec scripts and short films, rarely viewed but always returned, all those years of by-and-large ignored and unopened resumes had finally paid off.

The pre-mo director in DreamLand wanted **John "Charlie" Jackson** as his personal assistant.

He was on his way, alright.

He was finally on his way.

**Maybe.**

See, at the moment, Charlie was parked on the side of the freeway with a map in his lap that he couldn't read up-down-north-south-east-and-or-west. All he was really sure of was that he was somewhere in Arizona with two hundred and fifty dollars in the glove box and he was—

"—fucking lost…"

He lowered the map and with a resigned sigh looked around the landscape.

Sure, the desert could be beautiful, but sometimes—like now—it was just as disorienting as all get out.

"Where the fuck am I...?"

The situation wasn't completely hopeless. He wasn't in the *middle* of nowhere—

at least not what most would consider the middle of nowhere. There was a steady stream of cars, and he supposed that just a few miles down the road there would be all kinds of fast-food joints like there are on almost every freeway. If he had to, he could just drive on down the road, find an exit, and ask for directions.

It seemed simple enough.

But the fact was, he had done *just* that this morning—

and it had taken him nearly three hours just to find his way back to the freeway he was *currently* stuck on.

He didn't want to risk it again.

And although he knew that these days most folks had cell phones, he also knew it was damn unlikely anyone was going to stop for some long-haired kid in a rusted-out car.

Still, there was one alternative.

And it wasn't twenty yards behind him, nestled in the gravel lot at the side of the road.

But—*shit*—he didn't want to go in there.

Not the way he looked.

Sure, he was white. Don't ever think that doesn't get you *some* slack.

But the rednecks that had to be hanging out inside weren't going to be tolerant about the length of his hair or the tattoo on his right arm—an homage to his high school buddies that said simply:

**THE BOYS.**

He didn't have a coat (well, he had one in the trunk, but he'd play hell getting to it), and the tank top he was wearing showed said homage in all its glory.

If he walked in there, they'd figure he was just some hippy faggot.

But damned if he didn't have a whole hell of a lot of choice.

He gently rapped his head against the steering wheel.

**"Oh shit…"**

After locking his car—a self-deluding pretense at best—he started across the street, dodging the cars that wouldn't stop when he was moving, thereby cementing his earlier assumption that they sure as hell wouldn't have stopped for him when he wasn't.

Having run the gauntlet, he looked up at the building and let out a heavy, mental sigh. It was a redneck joint all right, no doubt about it. A two-story, striking white gas station that was also part hotel, part restaurant, and part curio shop—but one that did have its own folksy kind of charm.

A real slice of honest-to-goodness Americana.

**Unless you were a long-haired, lost hippy faggot with a tattoo.**

He went inside.

The smell of homemade chili wafted from the adjoining kitchen as Charlie entered the curio shop portion of the building, and if he had felt more comfortable about his current surroundings, he might have wanted to hang for a while. There was interesting shit everywhere—not the least of which was a counter up front that displayed what the sign claimed were **authentic Indian artifacts**. They were all animals that lived, or *used to* live, in the area, and dangled from horsehair looped over the rafters, gently swaying in the breeze from the rotating fan propped on an antique Coke machine.

These bone carvings—or at least that's what they appeared to be—were neatly arranged, beautifully rendered, and whether the handwritten advertising was true or not, the fact was, these pieces were **spellbinding**.

Charlie neared to closer examine them when he heard the woman's voice.

"I help you?"

He looked up. The old woman was watching him. She sat in a wicker chair, a cigarette dangling from her gloss-white lips, and appeared to be **older than dirt**. He had expected attitude when he walked in, but her expression wasn't just dismissive. It was genuine **contempt**.

No.

It was more than that.

She was looking at him like...

"I said, help you?"

He didn't respond for a moment—the dangling ornaments had stolen his attention—then looked down to her.

"I'm sorry?"

The Old Woman looked him up and down as if taking his innocent question as an apology.

"What do you want?"

Charlie glanced around the small shop again, seeming to find a new curiosity in every corner—some forgotten treasure left here to be discovered. This was the kind of place that turned seemingly rational people into mole-like collectors who browsed darkened little alcoves until their eyesight and, stereotypically, their sanity were gone.

But for the first time in his life, he was beginning to understand such behavior.

"This place is something else…"

She didn't remove the cigarette when she spoke, didn't even bother to knock off the inch-long ash.

"What do you want?"

Charlie looked back at her.

"Oh. I need directions."

Again she looked him up and down with that same unreadable expression.

"That's what you need?"

If he'd had a hat, he would have removed it and wrung it in his hands. She was one of those people that had that peculiar effect on others—the old-school-down-on-the-plantation-types. A dying breed to be sure, but this woman was still alive, somehow, and judging by her demeanor, still fully capable of kicking.

Charlie didn't have a hat, so he just did his best to look uncomfortable.

"Well, yes ma'am."

161

It seemed, after all, the appropriate response.

Again the Old Woman gave him that appraising look—as if she were committing him to memory. Or sizing him up.

"Spilly!"

He wasn't sure what that barked command meant until half-a-second later a man in a red-striped shirt stepped from the kitchen, wiping his hands on his apron.

"Yeah, Ma?"

She distastefully motioned at Charlie, and the man—Spilly—glanced at him, seemingly surprised to find someone else in the room. He also looked him up and down.

(An increasingly disturbing way to be greeted, Charlie thought.)

Then Spilly offered a wide smile—with a truly **remarkable** amount of teeth—and extended a hand.

"How you doin' today?"

For the first time since he'd walked in—actually before he'd walked in—Charlie felt relaxed and took the hand offered to him.

"Well, actually I'm lost."

Spilly had a strong, vigorous handshake, and when he talked, his smile never wavered and his eyes never left Charlie's.

"Lost, huh? Well, we'll just have to see what we can do about that."

He continued to shake Charlie's hand but, as he did, his free hand ran up and down Charlie's arm—**squeezing it softly**.

"By the by, folks call me Spilly and I own the place. Just in case you didn't see the sign out front."

The fact was, Charlie didn't notice any sign out front. He wasn't even sure it *was* a business at first—and if it hadn't been for the cars and trucks out in the lot (and the location, of course), he probably would've just kept going, holding out for one of those fast-food joints a little farther up the road.

Another fact was that Spilly was in very real danger of shaking off Charlie's hand.

"Nice to meet you. My name's John but,"

he finally managed to free himself,

"most people call me Charlie."

This seemed to briefly puzzle Spilly, then he smiled wider—something Charlie didn't think was physically possible.

"There must be an interesting story behind that."

Charlie shook his head.

"No. Not really."

"Well, live and learn, that's what I always say."

Spilly took him by the arm and gently guided him toward the restaurant.

"Why don't you step on in here and we'll see if we can't get you cookin'."

Charlie wasn't so sure he wanted to step inside that restaurant. There had been no one but the Old Woman in the curio shop, so the owners of all those vehicles—the ones with the lifted suspensions and *definitely* with the gun racks—had to be in there. Probably elbow-deep in bowls of that incredible-smelling chili, working up the strength and appetite to pound the shit out of someone who looked exactly like him.

Still, he allowed Spilly to lead him inside.

And sure enough—every ass-kicking, redneck trucker he'd imagined was sitting right there.

In fact, if his future boss had asked him to build a set and cast the extras himself, he couldn't have done a better job. Every one of them—every mother's son—was exactly where Charlie envisioned them. Perched on stools at the counter, flabby legs wrapped around chrome stems, flannel shirts tucked into jeans that hadn't seen a washing machine in at least a week.

Some glanced lazily at the wall-length mirror behind the bar that doubled as a beer advertisement. Others kept their eyes fixed on the pie display like it held answers to life's biggest questions.

But none of them looked at each other.

And every one of them was looking **right at him**.

Charlie glanced at the diners. None of them had looked up since he walked in. Same posture, same grip on their spoons, same methodical scooping and chewing. Like they were running on auto-pilot.

Or worse, like they were all **waiting** for something.

He cleared his throat, trying not to let the unease show.

"No really, I'm okay. I should probably get back on the road."

Spilly tilted his head, not unlike a crow sizing up roadkill.

"Long drive ahead. Sure you don't want to fuel up first?"

There was something odd in the way he said *fuel up*.

Like he wasn't talking about food at all.

Charlie offered a tight smile, standing from the stool, "I'll be all right. Appreciate the directions, though."

Spilly gave a slow nod, still smiling. "Well, just don't say I didn't offer."

He pulled a small notepad from beneath the counter and scribbled something, tearing the page and handing it over.

"Here. In case you forget the turns. That road can get… windy."

Charlie took the paper. Spilly's handwriting was neat. Almost *too* neat. Like the script of someone who hadn't written anything impulsive in decades.

Right at the fork.

Left at the lone cactus.

Stay on the gravel.

When you see the old windmill, **don't stop.**

Keep going.

**No matter what.**

Charlie blinked.

"What's that last part?"

Spilly waved a dismissive hand and chuckled.

"Oh, you know how folks are around here. Superstitious. Lotta stories about coyotes pretending to be people, lights in the desert, ghost trains—small-town nonsense."

Charlie didn't laugh.

Spilly leaned in, lowering his voice.

"But just between us… if you see anything weird, keep going. That road don't like hesitation."

There was a pause.

And then, as if someone hit the un-pause button on the world, the scraping of spoons against bowls resumed in perfect rhythm. Charlie looked around. No one had looked up. No one had moved.

He folded the note, slid it into his back pocket, and nodded once.

"Right. Thanks."

Spilly tapped two fingers to his temple. "Safe travels… Charlie."

Charlie turned to leave, but the moment he touched the doorknob, Spilly called after him one last time.

"Oh—and don't forget to reset your trip meter. Wouldn't want you to lose your way again."

Charlie didn't answer. He stepped out into the sunlight and suddenly, the air felt colder than it had been just ten minutes before.

Charlie took the bowl with a smile, but somewhere between his fingers and the ceramic, the warmth of the chili pot crept higher up his arms than it should've. Like the heat had hands. Still, he didn't pull away.

He took another bite. Maybe a little too fast.

"Damn," he muttered, "this *is* good."

Spilly chuckled behind the counter, folding his arms and leaning forward like a proud cook watching a kid enjoy his first home-cooked meal in months.

"That's the thing about chili," he said, tapping a long nail against the wood, "It gets better the deeper you go."

Charlie wiped his mouth with the back of his hand, chuckling, "Yeah well… you're gonna have to roll me outta here."

"You'd be surprised," Spilly said. His voice had shifted just slightly—lower, quieter. Like he was talking to the chili more than to Charlie.

"Most folks walk out of here just fine. Least the first time."

Charlie paused, mid-bite.

First time?

Spilly saw it. Saw the brief flicker of hesitation, the crease in Charlie's brow.

And he smiled that same steady smile.

"You never know when you'll be passing through again."

Charlie laughed, easing the tension. "Yeah, right. I guess it'd be one hell of a detour just for chili."

Spilly didn't laugh this time. He looked Charlie dead in the eye.

"Well, it depends on what's waiting on the other side."

Charlie froze.

Only for a second. But it was long enough. He wiped his mouth, set the spoon down, and gave a final nod. "I'd better get going."

Spilly nodded, slowly.

"Sure. Wouldn't want you missing your... big chance."

There was something strange in the way he said *chance*. Like it had quotation marks around it.

Charlie stood, dusted himself off, and turned to the door. The napkin directions still crinkled in his back pocket, a faint warmth pulsing from it like it had soaked in the heat of the chili. The patrons were still eating. Same posture. Same grip. Same mechanical scooping.

None of them looked up.

Not once.

"Thanks again," Charlie said, trying not to sound like he was in a hurry. "Really."

Spilly didn't say goodbye.

He just stood there with his arms folded and that all-knowing grin as Charlie pushed open the door and stepped into the late afternoon sun.

* * * *

Charlie followed the directions and found himself at the end of a dead-end dirt road, deep in the middle of nowhere—face to face with Spilly's father, who sat comfortably in a rocking chair. The old man ended Charlie's life with a single shot to the head.

Cousin Ned—who had a part-time job changing the road signs on the freeway—also owned a garage and salvage yard. And even though he had little use for a 30-year-old Delta, he towed it away as a favor to the family.

Spilly, of course, handled the butchering, careful not to scratch the bones so that his mother—a full-blooded Arapaho—would have suitable carving material. He also saved the scalp. Hair that long would be perfect for hanging the bone carvings on display.

And then there was the meat…

* * * *

Nibbles Tricket, a trucker out of Barstow, looked down into his bowl and said, "Hey Spilly? Come on over here."

With his usual wide grin, Spilly complied. "What can I do for ya, Nibbles?"

He pointed into the bowl. "There's somethin' wrong with this meat."

"Aw now, there ain't nothin' wrong with that meat." Spilly leaned over the counter to get a better look. "We choose only the best."

"Then why is that piece there blue?"

"Must be the USDA stamp."

"The what?"

Spilly leaned back and smiled wider. "Kinda like a meat tattoo. You can eat it. Won't do you no harm."

Nibbles poked at the piece with his spoon for a second, then scooped it up. "If you say so…"

Spilly kept smiling as Nibbles shoveled it in. "See? Now there you go."

Nibbles nodded. "Y'know, my wife makes chili—but it ain't nothin' like this. What's your secret?"

"Well hell, I'll write down the ingredients for you."

Nibbles looked surprised. "You'd do that?"

Spilly pulled a napkin from the pile and took out a pen. "Why sure." He started writing. "The hardest part is gettin' the right ingredients. Once you got 'em, it's just a hop, skip, and a jump to the pot."

He finished scribbling, slid the pen away, and handed the napkin over with a grin that somehow stretched even wider.

"Now you pay attention to that," Spilly said, "and you'll be just fine."

**"Just follow the directions."**

# NICE TO SEE YOU AGAIN

At precisely 7 p.m., the switch clicked, the lights blazed to life, the doors swung wide, and Julienne's officially opened its doors.

Tonight's dinner was by invitation only, and just the cream of New York's elite were here. It was black tie, of course, and every guest was ushered to their seats by an over-paid, well-groomed waiter who offered chairs to the ladies and polite nods and smiles to the gentlemen. As the menus were passed and the candles lit, the owner – Oscar Julienne – watched from the balcony overhead and smiled. This had been his dream since he was a boy growing up in the Bronx. A dream that was a long time coming.

A dream *finally* realized.

**A dream built on a lifetime of nightmares.**

Until just a year ago, Julienne was a professional killer—call it hit-man, hired gun, "mechanic," whatever suited you. He wasn't cheap, but his record was spotless: not once had he failed to finish a job. Maybe that success was simple—he loved the work. Vaporizing roaches and nobodies for a thick envelope of cash beat any other ticket out of the neighborhood, and the steady money let him leave the ghetto—and the people he despised—far behind. Could life get sweeter? Back then, he would've said no. Yet here he was now, exactly where he'd always felt he belonged.

With his *own* kind.

**The elite.**

With an exaggerated flourish, he straightened and picked up an oversized silver spoon that he had made for this very occasion. With a flourish he'd spent a lifetime rehearsing, Julienne tapped his crystal glass against the champagne punchbowl—sharp, deliberate raps that rang through the room. When the murmur below stilled, he lifted the glass high, flashing a wolfish grin.

"Ladies and gentlemen," he declared, "I am Oscar Julienne, and it is my profound pleasure to welcome you to my establishment!"

The silence that followed was thunderous.

Julinne froze. His smile fell. His glass hovered.

There was no roar of approval. None of the applause or the clinking of glasses that he had anticipated. There was nothing at all. It didn't make sense.

What was happening here? Where was the celebration of his lifetime achievement? Didn't these people realize the enormous favor he was doing by simply inviting them here? How privileged they should feel just to be at this event? They should be on their knees in gratitude to have even been considered for this honor.

Instead, below him, the guests merely sat in front of empty plates, blandly sipped from their glasses, and engaged in what he could only assume were meaningless conversations.

Julienne bristled. This was his night. The night he had waited for his entire life. What he had *worked* for his entire life! And suddenly, a comment from one of his former employers – Nino Carbelleri – came to mind. Though he had personally fitted him with cement shoes and sunk him in the bay, the man did have a way with words. And this particular remark seemed especially relevant now.

"Be loved, be hated, but don't be ignored."

Words to live by.

(Or die by.)

Julienne exaggeratedly cleared his throat and shouted in a loud, clear voice, "Excuse me! I don't believe you heard me!"

Although not a single guest looked in his direction, a faraway voice came from the room's darkest corner. "We heard you."

Julienne stiffened. Nobody did this to him. No-fucking-body. He had planned this event for over a year. Had sought out and invited only the very best. Had made sure that every paper in town knew that this would be *the* event of the year. And dammit, it was going to be! Nobody snubbed Oscar Julienne! Not anymore and never again! He had spent his entire fortune on this place. Every fucking dime he had ever earned – all of his blood money – was right here in front of him, and he wasn't going to sit on his ass and watch it go down the proverbial drain.

Unlike his previous life, Julienne kept his rage in check, but with gritted teeth, he made his way downstairs.

By the time he descended to the main floor, Julienne had regained his composure. He reminded himself: the killing days were finished. If he meant to belong here, he needed a new posture—something smoother, genial.

173

Drawing a steady breath, he adjusted his tuxedo jacket, let a practiced smile settle on his face, and stepped into the dining room. He paused to straighten his bow tie, then approached the nearest table. With a courteous pat on the diner's shoulder, he said, "Good evening. How are you tonight?"

The man flinched away from his touch. Even behind the incongruous sunglasses he wore indoors, Julienne could sense the distaste in his stare.

"Why are you touching me?" the patron asked, voice icy.

Being unaccustomed to apologizing, Jullienne briefly looked confused.

"I'm sorry. I just wanted to thank you for - "

The man roughly pushed Jullieen's hand away and said, "Well, you have done so, and now you can leave."

This man – whoever he was – had no idea who he was talking to. Julienne had killed a hundred like him and never batted an eye. This asshole was like every mother-fucker with money. Thinking they were better than him. That they were somehow on another plain. The kind of shit who thought that just because they had lived a privileged life, he was somehow above him. This prick was just like -

Jullienne froze as icy fingers suddenly tickled up his spine, and he squinted.

All of a sudden, this guy looked somewhat familiar to him. Very familiar.

Julienne's gaze flicked, skimming his memory like pages in a flipped book. Then—recognition. His eyes snapped wide.

174

Five years ago, he was sent out on a job. To visit a garment merchant who didn't want to pay the tax. A small Jewish man who attempted to unite the other local businesses against his then-boss. Well, a little after midnight, he and his partner – Arnie something – had slipped in through the back door of his shop and found him alone in his office doing the books. They then duct-taped him to his chair and suggested that he should mind his own business if you get the meaning. He didn't. Shit, the old man didn't even appear to be threatened but instead said to them that no matter what they did, he wasn't going to close his eyes to what was going on in his neighborhood.

So that's when Julienne took the ice-pick from his inside coat pocket and gouged them out.

He had done it before – just a job - but he remembered this because the old man didn't scream. Can you believe that? Not even a whimper. Instead, he continued to stare at him – at least in his direction – the blood and pus spilling down his face until he bled to death.

This guy in front of him looked just like that old man, and Julienne felt an overwhelming urge to pull off those sunglasses and see if there were still eyes behind them.

Julienne gave a brisk shake of his head. "I'm sorry… sir."

The man snorted and groped across the linen until his fingers closed around a water glass. "You never called me 'sir' before."

"Before?" Julienne's brow furrowed.

"We've met," the patron said, still refusing eye contact. "You came into my shop once."

Julienne leaned in, voice low. "Shop?"

Again, the man nodded, "I had a small shop at one time."

Julienne looked curious, but he wasn't sure he wanted the answer even as he voiced his question. "What kind of shop would that be?"

The man waved a dismissing hand, "It's not important. I've since moved on." And with that, he turned back to his dinner companion -

Julieene looked over and found his eyes widen again.

It was Myra. Myra Bingham.

He would have recognized her even in the dark. He had dated her – if you call the occasional suck and fuck a date – for two years. She had been a call girl out of O'Rielly's stable until he found her going through his books and had Julienne put a bullet in her head. That had been a tricky one – no prep time – and had barely gotten the body out of the office before the rent-a-cops came back from their donut-break.

Damned if she didn't look like Myra. Even more so when she smiled and raised her glass. "How have you been, Julienne?"

This couldn't be right. This couldn't be happening. It didn't make any sense, and he didn't even realize that he had begun backing away until he nearly tripped over the little girl behind him, who held up a small wicker basket filled with roses. "Care for a flower for the lady?"

He could feel his eyes widen again. He remembered this kid. She had been outside Mickey's Pub when he opened up on the old Stellman gang. That had been one messy hit, a bloody fucking mess, and she had been caught in the crossfire when she unexpectedly stepped from the bathroom. That was the first and only kid he'd ever killed.

But here she was, standing not a foot away, offering him a dead rose. She smiled even wider and a trickle of blood spilled over her lip. "They're only a dollar."

Julienne lurched backward, colliding with the next table.

"Hey! Watch where you're going, Mac!" a voice barked.

Mac. Only one man ever had the nerve to call him that.

Julienne swung around—and slapped a hand over his mouth. There, blotting at fresh wine stains on his trousers, sat Timber Goldberg.

Impossible. Two years ago, Julienne had kicked in the door of Goldberg's dingy apartment, jammed a shotgun between the old man's teeth, and blown the top of his head clean off.

And here he was. There was no mistake. He not only recognized the voice but he was just the way he left him. There was literally nothing above his nose. Just exposed gray tissue.

Julienne couldn't look away. He couldn't catch his breath.

"What's going on here...?"

He spun in a circle, but everywhere he looked, there was someone he now recognized. His long-dead victims who finally smiled and raised their glasses in a toast. This was impossible, and he shook his head, "You can't be here!"

All at once, they stopped smiling and rose to their feet. Julienne stiffened and turned to the nearly headless man, who said simply, "But you invited us."

Julienne was trembling. He had never been afraid of anything in his life, but now he felt like he was about to shit his pants. "I didn't invite you..."

Goldberg corrected, his jaw gibbering, the rotting flesh barely holding it in place, "But you did."

Julienne vehemently shook his head, "I didn't!"

The little flower girl – who now sported several bullet holes in her tattered dress – nodded and said, "Yes, you did." Julienne looked down at her and into her now dead, white eyes, "You wanted to be one of the elite." She raised her hands, dropping the basket , and shrugged, "That's what *we* are."

Her small smile fell, and he could actually see her begin to rot before his eyes, "Or were."

Julienne turned and ran, but if they were pursuing, they were in no hurry. Probably because when he reached the front door, he found that someone had chained it closed. A heavy rusted chain that bore the inscription St. Angelo's Cemetery. Julienne desperately pulled at it, hoping they had sufficiently decayed enough that he might pull it apart and escape. But it held fast.

"This isn't the back door to a garment shop. You can't just pick the lock with a credit card." Julienne turned to find the blinded old man holding up a skeleton key, an appropriate choice considering his current appearance. He grinned, "You need to have the key."

Again, Julienne spun and ran. The only other way out of the restaurant was through the kitchen – straight through a room full of his zombie victims. Still, he continued on, failing to notice that, again, none of these walking corpses made any kind of move to stop him. Instead, they only giggled, lightly brushing his shoulders as he passed—like well-wishers parting for a returning war hero.

He burst through the double doors and skidded across the empty room -

*(Where were his employees? Where were the chefs? Where were the waiters?)*

Finally, falling flat against the closed back doors. Even more chains rattled as he fell against them. Only these were brand, spanking new, and read 'Property of the New York City Morgue.'

He didn't bother to tug on these but instead turned to find all of his uninvited guests filing in behind him. They hadn't bothered to stop him because there was nowhere for him to go. This was the end of the line.

Tears streamed down Julienne's face, and like so many, many of his victims had said to him over the years, "Why are you doing this...?"

The blind old man lurched closer, clothes still caked with grave-dirt, a skeletal finger crooking Julienne's way.

"You didn't think we'd skip your grand opening," he rasped, his grin writhing with maggots. "Did you?"

They advanced. He screamed.

*****

179

Patrolman Thomas was on his routine patrol, one that he actually enjoyed. It was a low-crime area, and he was usually greeted with waves and hellos instead of the crap often complained of by other officers in the station house. That's why it puzzled him to find the same Mercedes parked in front of Julienne's restaurant three nights in a row. Even if the car failed to start – as foreign cars, even such expensive ones – are prone to do, it should have been towed by now.

He made a U-turn and pulled to a stop behind it. He ran the usual checks, registration, license plates, etc., and found that it belonged to Oscar Julinne, owner of said restaurant, so he tried the front door and was surprised to find it open.

He entered, looked up – and promptly fainted.

****

A passerby spotted Thomas slumped behind the glass doors and, mistaking the crimson blossom on his shirt for a fresh gunshot wound, dialed the station in a panic. The dispatcher heard the words "officer down," and within five minutes, a dozen patrol cars screeched to a halt at the curb, lights strobing red-blue across the façade.

And not five minutes later, two dozen cops were seated on the curb outside, most with their heads between their legs, trying to catch their breath or keep their dinners down.

Only detectives Hacker and Cecerrelli were still on their feet, both figuratively and literally scratching their heads.

Because the restaurant was filled to capacity with long-dead corpses seated at their tables, seemingly strung together by miles of cobwebs. At first glance, it would appear that they had died at a party. They were all dressed to the nines,

180

their arms raised in frozen up-raised toasts and all of them smiling, as skulls are prone to do.

In the manager's office, there were several moldy invitations to very important people that had never been sent. In fact, they had been addressed and stamped but then apparently squirreled away in the desk's bottom drawer. According to the employee schedule posted against the wall, well, shit, no one was set to work. No one at all.

But what puzzled the detectives most of all and what accounted for the legion of policemen steeling themselves outside was what they found in the kitchen. Namely, a line of knives and meat cleavers covered in the victim's blood. The ones used to cut the owner into bite-sized pieces that were now being deep-fried in an oversized cauldron.

Though the case would never be fully solved, it did offer some twisted clarity regarding the chilling message scrawled in blood on the chalkboard menu in the foyer. The words, bold and unsettling, read:

**"Today's Special! Julienne Fries!"**

# THE TWILIGHT'S LAST...

A timid knock.

Corporal Benton leaned into the spacious—if somewhat Spartan—office.

"Sir? He's still outside."

General Irons sat behind his massive oak desk, the one luxury he allowed himself. Upon seeing the young man, he let out a sigh—long and well-practiced, the kind only perfected by a lifetime of chastising subordinates.

"How's your hearing these days, son?"

The Corporal blinked. "Sir?"

Irons made a circular gesture beside his head. "Your hearing, Corporal. Still functioning, is it?"

"Fine, sir."

"Then it must be the memory. Giving you trouble, is it?"

"No, sir."

Irons leaned forward, steel in his voice. "Seems like an either-or situation to me, Corporal. Either you didn't hear me tell you to get rid of the old man—" The Corporal winced. "—or you don't remember me telling you to get rid of the old man. So which is it?"

"Well, sir, we have had him escorted from the building before—"

Irons waved a hand, already exhausted. This guy in the outer office—some shriveled relic named Webbersmith—had been a burr in his side for a month. At first, they'd assumed he was just some harmless old fool who'd wandered off from a tour group. Then, inexplicably, he began showing up during off-limit hours. Gates locked. Cameras running. Armed sentries posted. And yet, there he was—always inside. Always asking for him.

A miracle weapon, the old man said. Some kind of top-secret tech only fit for the upper brass. And on this base, that meant Irons.

Lucky fucking him.

He rubbed his temples. "Fine. Show him in, Corporal."

Less than a minute later, the door opened again. Webbersmith shuffled in, hunched over a cane that looked older than he did.

"If you'll have a seat, sir," the Corporal said.

Webbersmith patted his shoulder, all gentility. "Thank you, son. Mighty appreciated."

"You're welcome, sir."

Irons, already regretting this, nodded without enthusiasm. "You may leave now, Corporal."

The smile vanished. "Yes, sir."

"And close the door behind you."

"Yes, sir." He did.

Irons sighed and stood—military courtesy, nothing more. If not for protocol, he would've left the old bastard in the lobby to decompose.

"Mister Webbersmith, is it?"

He stretched a wide grin—perfect teeth, surprisingly remarkable for a man his age.

"Simon Webbersmith, yes sir." He extended a hand. "And how are you today?"

Irons glanced at the hand, then shook it. The old man's grip was surprisingly strong.

"Fine, sir. And yourself?"

"Fit as a fiddle and ready for love." His grin widened. "That was a song, wasn't it?"

Irons sighed. "I wouldn't know."

As Webbersmith pulled up a chair, he gestured toward Irons's own.

"Oh please, take your seat."

Irons responded with dry sarcasm. "Why thank you."

It went unnoticed.

"Think nothing of it."

Irons sat. Under his breath, he muttered, "I won't…"

Unaccustomed to civilian interaction, he folded his hands on the desk, cleared his throat, and asked in the most even-tempered voice he could manage,

"What is it I can do for you today, sir?"

Webbersmith waved a hand in good humor. "Oh, you can call me Simon."

He reached into the pocket of his worn green jacket.

"It's just the two of us here."

"Yes, it is just the two of us." Irons leaned forward, not smiling.

"And why do you think that is?"

Webbersmith didn't seem to hear him. Instead, he pulled out a pipe and held it up.

"Do you mind if I smoke?"

Irons sighed and rubbed the bridge of his nose—the telltale sign the headache had graduated to a migraine.

"Go ahead."

Webbersmith drew a small pouch from his jacket and tapped a modest amount of tobacco into the bowl.

"I grow this myself."

Irons couldn't have cared less, but said,

"Is that right?"

"That's right." He packed it tight and looked up with another grin.

"Got myself a little parcel outside Starts Creek, Georgia."

He paused mid-pack and asked, "You ever hear of it?"

The old man must've noticed Irons was only half-listening.

"Heard of what?"

"Starts Creek."

"No. No, I haven't."

Another friendly wave. "Well, I wouldn't worry none. Not many have."

He pulled out a matchbook, struck one with a practiced thumb, and lit the pipe with strong, unshakable lungs. The aroma rose—a sweet, rich smell—and Irons, despite himself, inhaled it with mild surprise.

Webbersmith caught the look. "Better than store-bought." He shook out the match and dropped it in the ashtray. "Yes sir, if you want something done right, you got to do it yourself."

Irons, already tired of the old man—hell, he was tired of him before he even walked in—said,

"I always thought the quote should be: 'If you want something done your way, do it yourself.'"

Webbersmith gave it a moment's thought, then nodded.

"You know, you might just be right."

Irons rubbed harder at the bridge of his nose. "Mister Webbersmith—"

He raised a finger, interrupting. "Simon."

In a conceding voice, Irons repeated, "Simon... what can I do for you today?"

Without missing a beat, the old man replied,

"Surrender."

Irons froze mid-motion. He must've misheard.

"I'm sorry. Run that by me again?"

Webbersmith casually glanced into his pipe, satisfied with the burn.

"I'm saying," he said simply, "I expect you to surrender."

"Surrender?"

He puffed and nodded. "That's right, General."

The guy was nuts.

"To you?"

He nodded again. "Yes, sir."

The guy was *fucking* nuts.

"Just me, or—?"

Instead of shaking his head, Webbersmith wagged the pipe from side to side. "—All of you."

"All of us?"

He took another drag and nodded, "Yes, sir."

186

Irons gave a slow smile and rolled his hand in the air. "Meaning... the army?"

Webbersmith sat up straighter. "No, sir."

"Who then?"

He began ticking them off on his fingers.

"The Army, the Navy, the Marines, and the Air Force."

He leaned back, smiling contentedly as he puffed on that old wooden pipe.

Irons remained relaxed, reclining in his chair.

"I see. And what exactly would make us do that—" he added quickly, "—if you don't mind me asking?"

Webbersmith waved the pipe casually. "No, of course not."

"Oh good."

"Well, the reason you'd do that—" he raised his cane, "—is because of this."

Irons gave a polite nod. "So you intend to beat us with that if we don't... what did you say? Surrender?"

Webbersmith shook his head. "No, sir."

Irons pointed at the cane. "But that *is* the weapon you were talking about?"

"That it is," he said with a puff.

Irons nodded again and made a mental note to find out which incompetent morons had let this lunatic onto the base.

"And just what does the magic cane do?"

Webbersmith didn't flinch. "It explodes light."

"Light?"

"That's correct, sir."

*Absolutely fucking nuts.*

"And how does it do that?"

Webbersmith held up the knotted wooden cane and spun it easily, like a baton.

"You know, I ain't quite sure. It's what you'd call an heirloom. Passed down from daddy to son, 'til it come to me. I'm the last one now. And what we was all told is this—" he pointed at the handle, which looked eerily like a snarling face, "—if I twist this off, you'll see one big boom."

He chuckled. "Or not."

Irons rolled his hand again. "And you can prove this? I mean, you can give us some form of demonstration?"

"That's why I'm here."

"How?"

A stupid question to ask a crazy man.

"Well, I figured with all the machinery you got around here, you must have some kind of light-splitter or something."

"A light-splitter?"

"See, all I need to prove this to you is…" —he paused, searching for the word— "just an atom of light. Real small."

"You can't just open it here?"

He shook his head adamantly. "Oh no, no, no!"

He held the cane up like a live grenade. "I told you, this explodes light. *All* light. If I were to open it here, everything the sun touches would be gone."

Irons nodded slowly. "Is that right?"

Webbersmith bobbed his head vigorously. "Yes, sir. It is, and I ain't lying."

Irons rubbed his temples. His head was splitting. "Then how do we test it?"

"All I need is a dark room and one of them light-splitters."

Irons sighed. "Okay…"

He could already see the future—this old kook showing up day after day, babbling about light-splitters and doomsday canes, and his migraine blooming bigger with every visit.

He pushed himself up from the desk and gestured toward the door. "After you, sir."

Webbersmith smiled and stood. "Just call me Simon."

The old man shook his head as he looked around the empty warehouse. "This won't do."

Irons rubbed the bridge of his nose. His skull felt like it was about to split. "Why not?"

Webbersmith spun in a slow circle. "It's too bright. And it's too close."

"Too close to *what*?"

The answer was almost too obvious to bother stating.

"To everything. If I was to twist off this cap,"—he shrugged—"everything would go up. And I do mean *everything*."

Irons gritted his teeth. "So where do we go?"

\* \* \* \*

It was twenty minutes later and they were out on the Salt Flats. Sergeant Benton had agreed to drive the old man to an abandoned receiving station, and that's where he was now—equipped with an electron light-splitter. The station's underground bunker, the old man had said, would be perfect for their purposes. He'd also claimed that despite the awesome fury of the impending explosion, he would be just fine. Something akin to being in the eye of a hurricane.

It was all bullshit anyway. So Irons had swallowed a substantial amount of aspirin and waited in his jeep until the good Sergeant wheeled up and said, "He's ready, sir. Five minutes."

Irons nodded wearily. "You have the remote?"

Benton held it up. "Yes, sir. But I'm not sure it's going to work from this distance. We're a good ten miles from the site."

Irons tossed the empty aspirin bottle aside. "Like it's going to make one bit of fucking difference."

"I don't understand physics, sir, so maybe you can explain this to me—what exactly is one electron particle of light supposed to do here?"

Irons shook his head. "Absolutely nothing. Except keep that idiot out of my office."

Five minutes later, Benton pressed the remote—and both men were blown twenty yards out of their jeeps.

In that brief glimpse before the world went sideways, Irons witnessed an explosion not seen since the hydrogen bomb tests of the fifties. A colossal column of flame, miles high, rose and fell. The shockwave fractured his ribs and snapped the poor Sergeant's neck like a twig.

The old man hadn't been lying.

He wasn't crazy.

With a single atom of light, he had destroyed ten miles of land—thankfully unoccupied—and left a crater hundreds of feet deep.

"I'll be damned…" was all Irons could manage as he clutched at his side. One particle of light. A wooden cane. And an old man had done what an army of scientists and defense contractors had never managed: produce an explosion of unfathomable magnitude, without nuclear fission. Without radiation. Without fallout.

He wasn't sure how long he'd been unconscious. But when he finally turned away from the smoking abyss, the old man was standing over him.

Cane in hand.

"Convinced?"

* * * *

It was twenty minutes later, and they were out on the Salt Flats. Sergeant Benton had driven the old man to an abandoned receiving station, where he now waited—equipped with an electron light-splitter. The station's underground bunker, the old man said, would be perfect for their purposes. He'd also claimed that, despite the impending explosion's awesome fury, he would be perfectly safe. Something about being in the eye of the hurricane.

It was all bullshit anyway.

Irons had downed a heavy dose of aspirin and now sat in his jeep, rubbing his temples, until the Sergeant wheeled up beside him and said, "He's ready, sir. Five minutes."

Irons nodded wearily. "You have the remote?"

Benton held it up. "Yes, sir. But I'm not sure it'll work from this distance. We're a good ten miles out."

Irons tossed the empty aspirin bottle aside. "Like it's going to make one bit of fucking difference."

"I don't understand the science, sir," Benton said, "so maybe you can explain this—what exactly is one electron particle of light supposed to do?"

Irons shook his head. "Absolutely nothing. Except keep that old bastard out of my office."

Five minutes later, Benton pressed the button—

—and both men were blown twenty yards from their jeeps.

In the instant before the world flipped, Irons caught a glimpse of it: an explosion unlike anything since the hydrogen bomb tests of the fifties. A towering column of flame erupted, miles high. The blast wave shattered ribs and snapped Benton's neck like a toothpick.

The old man hadn't been lying.

He wasn't crazy.

With a single atom of light, he had destroyed ten square miles of land—thankfully uninhabited—and left behind a crater hundreds of feet deep.

"I'll be damned..." was all Irons could mutter, clutching his ribs.

One particle of light.

A wooden cane.

And an old man had done what teams of scientists hadn't: unleashed a cataclysm without nuclear fission, radiation, or fallout.

He didn't know how long he'd been out. But when he turned away from the smoldering abyss, the old man was standing over him.

Cane in hand.

"Convinced?"

# THE HANGING TREE

I had never seen this part of the South before—except maybe in Depression-era movies—and frankly, it made me a little sad. I passed worm-eaten shacks that would've been condemned long ago if anyone had been around to care. Stately homes that were once called mansions now stood in ruin, slowly rotting into the earth. Businesses were shuttered and buried in weeds, abandoned since the freeway rerouted traffic and life away from them.

It made me wonder why anyone would stay in a place like this instead of seeking a better life somewhere else. Maybe it was financial—just simple economics. Maybe they just couldn't afford to leave. And so the residents, like their homes and storefronts, simply waited. Watched. Decayed. Until, like everything else, they quietly slipped away and were forgotten.

I used to think that.

I don't anymore.

See, I had gotten royally lost—which, if I'm being honest, was kind of the plan. I didn't want to see the "New South," the one overrun with McDonald's and Ramada Inns. I wanted history. I wanted those quiet towns time forgot, the ones that clung to their old bones and whispered of days long gone. Americana, they call it. The good old days. People and places the world had passed by.

But what I found was different. Time hadn't just passed them by—it had *ravaged* them. There was no gentle charm, no sepia-toned nostalgia. Just mile after mile of despair, and a quiet kind of grief that hung over everything like a humid fog.

It got to me.

I decided I'd seen enough. I'd gas up, head home, and forget the whole thing.

That was a terrible mistake.

You see, I ignored the signs—literally. Not the old weathered billboards advertising products that didn't exist anymore. Not the ghost signs on brick walls or the rusted metal ones for diners long since burned out. No, these were different. Newer. Clear. Warned me in plain language:

**DO NOT STOP IN HANGMAN'S BLUFF.**

**NO GAS – NO LODGING.**

I should've listened.

But I didn't.

At first, I thought the name was just southern flair—picturesque, if a bit grim. Hangman's Bluff. Sounded like something out of a tourist brochure. And anyway, I didn't have a choice. My tank was dry. Something—or someone—in this town *had* to have gas.

So I rolled in.

And it didn't take long to see that the name was a lie. There was no bluff. No view. Just a crumbling little town with a single massive oak tree in the middle of the square. And as I slowed the car beside it, I looked up—and froze.

There was a man hanging from the tree.

At first, I thought it had to be fake. Some kind of protest or effigy. I'd heard about things like that—southern politics, small-town theatrics. Maybe someone was making a point about taxes or town leadership.

But this wasn't that.

This wasn't staged.

This wasn't political.

This was *real*.

And he was still swinging.

This was an *actual corpse* strung up in a tree.

His black tongue jutted between cracked, purple lips, and his head—blotched blue and gray—lolled crookedly to one side. Whoever had done this hadn't even bothered with a hood. If the man had still had his eyes (and from the looks of it—confirmed only after a stomach-churning glance—he didn't), they would have been fixed on the old bearded man sitting on a bench nearby. The one smiling. The one casually whittling.

The one who gave me a small wave.

"Mornin'."

I could barely nod. My eyes were locked on the horror swaying gently above us. "…what…?"

The old man didn't seem to notice my voice or the body. He just glanced up at the sky and said, "Looks like it's gonna be a good day. Weather folks said rain, but I don't see none comin'."

None of this made sense.

Not ten feet from him was a corpse—an actual dead man swinging from a tree—and the old man was just sitting there, whittling. *Whittling.*

I circled the scene in a wide, cautious arc and asked, trying to keep my voice steady, "What... happened here?"

He blinked up at me, puzzled. "Where?"

Absurd. I pointed at the corpse. "*Here. This.* Who is responsible for this?"

The old man nodded toward the tree with his knife. "You mean him?"

I couldn't contain it anymore. Rage flared in my chest as I stepped toward him. I've never supported the death penalty—not for *any* reason. But this... this was medieval. Barbaric. It wasn't just that someone had been lynched—it was that he'd been *left*. Left to rot in the middle of the town square like a warning.

"Yes," I snapped. "*Him.* Who did this?"

The old man didn't flinch. "We all did."

I stared at him. Then back up at the body.

For the first time, I noticed something strange—he'd been dressed. Someone had put him in a clean suit. His boots were polished.

"You all... did this?"

He nodded, casually brushing away wood shavings from his lap. "He know'd the rules," he said matter-of-factly. "Just figured they didn't apply to him."

I stepped closer, something pulling me toward him despite every instinct screaming otherwise. "Where's the law?" I demanded.

He didn't even look at me. Just pointed lazily over his shoulder with the knife. "'Bout two blocks up. Can't miss it."

I looked again at the body—at the grotesque arc it traced, like some human pendulum in the midday breeze. "Why is he still hanging there?"

At this, the old man chuckled. For the first time, he actually seemed amused. He set his carving aside and looked up at me with a grin that sent a chill down my spine.

"A lesson, son."

I blinked. "A… lesson?"

He nodded. "You betcha."

I stood there for a long moment, unable to move. Because suddenly, I wasn't sure if I'd taken a wrong turn somewhere outside town…

…or if I'd driven straight into *The Twilight Zone.*

"A lesson?" I repeated.

He nodded again. "For the children, yessir."

I didn't think I could be more shocked. I was wrong. Again. "*Children?*"

He calmly returned to whittling. "Yessir, that's right."

For a moment, I couldn't breathe. I couldn't begin to understand how anyone—let alone a *child*—could learn anything from such a grotesque display.

So I asked him.

He sighed and once more set aside his knife and block of wood. "Rules gotta be followed," he said slowly, like he was explaining basic math. "If there ain't no punishment, what's the point of havin' rules?"

I turned in a slow, disbelieving circle, completely flabbergasted. This town hadn't just taken it upon themselves to hang a man—they left him there. Rotting.

Swinging. As a *warning*. To children. *To children,* who now got to watch a body decompose in the town square. Birds had already eaten his eyes, and someone thought *this* was part of growing up?

I turned back to the old man, rubbing my own eyes as if I could blink this all away. "What did he do?"

He shrugged. "Why, son... he tried to leave."

"...Leave?"

He nodded. "Yessir."

"Leave *what*?"

He gestured lazily with the knife, motioning to the overgrown buildings and boarded-up storefronts around us. "Why, *here*. Hangman's Bluff."

I sat down beside him without asking. My knees were weak and my mind weaker. "That was his *crime*?" I asked, incredulous. "He wanted to leave *town*?"

The old man didn't look up. He just blew the wood shavings off his hands. "Yessir."

I fell back against the bench, eyes drifting to the swaying corpse. "How is that a crime? Just *wanting* to leave?"

He answered without hesitation. "This here's a farmin' community."

"What?" I blinked. "What does that have to do with *anything*?"

Again, he nodded. "We make our livin' farmin'."

Like everything else out of his mouth, that made no sense. I hadn't seen a crop in twenty miles. Hell, I hadn't even seen a *field*—just dust and vines and rot. But even if there were crops...

"What does *he* have to do with farming?" I asked, pointing at the corpse. "How does a man leaving town hurt the crops?"

He gave a small shake of his head. "If he'd been leavin', it would've hurt the yield. Can't be havin' that."

"You're telling me the whole town depends on one farmer—"

The old man cut me off. "Who said anything about him bein' a farmer?" He jabbed his knife toward the hanging body again, and I flinched. "He was the president of the bank. Up the street there."

That made even *less* sense.

"I get that some farmers might think they've got good reason to hang a banker," I said, trying—failing—to lighten the moment. "But what, exactly, would *he* do to the crops?"

The old man didn't look up. He just kept carving and said, without a hint of humor:

"You might say we raise the dead."

I froze. "Say that again?"

He nodded slowly. "That's where the old expression comes from."

"What expression?"

He looked at me now, eyes steady and bright. "*We're gonna plant him.* Heard that one before, ain't ya?"

I suddenly realized how close I'd leaned in. I pulled away, and my voice cracked just slightly. "Yeah... yeah, sure I have."

But not like this.

Never like this.

"Well, there you go." He went back to whittling.

I stared at him. "Where am I going?"

He sighed so deeply it sounded like it shook something loose in his chest. "Look, son, ain't you ever wondered why we bury folks?"

Even though it's generally a bad idea to be sarcastic with someone who might be unhinged, I couldn't help myself. "I always assumed it was because they were *dead*."

He chuckled. "That's what most people figger. But it ain't so."

"...Then why?" I asked, thinking it was a simple question.

He turned toward me, and I instinctively shifted away. But he wasn't threatening. He was just settling in—a storyteller's ease falling over his frame like an old quilt. "Fact is, we didn't even start buryin' folks 'til recent times. Historically speakin', I mean. We used to *burn* 'em. That was before we knew better. Before we figgered out we were the farmers."

He tapped the bench for emphasis. "*We* do the plantin'. *They* do the eatin'."

"...Who's *they*?" I asked, chilled without knowing why.

"Them that lives below."

"Who?" My voice was quiet now.

He turned away, tone flat. "Don't rightly know who they are. They older'n dirt. That's why they live *under* it."

I raised a hand. "Hold on. Are you saying we bury our dead so that something—*some thing*—underground can... can eat them?"

He nodded. "Yep. I don't know when we started makin' such a show of it. All the songs and preachin'. Kinda like when they started puttin' burgers in them Styrofoam containers. Used to just slap 'em on a plate. Now it's harder to get at, that's all."

He resumed his whittling. "Truth is, we oughta just toss 'em in the ground, cover 'em up, and let them eat in peace."

That was it. Not only was he insane, but the entire *town* had to be. This was a cult. Some long-rotting belief passed down from generation to generation until everyone here had forgotten it was madness.

I stood up fast and staggered back. Something in me refused to touch anything around me—as if insanity could spread through contact.

"You're insane," I said.

He let out a short chuckle, collecting his wood shavings. "Might just be."

He stood and pocketed his knife. "But if I were you, I wouldn't be tryin' to leave." He looked at the tree, then back to me. "Might find yourself at the end of a rope."

I blinked. "What did you just say?"

But he was already walking away, pausing only to dump the shavings into a rusty barrel near the curb. "You shoulda abided by the signs," he called back. "They was plain enough."

My mind reeled. I half-stood, knees shaking, then collapsed back onto the bench. I looked from the swinging corpse to the old man now crossing the street—the street I suddenly realized was lined with nothing but *weeds*.

No shops. No cars. No people.

Just my car.

And a tree full of birds.

"Hey!" I called out. "All I wanted was gas!"

He didn't turn around. "Ain't got no gas here," he said over his shoulder. "Ain't got no use for it. Ain't nobody goin' anywhere."

He kept walking.

"That includes you too, son."

I was trapped.

Trapped in a town where the rules were madness and the dead fed the harvest.

"Wait!" I shouted, a final, desperate plea.

He didn't stop. "You really shoulda paid them signs some mind."

And then he disappeared down an alley I hadn't noticed before.

And I was alone.

Except, of course…

For the man in the tree.

And whatever lived *beneath*.

\* \* \* \*

I've been here about a year now, but the townsfolk still keep a close eye on me.

They peek through curtains. Offer the occasional nod and tight-lipped smile when they pass me on the bench where I spend most afternoons whittling. I'm always careful to gather up my shavings before I take up my crutches and hobble back to Sarah's Boarding House. I rent a room there. It's small, sparsely furnished—but it's home.

It has to be.

See, I took the Old Man's place after he became the latest meal.

Lately, I've been thinking—maybe I've made too much of this. Maybe they're right. Even if they aren't, what does it matter? When you're dead, you're dead, right? Whether it's worms or... *them*... something's going to eat you.

Still, I miss things. Even the things I used to hate. Traffic noise. Wrong numbers. The sound of a train in the distance. The relentless hustle of the city. Hell, I even miss my old job.

Not that I need one anymore.

Everything's provided here—by those with no name. As it is for everyone else in this godforsaken town. And I can't complain about the sex life, either. Not that I ever could before. But, hey... we're farmers now, right?

So I sit. Watching the UPS man swing gently from the tree in front of me—just another burger on a plate—and I think, sometimes, about running.

But then again, how far can you get without your feet?

Maybe tomorrow I'll think harder about it. Maybe I'll hatch a plan while I sit here and whittle another stick down to nothing.

Maybe.

But let's face it.

I'm not going anywhere.

# MAKEOVER

She came into my office at 2:15.

I remember that because I had a tee-off time at three and had purposely left my schedule open. You see, I've been a plastic surgeon here in Beverly Hills for twenty years and have built up quite a substantial practice. I tell you that so you'll know that I don't accept walk-in trade—appointment only—and had already told my receptionist, Louise, that she could go home for the day. I suppose she forgot to lock the door on her way out, and I can only assume the woman simply walked in and, finding no one at the reception desk, helped herself into the outer office and finally into my own.

"Doctor Walcot?"

Having practiced here for as long as I had, I was used to beautiful women—read: high-maintenance women—and by now saw even the most striking of them as little more than a collection of technical check-points. Some wanted a tuck here or there, maybe a new nose, but as anyone in my profession would tell you, the best sellers were, of course, breast implants or the ever-popular liposuction. And I guess that's what fascinated me, because I couldn't think of a single thing I could do for her.

The long and the short of it is that she was perfect.

Absolutely perfect.

I stood. "I'm Doctor Walcot."

She offered a small smile and closed the door. "I've heard a lot about you."

I was momentarily entranced—any man would be. It wasn't just her body but her voice and the way she moved. She had the elegant grace of a '40s starlet. The way her dress clung to her exquisite frame and that soft, whiskey voice... She could have easily stepped right out of the screen and into my office.

"You have?"

She nodded. "Good things. Very good things."

I have to admit that I was getting a little turned on, and if you knew me, you'd know that was virtually unheard of—in my professional life, that is. As a doctor, I'm proud of my ability to detach business from pleasure, and this was not a bar or a cocktail party. I couldn't afford to indulge in even idle fantasies. I took a step back—not literally but figuratively—and said in my most even voice, "That's very flattering, but right now I have an important appointment and I—"

She interrupted with the ease of someone used to doing so. "—You have a tee-time at three. You're playing golf with a Doctor Kirschbaum. He's a chiropractor, isn't he?" She sat down and crossed her legs.

"How did you know that?"

She opened her purse and took out a cigarette case. "I took the liberty of looking through your appointment book." She lit one with a small, gold lighter and sighed smoke. "I hope you don't mind."

"You can hope all you want, but I do mind."

She briefly perused the room, looking unimpressed, and said, "I'm so sorry."

She wasn't, of course. She had the demeanor of someone who honestly didn't understand what the word meant, and that made me bristle. Now, I'm used to attitude—it comes with the location—but I was beginning to realize that this woman wasn't going to leave until I dealt with her. I sat back down, and though I didn't yet know her name, I did know that she didn't come in for a sex change.

Because she had already proved that she had an enormous set of balls.

"Well, since you've already gone to the trouble of examining my personal itinerary, why don't you tell me what you want."

I was intentionally trying to be sarcastic, but if it fazed her, it didn't show. It never does with people like her.

"I waited until your schedule was clear. I didn't want anyone to see me come in."

So she was vain. "And why is that?"

She momentarily avoided the question. "I hope you don't mind if I smoke."

"Actually, I do. It's not healthy."

She took another puff and offered the same small smile she had upon entering. "I suppose you're right. But then again, this isn't a lab or an operating theater."

"I meant, it's not healthy for you."

"I understand what you meant, but advice isn't why I'm here."

I sighed. The extremely wealthy and the extremely attractive can also become extremely tiresome in a short span of time, and frankly, hers was about up. "Then why don't you tell me why you are here."

She exhaled a thick cloud of smoke, paused, and then said simply, "I need some work done."

Again I looked her up and down. "Where?"

She smiled—a riveting smile—and I noticed, with a doctor's curiosity, that her teeth weren't stained with nicotine. Most probably caps, I thought. Recent ones.

"Thank you," she said. "It appears you can be flattering yourself."

"Please, Mrs—"

She tapped her ashes into an empty beaker on my desk and, while it briefly angered me, I also understood it was because I hadn't offered her the courtesy of an ashtray. "—It's Miss. I never bothered to marry."

(*Bothered? Kind of an odd term.*)

She looked back at me and added, "But the rest of it is Kelsey. Myra Kelsey."

I offered a polite nod in her direction. "Miss Kelsey, then. If I am to take you on as a patient,"—I quickly raised a hand before she had a chance to interrupt—"and I'm not saying that I will—"

She interrupted anyway. "—You will." She smiled again. "Trust me."

"And what makes you think so?"

"You're the best. I insist on the best." Again she tapped her ashes. "I always have."

She spoke like someone older, someone with life experience, even though she was probably all of twenty-five.

"Even if I were the best, why would you need the best?"

She leaned over and opened a rather expansive bag that I had failed to notice her carry in. "Because I'm going to need some rather extensive reconstructive work."

That answer didn't make sense. "What?"

She passed me a file. A thick one. "I think you heard me."

I didn't take it at once, and she didn't lower it. When I finally did accept it, I found it to be full of X-rays. Full body shots—and when I say that, I mean that they had been taken from every angle. Every conceivable angle. I looked up at her and she smiled back at me.

"What exactly am I supposed to do with these?"

"Very soon, I'm going to need a full body reconstruction."

I leaned forward. I had to have heard her wrong. "Excuse me?"

She took another brief puff. "Again, I think you heard me."

I dropped the file and it hit my desk with a thud. "You're telling me that you—"

She nodded. "—Yes."

"Do you have any idea what that would encompass?"

"I understand very well."

She couldn't. "Any surgery this extensive would take years and run into—"

She interrupted again. "—I don't have years."

"Excuse me?"

"I sought you out because the work must be done quickly."

"Why?"

I watched as she sadly dropped the cigarette into the beaker and said, "I'm afraid that time is a commodity I don't have."

Like I said, she was young, rich, and arrogant—a very bad combination—and so I felt I should explain things very slowly. The way you would to a spoiled child, which she certainly was.

"You can't rush the body's natural healing process." I motioned at the X-rays. "Particularly something like skin grafts, bone grafts—"

She interrupted yet again, this time sounding more impatient. "—I have the money."

I had had just about enough of Miss Kelsey, and so I made no attempt to disguise my anger. "We're not talking about money here! I want you to understand that!"

She sighed and looked bored—something that further enraged me.

"There are not only medical considerations but ethical ones as well."

She lit another cigarette and, in a dismissing tone, said, "Please…"

I threw up my hands. I didn't know what else to do. "All right, then let me ask you a question."

She sighed smoke again. "Fine."

"Why?"

The question didn't make sense to her. "Why?"

I nodded. "Why do you say you need this surgery?"

At that, she laughed. I mean, she actually laughed. The kind of laugh that makes your chest heave—and it wasn't for a moment—a long moment—before she could control herself.

"I'm sorry, but I thought you were the best."

I was confused. "That aside, you haven't explained why you want surgery," I thumped the file, "surgery this extensive."

"You really can't tell?" She took another drag on her cigarette. "Maybe you need glasses."

I was not only losing patience—it was gone. I had a tee-time in twenty minutes.

"WHY?"

"Because I'm beginning to rot again," she said simply.

I leaned forward, my chin damn near resting on her file. "Rot?"

She nodded and smoked. "You know? Decay?"

(*What the hell was she talking about?*)

I thought I'd ask her.

"You don't remember me, do you?" she asked.

I didn't have a clue. "Should I?"

She sighed and tapped her ashes into the rapidly filling beaker. "Maybe not. I was only a bit player." She looked at me and smiled. "But at one time, they said I was going to be the next Lauren Bacall."

I shook my head, uncomprehending, and she continued, "That was before my boyfriend at the time killed me."

I shook my head as if to clear it. She had to be nuts. "Killed you?"

She leaned back in the chair. "In 1947."

I was right.

She was out of her pretty little fucking mind.

I was going to be careful. "You were killed in 1947?"

"Um-hmm." She smoked.

Now, I grew up in L.A., and so I knew that this town attracts all manner of loonies. It always has. That's why we have so many psycho killers out here. As I looked at her, I thought about that but decided she wasn't a killer.

She was just plain fucking nuts, and I didn't have time to deal with her dementia even if I wanted to.

I had a tee-time.

I started to push myself up, and that's when it happened. I mean, I was looking right at her when it did.

The cigarette was stuck to her lip, and when she pulled it away to tap off the ashes again, her lower lip came off with it.

You heard me right.

Her lower lip just fell from her face and hit the floor at her feet. And although I reacted in horror, it didn't seem to surprise her. She just looked at me and grinned, her white caps gleaming over dead-gray gums, and said, "You can fix that. Right?"

# JEFFY

The boy's name was Jeffy, and he lived down the street from me in a small colonial badly in need of paint. I didn't know his exact age, but judging by his height and weight, I'd guess he was nine or ten. He looked the part of a small-town American boy—one straight out of the fifties. Straight out of *Mayberry*. The striped shirt and freckles, the tousled red hair usually hidden beneath a tilted baseball cap. You'd most often glimpse him on his bike, racing down the street with the kind of urgency only children possess.

In every sense, he was the typical kid. The perfect child. The kind of kid every couple dreams of having. Sometimes, when I looked at him, I swear I could see a Norman Rockwell painting come to life: a grinning family in a warm embrace, the parents dreaming of a doctor or lawyer in the making, while he merely dreamed of going outside to play ball.

That's what made Jeffy such a great actor—such an artful dodger. He could summon those innocent fantasies, trigger those nostalgic daydreams of a golden past that likely never existed. He made you picture the kind of Americana old people speak of with reverent sighs, even though you know the past wasn't really like that. Still, it made you want to pull your feet up under you and listen, mouth open, eyes wide.

Jeffy brought those images to life—and that's what made him dangerous.

He made you feel safe. He lulled you into a false sense of security. No—complacency. The kind that lands you in a rocking chair or porch swing for the rest of your life, offering mindless nods and smiles to strangers who do the same.

No, Jeffy was just *too* perfect. And to me, it was clear he was hiding something. I had to know where he was always going on that bike, riding like his life depended on it. His butt raised off the seat, legs pumping hard to gain more speed—always racing toward some unknown destination.

It's a simple truth, but rarely voiced: adults usually have no idea where children are going or where they've been. But Jeffy was different.

I *had* to know where Jeffy was going.

So I followed him.

I don't know if you've ever tried to trail a kid—especially one on a bike—but it's no easy feat. Kids have their own ingenious routes, often bypassing every paved road and sidewalk. They favor narrow, overgrown trails that border on criminal trespass. For a while—briefly—I tried following him in my car, but that was hopeless. So I continued on foot.

Damn, kids can move when they want to. They're like cats. They can sit around doing nothing for hours, and then suddenly—they're gone. Gone like the wind. But I was determined not to lose Jeffy.

I followed.

Even after I found his abandoned bike, half-hidden in a hedgerow, I kept going. I ducked through broken chain-link fences, crawled over low stone walls long-neglected, and even squeezed through a narrow sewer pipe that had clearly been dry for years—but felt designed by children for the very purpose of avoiding adult pursuit. Maybe it was. I don't know.

Still, I pressed on. Crouching. Crawling. Until I found him.

The pipe opened into a surprisingly cavernous chamber—one that felt almost medieval. Dark, smooth marble walls capped by snarling gargoyles. Flickering torches lit the space. It was like a Gothic horror set, befitting Bela Lugosi himself.

*(This is under our town?)*

"Hi."

Startled, I looked up. Jeffy sat comfortably in a small wooden chair, an adult smile curling on his face. He wasn't surprised to see me. In fact, another chair sat across from him, and he gestured toward it.

"Come in. Be welcome."

I was so unsettled by that eerie smile, I didn't immediately notice the rats—dead and dangling overhead, gently spinning like mistletoe at a Christmas party.

Icy fingers tap-danced up my spine. I wanted to run— but I didn't. Maybe it was the thought of crawling back through that filthy pipe, or maybe it was just my damnable morbid curiosity.

Whatever the reason, I stayed.

I pulled myself fully from the tunnel, my eyes locked on the grotesque surroundings. I don't remember speaking, but

I must have, because I heard myself say, "Is that chair for me...?"

Jeffy nodded. "For now."

I didn't like the sound of that, but I stepped forward anyway. Maybe I was overwhelmed. Like most people—especially in small towns—I had no idea what existed beneath the streets we walked on. This chamber was as big as any house I'd lived in, and it smelled like urine and shit—the stuff we flush away without a second thought.

Still, Jeffy seemed right at home.

**Right at home.**

"You've been watching me," he said.

I didn't know how he knew that—but he did. My reaction made him smile wider.

"Can I ask why?"

I paused. I wasn't going to play by his rules.

"Why the rats?" I asked instead.

He looked puzzled, glanced up at the rodents dangling above. "Oh, them." He shrugged. "When I first got here, they were everywhere. I had to do something with them. Besides,"—he playfully tapped one—"they make nice ornaments, don't you think?"

I shook my head. "No."

He looked more than confused. He looked... insulted. Like I'd just criticized his home. Or his children. It wasn't the expression of a child. It was something more... sinister.

But then—just like that—he smiled. A child's smile.

Jeffy again.

216

"Why don't you sit down?" He patted the chair. "You know you want to. Come on."

Now, Jeffy was half my size. No match for me. But I didn't want to get any closer to him.

**If** he was a kid.

He patted the chair again. "Sit. Then we can talk. I mean, that's why you're here."

His smile stretched. His eyes gleamed.

"Isn't it?"

It was. I didn't want to admit it—but it was.

So I sat. And in that steaming tunnel, it felt cold.

"See? Isn't that better?"

"No." That was all I had.

He sighed—an adult sigh—and asked, "I guess there's something you want to ask me?" He shrugged. "What is it?"

I knew what I wanted to ask. The question that had haunted me since I first saw him racing off on those relentless journeys. But I'd buried it, afraid of the answer.

I don't even remember saying the words:

"What *are* you?"

With the innocent expression of a child—of which he certainly wasn't—he replied, "My name's Jeffy. I live down the street from you."

I nodded. "That's not what I asked."

He braced a small fist under his chin. "What if you don't want to know? A lot of adults ask questions they don't really want answers to. Do you?"

He smiled again. His eyes shimmered in the dark.

As disturbing as it was, I leaned in. "I want to know."

He laughed and straightened up—suddenly looking taller than I remembered.

"What if I don't tell you? What'll you do?"

I didn't have a solid answer. All I had were suspicions. To everyone else, he was just a kid. A perfect kid.

Except he enjoyed hanging rats that got in his way.

That thought made me swallow hard. I was surprised to hear myself say, "Maybe I'll wring your neck..."

It didn't faze him. He kept grinning.

"No you won't. You'd be a child murderer. And I'm betting you know what happens to them in prison."

In any negotiation, you've got to keep your opponent guessing. So I leaned back in the chair and folded my hands behind my head.

"That is, if they caught me."

His smile faltered. Just slightly—but I saw it. That flicker of fear.

"What?"

I smiled. I had him.

"You made it damn hard for me to track you. Your bike's half a mile from here. My car's even further. Why would they look for *me*? I don't even know you."

The rules had changed.

"Right?"

Jeffy looked around the chamber, then back at me. A slow, sideways nod.

"Good point."

**The worm had turned.**

218

"So here's how it goes from now on, Jeffy. I ask the questions. You answer. Clear?"

He chuckled—and I'll admit, that confused me.

"You're like a lot of adults. Got all kinds of questions. But when you get the answers—you don't really want 'em. Not the *real* ones."

I swallowed again. "Tell me anyway."

"To me, it's obvious," he said, shrugging. "I'm here because I'm a kid. I don't ask questions."

I frowned. "What?"

Jeffy met my eyes, his gaze sharp and steady.

"I'm a kid. We explore. That's what we do. One day I found this place. And I was told to watch the gate." He gestured behind him—and for the first time, I saw the rusted iron gate. Hidden in shadow. Suddenly gleaming in the dark.

"He told me to watch it. I didn't ask why."

I looked at him. "Who told you—?"

He smiled wider. "Ask him yourself."

The gate creaked open.

I looked up.

I screamed.

Jeffy laughed.

\* \* \* \*

Well, I've told you my story—as much of it as I could, anyway. I hope it makes sense. I couldn't write it myself, you see, because Jeffy has my fingers now. I imagine they're hanging alongside his rats. Maybe by my tongue.

So, if there's a moral to any of this—and I'm not saying there is—it might be this:

If you see a child, even if something deep down tells you he's not really a child, don't ask where he's going. He might just be off to a job. A paper route. A shift as a bag boy at the local market. That kind of thing.

I just didn't realize some kids have jobs.

Jeffy does.

He guards the gates of Hell.

# THE PRACTICAL JOKER

The thief was out of practice.

It had been ten days since his last job.. Even a thief has a private life and so he – him being Sammy Jacobs – had been down to Orlando for a family reunion. But now he was back and he had a job to do. The same job he had done for the past three years.

As always, he woke at five that morning to case the place and even though he hadn't seen the delivery boy, he knew it had to be there. It always was. Every day. As quietly as he could, he crept along the hedges that separated his trailer from his neighbor's. He was skilled and as he walked, he was careful that no one saw him. There were no lights on in the many summer homes that lined the river, the ones that were usually there this time of the morning and so today there would be no witnesses.

It would be so easy.

He swung around the last of the hedges and as quietly as he could, opened the gate

that led to Mad's place. The owner's name was actually Madison but everyone called him Mad. If you knew him, you knew why.

He would have to be careful.

He was.

As silent as a mouse, Sammy snuck down the drive, careful to avoid the broken concrete that threatened to snub any one of his bare toes. He couldn't risk crying out. Mad sometimes got up early – hell, sometimes he stayed up all night – and he might be lying in wait just inside the screened-in porch. Just sitting there waiting, maybe with a beer in hand, ready to catch him.

Careful.

It wasn't until he was almost to the porch that he noticed and he even counted

them twice to make sure. There were nine of them. Nine newspapers lying across the lawn. Now Mad was well aware that he made a daily routine of swiping his morning paper – it was always returned of course – but this didn't make sense. Mad's car was in the driveway and even if he had left with someone else, there was still the matter of his two dogs, Smith and Jones –

(Where are they?)

– and he would never leave them unattended. They were the only children he had and no pet could ever ask for a more attentive parent.

Sammy turned and looked out at the lawn. Nothing seemed out of the ordinary

but something had to be. Mad wasn't a young man but he wasn't an old man either. He kept a .45 on his night stand and a sawed-off in his closet and if he had fired them, someone would have heard the shots if some ignorant jackass had decided to break in. That couldn't have been it but there was definitely something wrong here. Maybe Mad had suffered a heart attack or a stroke and was lying inside, unable to reach a phone that Sammy knew had all of the emergency numbers on speed dial. It explained the present circumstances and quite frankly, the possibility scared the hell out of him.

"Oh shit…", he said, opening the screen door.

(Not locked. That's not like Mad.)

Mad wasn't on the porch, beer or no, and that scared him all the more. His recent

fears must have been right and he could feel a chill run through him as he called out. "Mad?"

The voice from inside was calm and unmistakably Mad's, "The door's open. Come inside but close it behind you." He added, "And do it quick."

Sammy did what he was told. He crossed to the trailer door, swung in quick,

closed and locked it. And when he turned back to view the kitchenette, he was astonished by what he saw.

Mad was an unusual guy – a practical joker by nature – but he was also as neat pin. He had been in the service for over ten years as an M.P. and upon retiring, became a cop, eventually working his way up to Captain. Even though he was, shall we say, a unique individual, he also had a passion for cleanliness and that's why Sammy couldn't understand why his friend of some thirty years was sitting in the middle of discarded cans and empty frozen food boxes, the trash cans on either side of him filled to the brim and boiling with maggots. He was smoking a cigarette, his feet resting on the cluttered table in front of him when he looked up and said, "How was Orlando?"

The smell was overwhelming. Mad didn't believe in air-conditioning, saying that he wasn't going to shell out good much for so much cold air and instead opted for a simple rotating fan, the one resting beside the closed window. In fact, all of the windows were closed and it only succeeded in blowing the foul air from one side of the room to the other. "What did you say...?"

Mad tapped his ashes on the growing pile on the floor, "Orlando. That big city in the middle of the state. The one you been in for the past week."

"Nine days...", he said absently. "You want to tell me what the hell's going on?"

"Not especially."

"Yeah?" Sammy pulled up one of the kitchen chairs, pushed the trash resting on it to the floor and sat down. Normally he would have never done such a thing, particularly in Mad's house. But this wasn't the Mad he knew and he had to know why. "Well tell me anyway."

Mad ground out the cigarette beside at least two dozens others, "I sprayed my trees."

The answer was nonsensical and typically Mad. "You sprayed your trees?"

He nodded and lit another cigarette, "The day you left."

"Why?"

"Had chiggers." He tossed the match to the floor, "Don't have 'em no more."

Yep, this was typically Mad. See, he had never heard of or chose to disregard the phrase 'to make a long story short'

224

and so whenever you wanted to get to the point, you'd have to take his route. Sammy nodded, "That's fine."

"You'd think so, wouldn't you?"

"But it's not? Is that what you're saying?"

"I used this new stuff."

Sammy rolled a hand, "You used a new spray?"

Though it was too soon to have any ashes, he tapped anyway, "Try and keep up, Sam."

"Sorry."

"I picked it up over to Harley's. He'd just got some in. Some kind of environmentalist stuff."

Sammy shook his head, "You want to run that one by me again?"

He nodded, "You heard me right. It was invented by them GreenPeace people or some such group. I don't really know. I threw the canister away."

Sammy looked around the impossibly cluttered room and then to Mad sitting amid the dozens of discarded beer cans and empty packages. Now Mad wasn't exactly an avid shopper – he only went on grocery runs maybe six times a year – and so he kept his frozen food in his two lie-down freezers out back. This stuff, this trash, had come from the fridge right here in the kitchen and by the amount, Sammy figured it must be darn near empty. "Why didn't you throw this other stuff out with it?"

"Because I'd have to go outside.", he said simply.

"What?"

He shrugged, "That's where the trash cans are."

(What the hell was he talking about?)

Sammy shook his head as if he were trying to rattle something back into place,

"Okay, so the trash is in here, the trash cans are outside and the chiggers are gone –"

Mad interrupted, " – That's not all that's gone."

"What's say?"

"Just quiet down and listen a minute."

They did. For a full minute. And if you don't know how long a minute can be, just sit in the dark for a full sixty seconds in a room like that and find out. Sammy finally sighed, "Would you tell me what we're listening for?"

Mad motioned at Sammy's watch, "What time you got?"

He sighed again. Damn if Mad wasn't taking the scenic route this time. He glanced at his wrist. "Coming up on six."

"Kinda quiet for six, don't you think?"

Sammy cocked his head to one side and this time actually listened. Living all your life in Florida, you sometimes take for granted the sounds of nature just like he done only a moment before. But Mad was right. There was nothing at six in the morning when the river should be teaming with life. Bullfrogs, gators, crickets and horseflies, all manner of birds. Literally teaming with life.

It wasn't.

Sammy shook his head, "I don't get this." He looked back at Mad who was staring at him, appearing not to blink in the dim light, "What's going on here?"

"I told you, ", he said, exhaling a thick cloud of smoke, "I sprayed my trees."

It was all suddenly very clear to him and Sammy felt his eyes widen. "What kind

of poison did you use?"

Mad shook his head, "It wasn't poison." He casually pushed the butts out of the ashtray and laid the newly lit cigarette inside, "I told you, this was environmentalist stuff. All natural." He sadly watched the smoke swirling upwards, "All natural…"

Sammy looked toward the lifeless river and then back, "You want to cut to the chase and tell me what this is all about?"

"That stuffed I sprayed, the spray itself, was alive."

He leaned closer and offered his ear again. Even though there were no other sounds, Sammy figured he couldn't have heard him right. "You wanna run that one by me again?"

"Some kind of biological thing. A liquid fungus." Ignoring the other cigarette, he lit a new one, "Environmentally safe. Good for the ozone.", he waved a hand, "All that happy horseshit. See, like I said, this stuff wasn't poison. It would feed on the chiggers. Survival of the fittest, right? And poof! Problem over."

"What's wrong with that? I mean it sounds, ", he searched for the right word, "Reasonable."

"That's what I thought. Good, solid American-made natural shit." Mad paused a moment to stare at his glowing embers and Sammy realized that was the only real light in the kitchen, "Only we both made the same mistake. We ignored the same thing."

"What's that?"

227

He paused and looked Sammy straight in the eye.  He didn't smile as he said,

"Everything that feeds grows, Sam."

Now it was clear.  Oh yeah, he got it now.

Mad had done it again.

He had had nine straight days to come up with this one and that was more than enough time for a joker like him.  His reputation here in Deland was legend and even though the locals respected him, nobody believed a word that he said.  You didn't dare.  Still, there were the tourists,  Those poor innocent victims from up north that would occasionally bumble into Mad and ask for something like directions or just some innocent question.  There was that fellow who was trying to get to Daytona Beach who was probably now in Cuba and a woman he warned about the infamous 'Red Hat Killer' when the Shriners were in town.  Even animals weren't safe from Mad when that grin appeared and those eyes gleamed with mischief.  On more than one occasion, Sammy himself had witnessed Mad gleefully spraying WD-40 on the metal post to his bird feeder just so he could sit back on his porch and watch the squirrels slip and slide in their vain attempts to reach the bird seed.

Sammy started to smile but fell short.

There weren't any squirrels. There wasn't anything. Sammy looked toward the river again.

"Why don't you ask me about my dogs, Sam?"

Sammy turned back, suddenly reminded of his favorite co-conspirators. His partners who greeted him every morning with yelps and kisses until he rubbed their bellies, their legs kicking playfully before finally letting him steal their master's newspaper.

Every morning.

Except today.

Mad sadly nodded. "That's right. It took them."

This had to be a joke, and Sammy thought he could prove it. He had him on a technicality. He leaned closer and looked into Mad's eyes. "So how did I get in here?"

He smiled. Mad didn't.

"Everything alive sleeps, Sam. And the real question now is, how do you get out?"

Mad was playing. Sammy kept smiling. "How about if I just call myself a cab?"

"Don't you think I've tried that?" Mad motioned toward the phone on the wall. "Go ahead. You won't get anything. There's no one there." He leaned forward, his voice serious. "See, Harley stocked half his store with that new stuff, and I got the last canister. He was sold out, Sam. How many other folks do you think used it?"

Sammy shuddered involuntarily. If this was a joke, it sure as hell wasn't funny. "You can stop this now..." he said quietly.

Mad leaned back. "I wish I could..."

Sammy stood up. "No, really. I mean it now. Stop it."

"I can't even get to my freezers. I figure I'm going to starve to death in a week or so—"

Sammy interrupted. "What about the neighbors?"

Mad blew smoke rings. "You see any lights on?"

Sammy turned and leaned closer to the window. He already knew there were no lights on—no witnesses, remember—and he was right. Nobody was home. Not anymore.

Sammy turned back. "Where are they?"

Mad shook his head, the way people do when others don't seem to understand what they're being told. "Most of those houses are rented out to tourists."

"So?"

"So we both grew up here. We're used to the heat. They're not."

"So?" Sammy repeated.

Mad looked at him as if the answer were obvious. "If they don't have air-conditioners, they leave their windows open."

(Oh man, this has to be a gag. Please, let this be a gag. A bad joke from a good friend. Please...)

As if reading his thoughts, Mad shook his head. "It's not. I'm sorry, but it's not."

"Then how did the paperboy deliver all those papers outside? Tell me that!"

He had him. This time, he had him.

Mad didn't look away from him. "How many papers did you see out there?"

"Nine!" Sammy said triumphantly. "Nine papers, nine days!" He chuckled. "Gotcha!"

Mad shook his head. "This is the tenth day, Sam." He looked up at him sadly. "So why aren't there ten papers?"

This was bullshit. It had to be. Typical Madison bullshit. Only Sammy wasn't a tourist and wasn't going to fall for it. He turned to the door. "I'm going home."

Mad nervously puffed on his cigarette. "I wish you wouldn't try that."

"You're not going to try and stop me?"

He shook his head. "I'm not leaving this chair. I tried that once, and it almost got inside." He ground the cigarette out beside the others. "I'm not leaving this chair."

For the first time, Sammy noticed two things. Sure, the kitchen smelled—it was a friggin' hothouse—but it shouldn't smell this bad, unless someone had urinated on the floor, which Mad had certainly done. Sammy could even see the dried yellow stains. The second thing he noticed, barely visible beneath the trash on the table, was Mad's .45.

Sammy looked at Mad, who nodded. "That's right. I've shot at it, but it didn't do any good." He picked up the gun. "And right now, I've got one bullet left. That's for me. I have other clips in the bedroom, but like I said, I'm not leaving this chair."

Sammy thought that maybe—just maybe—he finally understood what was happening, and he frowned. Mad had finally earned his nickname and had actually lost his mind. Maybe he had killed his neighbors, the visiting tourists he'd always loathed. Maybe he'd even killed the paperboy.

"I'm going home now, Mad..."

Mad offered a sideways nod. "I'm wishing you luck."

Sammy took the doorknob. "I'm going next door to see if I can get you some help." With his other hand, he unlocked it. "If that's okay with you."

Mad sighed. "I'm going to miss you, Sam."

He pointed at the door. "Can I leave?"

"You can. I wish you wouldn't."

Sammy opened the door, and Mad tensed. "I'll get you some help. I promise."

Mad sadly shook his head. "Just make sure it locks behind you when you leave."

Sammy did as he was told, and when he stepped out onto the porch, he was gone.

No joke.

# SPILLWORTHY JONES

I've never liked Spillworthy Jones—not since the first day I met him, some twenty years ago. And I've made no secret of it, from that time until now.

Right off the bat, his name: 'Spillworthy Jones.' What kind of name is that? Don't get me wrong, it wasn't a nickname. No, sir. His parents actually named him 'Spillworthy.' I mean, what were they thinking? When he was born, did they look at their infant son and say, "Hey, let's give him a name that will almost certainly get him beat up throughout his school years and screw up the rest of his life?"

Well, whether that conversation ever happened or not doesn't matter. Because that's exactly what happened. He was a punching bag all through school—one of his chief tormentors being yours truly. And get this: right out of high school, he became a chimney sweep. A damn chimney sweep! I didn't even think those things existed outside of Dickens' novels. But there he was, in a long black coat and stove hat, with brass buckles on his boots that he never bothered to polish.

And the worst part? He lived across the street from me. ME! The owner of the biggest brokerage firm in all of Wellston, and this guy had to live in that crappy little tenement right across from me. Think about that. No, seriously, think about it. I'm probably the most respected man in this town—certainly the wealthiest—and every damn day, I have to watch through my living room window as this idiot strolls down the street, whistling some insipid tune, usually with a line of children following him.

Oh, right. I didn't tell you about the children. They follow him everywhere, like some kind of Pied Piper. I never liked kids—hell, I didn't even like being a kid—but every day, I had to listen to a gaggle of them trotting down the street after him, all whistling the same damn tune. He had some kind of bizarre rapport with children, maybe because he never bothered to grow up himself. I had to endure it every day at five o'clock. Every. Damn. Day. But I haven't told you everything. No, you need to hear this. You know why they like him? You're going to love this, even if I don't.

It's because he can talk to ghosts.

See? I knew you wouldn't believe me. But that's what he claims. And kids, being the gullible little creatures that they are, actually believe him. Even though I've tried several times to buy his house—just to get him out of my neighborhood and especially out of my face—I've never been inside. Still, the kids had been. (Why don't the parents complain? He's never been married, and in all probability, he's some kind of pervert.) And they'd often tell others about their ghostly encounters inside Jones' house—stories about former statesmen, presidents, actors, and the like. Hell, there were even a few who swore they'd sat around and chewed the fat with fictional characters. Yeah, that's right—fictional characters. The kind from books.

What am I saying? I'm sure you know what fictional means. It's just hard for me to believe that any kid would actually think they sat in his house and spoke to the Velveteen Rabbit. I mean, is that the most ridiculous thing you've ever heard? It has to be! These kids swore he could bring any character they requested to life. It was crap, of course. But I had to see it for myself. I needed to know what kind of storyteller Jones was, what kind of magic he was weaving to convince even a stupid child that he could do such a thing. But his damn dogs, those stupid, yelping mutts, always chased me away before I could get close.

That's why I set up the meeting.

Well, that's not entirely true.

I set up the meeting so I could kill him. I even had a gun in my desk drawer when he arrived, under the pretense of trying to sell me his house again. I knew Spillworthy was a gentleman—(Read: 'idiot')—and so I knew he'd be on time. At exactly ten o'clock, on the dot, he was sitting before me, dressed in his ridiculous costume.

"I really can't stay," he said, glancing at a wrist that bore no watch. "I've got to be at the Wilkinsons' in half an hour."

I smiled. "It won't take that long." I motioned to the decanter on my desk. "Would you care for a drink?"

He made a brief gesture. "Thank you, but I never touch it."

Another smile. "Good for you."

He shrugged, as if unsure whether to speak his mind. But he did anyway. "Besides, it's a little early, don't you think?"

I sat on the edge of my desk and folded my hands in my lap. He had no idea how late it really was. "Do you know why I asked you here?"

235

He sighed. "I assume—"

I waved a hand. "The first thing they teach you in business school is to never assume." I smiled again. This was fun. "But then you wouldn't know that, would you? You never went to college, right?"

He didn't seem offended—something that briefly annoyed me—and said, "No. I'm afraid all my parents could afford was a general education." I was about to interrupt when he added, "That and the house across the street from you." My smile dropped, and his appeared. "That's why I'm here." He crossed his legs. "That is, if I'm not being presumptuous."

I glared at him—a bad business move—but if he noticed, he didn't let on.

He was one-upping me, and I didn't like it. "Maybe I just wanted to get to know you."

To prove my suspicions, Jones lazily removed a piece of lint from his pants, and to irritate me further, he rolled it into a neat ball before dropping it in my ashtray. "It's possible," he said. "But not very likely."

I inhaled deeply, the breath only serving to remind me how badly I needed a cigarette, so I lit one. I turned back to him. "I hope you don't mind."

(Though I didn't care one bit if he did.)

Still, he shook his head. "I'm used to smoke. I work in chimneys, after all. In case you haven't noticed."

I sat back down in front of the drawer. "I've noticed, and no, that's not the reason I invited you over." I began to open the drawer when he interrupted.

"Do you know anything about the afterlife, Mister Sawyer?"

I stopped. "Excuse me?"

He looked amused. "You don't, do you?"

I was genuinely confused and shook my head. "What are you talking about?"

He leaned back in his seat, looking pleased with himself. "You don't know anything about life, period." He laced his hands behind his head and chuckled. "You don't even know about the life you can create."

I could feel my fingers brushing against the gun's butt. But instead of pulling it, I leaned forward and asked, as absurdly as I could, "The life I can create?"

He nodded. "People can create life, and I'm not talking about procreation."

This was the kind of mumbo jumbo I was talking about. I realized I was about to hear his carnival-barker spiel without having to buy a ticket or risk a dog bite. I crossed my arms. "Is that right?"

He grinned. "Of course it is."

"And how, pray tell, would one go about doing that?"

He raised one finger. "Ah, therein lies the rub."

I sighed. "What the hell does that mean?"

His self-satisfied smile dropped, and he said simply, "I don't care for profanity."

I didn't apologize. "What does that mean?"

"You should know. Like you said, you're the one who went to business school."

I was getting tired of asking the same question. "What does that mean?"

He smiled—this time without humor. "I mean, how much is it worth to you?"

He was bargaining with me. This piss-ant little son of a bitch was sitting there trying to bargain with me! The little bastard, who didn't care for profanity and who had no idea I'd called him here to kill him, was trying to bargain with me!

I almost laughed. "What?"

"How much would you," he pointed at my chest, "Pay me," he pointed at his own, "To tell you?" He pointed at me again.

I wanted to snap that finger off and shove it up his ass. "You aren't serious."

He mockingly smiled wider. "How much in dollars for that information?"

I openly glared at him. "You mean how to bring people back from the dead?"

"Yes."

I rolled my hand. "And how to pull them out of books?"

He rolled his hand, mimicking me. "Yes."

I smiled. "You're crazier than a shit-house rat." My return to profanity seemed to offend him, but I continued smiling. "I mean, I've heard the stories about you, but who would have believed they were true?" I slapped the desk. "You're one triple-flippin' fucking nut!"

I laughed—hard and long. I laughed until my sides ached. I laughed until I felt the gun at the base of my neck.

And then I froze.

Because it wasn't funny anymore.

"That's right, pal," the unfamiliar voice said from behind me. "Knock off the noise."

I had planned exactly this kind of fate for Jones, but I never imagined he could turn the tables on me. He wasn't the type. And how his accomplice had gotten into the closed room without me hearing or seeing him seemed impossible.

As if sensing my thoughts, Jones grinned. "I don't think you two have met." He gestured to the man behind me as if introducing him at a cocktail party. "Mister Sawyer, meet Mike Hammer."

Mike Hammer? He was a fictional detective—one I had been reading just the night before. In fact, the book was still on my nightstand. How could Jones have known?

I slowly, cautiously turned to face the man standing there. He wore an old trench coat and tipped his hat, though his eyes never left mine, and the gun never left my throat. "I'd like to say it's a pleasure, but it's not." He replaced his hat. "Yet."

Jones smiled—at least, I assumed he did, since there was no way I was going to take my eyes off the guy—and said, "It's okay, Mike. You can go now."

The guy Jones called Mike didn't look away from me. "You sure?"

"I'm sure. Thanks."

He glared at me for a moment, then slowly pulled the pistol from my throat, sliding it easily back into its holster. "If you say so, pal."

And then he was gone.

I don't mean he left the room. I mean he was gone. I was staring right at him, and then, in the blink of an eye—believe me, I wasn't blinking—he simply disappeared.

Poof!

For a moment, there was no air in the room—or at least it seemed that way. Maybe I just couldn't catch my breath. Whatever it was, it took me a second before I could breathe again, and then I turned to Jones.

He was smiling. "See?"

No. I didn't see. I had indeed seen what had happened, but I didn't understand it. But I had to know.

"How did you do that?"

"I can do that whenever I want." He shrugged.

"But Mike Hammer," I looked from where he stood to where Jones was sitting, my voice stammering, "He's—he's—not real!"

"He is if you want him to be."

None of this made sense. None of it. And the only question I could ask—the one I had to ask—was this: "How?"

He sat up and, in a very even voice, asked me again, "How much is it worth to you?"

He was bargaining again, but this time, he had something to bargain with—something beyond price, beyond riches. For this—for this!—I would pay:

"Anything!" I blurted out.

His eyebrows raised. "Anything? Are you sure you mean that?"

I was sweating. Shit! I had a hard-on. "Yes! Yes, I'm sure I mean that!"

And then it hit me. In business, you naturally seek the best possible deal for yourself, but even then, there are always hidden clauses. Call it a sixth sense, but I could sense one here—one that smelled a little like sulfur and brimstone.

Again, he seemed to read my thoughts—or maybe my expression was just that transparent—and shook his head. "I'm not the devil, if that's what you're thinking. I don't want your soul. Hell, I doubt even he'd want that rancid thing by now." He smiled again, this time unquestionably genuine. "What I want is this. What's happening right now. To dangle something in front of you that you desperately want, just to take it away. I've watched you do it to others my entire life, but you never seemed to get the joy out of it that I feel now. I guess it's because in your case, it was done out of cruelty. Out of greed. An empty, unfulfilling greed. In my case, it's retribution." He uncrossed his legs, brushed at his pants again, and stood. "You see, what I have is an ability. That's all it is. But it's something you can't buy. Not for any amount of money. It's like my house. It's just plain and simple—something you can't have! Ever!"

I could feel my hand tighten around the grip of the pistol. I had never seen anyone look so pleased with themselves in my life—not even me at the end of an especially lucrative business deal. Somehow, he had set this whole thing up. He had devised this entire scenario just to make me look foolish. He had gotten the best of me—something he'd probably been dreaming of since he was that skinny little fuck I left bleeding in the schoolyard.

But what he didn't know was that nobody bests me, and nobody—absolutely nobody—humiliates me.

NOBODY.

I pulled the gun from the drawer.

A single shot rang out.

So here I sit now, on a homemade stage, beside a Velveteen Rabbit, Charlie Chaplin, and an actual dinosaur the kids in front of me call Barney. He seems to be their favorite.

You see, I finally got that glimpse into Spillworthy's home. In fact, I'm here quite often, and now I finally understand why he guarded his privacy and this house so fiercely. It's actually a school where he teaches his ability— his skill—to the children. He teaches them for free. That was the reason they were so enraptured by him.

He teaches them magic.

Genuine magic.

Barney teaches them songs and how to dance, Chaplin makes them laugh, but I have a purpose too.

I'm the bad example, and of course, I'm helpless to do anything about it. Jones calls me whenever he needs me, ever since John Wilkes Booth put that bullet in my head. And I can't complain, even when he talks about me. He brings up things from our past that, although true, I'd rather not hear. But I can't protest, and he certainly doesn't let me swear.

He doesn't care for profanity, remember?

That's why, whenever he calls me back from the grave, he doesn't give me a mouth.

# ARE YOU RECEIVING ME?

There was a loud pop, and Lauren urgently looked at Colin, who continued gripping the plane's wheel with white-knuckled hands. "What was that?"

He didn't look away from the ocean rushing past beneath them. "We just lost an engine."

Behind them, Arnie sprang from his seat and, in a panicked voice, cried out, "What did you say?"

Colin didn't turn. "I said we just lost an engine."

Arnie ran a hand through his already disheveled hair. They had barely made it off the islands with their stash, and he'd hoped the shots fired by the police had missed anything vital. He must have been wrong. "Shit!" he paced, wringing his hands. "Shit and shit!"

Colin looked at Lauren in the seat beside him and motioned to the radio. "You might want to get on the horn."

"What?" He gave a curt nod toward the console, and she realized, "Oh." She snatched up the mic, flicked the switch, and leaned into it. "Mayday! This is C-49er! We have a Mayday!"

Arnie turned back, sweating. "How far can we go on one engine?"

The wheel trembled under Colin's hands, and he gripped it even tighter. "That's not the problem."

The remark didn't make sense, and Arnie threw his hands up. "How can that *not* be the problem?!"

Colin didn't bother to look back. "The problem is, we've got pressure dropping on number two. In a minute, we're going to lose them both."

In the back of the plane, Phil—the guy they laughably brought along in case they needed a little extra muscle—dropped his head between his legs and looked close to tears. Beside him, standing guard over their neatly stacked piles of cocaine, the youngest member of their merry band, Ian, swallowed the lump in his throat and gasped, "Oh man..."

Arnie hurried to the cockpit and looked out the window at the sea, seeming to come ever closer. "Are you saying we're gonna have to ditch?"

Colin briefly glanced at Arnie and asked the obvious question, "Do you mean, are we going to crash?" Arnie nodded. Colin nodded back. "Yep. Seems damn likely."

Lauren covered her left ear to better hear any response as she continued, "Mayday! This is C-49er. We've got ourselves a Mayday!"

Arnie massaged the sweat into his face and asked a question to Colin that he didn't want answered. "Have you ever ditched before?"

Again, Colin didn't bother to turn. "I've been flying exactly two months. What does that tell you?"

Lauren switched channels, her voice sounding even more desperate. "Mayday! This is a Mayday!"

While gripping the back of a passenger seat as if for support, Ian offered a timid question. "Isn't Mayday just for boats?"

Lauren shot him a chastising glance—*What the hell was this kid doing on their run anyway?*—then returned to the mic. "Mayday! This is flight C-49er, and it looks like we're going down! Repeat, this is C-49er, and we are going down!"

Arnie covered his face and paced away. "Oh man, I don't want to die..."

If possible, Colin's grip tightened even more on the wheel as he attempted to steady the see-sawing plane and muttered under his breath, "Yeah, well, who the fuck does...?"

Lauren's eyes widened. She looked at the console and then brought a hand to the headset. She sounded unbelieving as she said, "I think I've got somebody...!" She spun to Colin, her voice rising excitedly. "I think I've got somebody!"

There were quick turning heads and wide, hopeful eyes.

Colin briefly took his hand off the wheel and flicked on the overhead speaker, the one that spat static like his dead engine spewed black smoke.

"C-49er. This is Belle Island Tower. Do you read? Mayday? Over."

Arnie looked confused. "Belle Island? I've never heard of that. What the hell is Belle Island?"

Lauren ignored him and spoke into the mic. "Yes, Belle Island! This is C-49er, and we're in pretty bad shape. If we have to ditch—"

The crackling voice interrupted. "We have you on radar, and we've got a runway waiting."

Colin and Lauren exchanged a look. Arnie turned back, utterly baffled. "Runway?"

Lauren shook her head, looking equally confused, then spoke into the mic. "Belle Island Tower, did you say runway? Over."

Another crackle. "That's a roger, C-49er. We are Belle Tower Naval Base, and we are awaiting your approach."

Again, quick turning heads, but this time, the hope in their eyes had faded.

Colin glanced over his shoulder and, in a stern and even voice, said to Ian, "Ditch the shit."

Even though Ian had clearly heard the command, he looked at the cache of coke and said in a disbelieving tone, "What...?"

"I said ditch the shit."

The overhead speaker sputtered again. "You just follow our coordinates, and we'll lead you right in."

Lauren replied, "Copy that, Belle Tower."

Ian continued to look unbelieving. "Copy that? No, it's *fuck that*!" He motioned at the coke and added, "This isn't going anywhere!"

Colin turned but didn't take his hands off the wheel. "Phil, deal with that asshole."

Phil looked confused. "What do you mean?"

Colin glared. "Give him a hand with the cargo."

Suddenly graced with understanding, Phil nodded and pushed out of his seat. "Done."

Ian's face went ashen as Phil moved down the aisle toward him. A good head taller and nearly twice his weight,

Phil was an imposing sight—exactly why he was on board to begin with. "Come on, man, I've got twenty grand invested in this."

Phil continued toward him and shook his head. "Move."

Ian pleaded. "I had to sell my Jag!"

Phil didn't even glance at Arnie as he passed but merely said, "Open the bay door."

Ian nodded. "You got it." He stepped over, attached a tether line to his belt, summoned his courage, and then popped the catch to open the door. Hot air immediately rushed throughout the cabin, and he found that even with the safety line, he had to hold on to avoid being sucked into the sea below.

Ian bounced from foot to foot like the frustrated, petulant child he actually was. "You aren't fucking doing it!"

Phil easily grabbed him under the arms and tossed him into the cheap seats before beginning to fling the one-pound bags out the open door and into the ocean below. Tears streamed down Ian's face as he cried out to Colin, "That's two hundred grand on the street! Think about what you're doing!"

The wheel trembled wildly in Colin's hands. "Ian, if we make it out, we're landing on a naval base. I don't think they'd be real understanding about our cargo." He briefly glanced back. "Do you?"

As the last of his coke flew outside and Arnie closed and sealed the door, Ian fell to his knees and covered his face. "Fuck..."

Lauren flicked off the speaker, placed a hand to her headset, and said to Colin, "He says we have to go two degrees east."

He shook his head and watched the fuel gauge fall almost as fast as his altimeter. "They better be close."

Lauren again touched the headset. "We're two miles out."

There was another loud pop, and she looked to her right. The second engine belched smoke, and the propeller quickly came to a stop. Her eyes widened, and all the color drained from her face. "Colin...?"

"I know." He let out a loud, resigned sigh. "Looks like we're going to be gliding in."

Arnie made sure the door was indeed secured, then realized what he'd said. He looked confused. "What did you say?"

Colin grimly added, "You fellas might want to strap yourselves in."

Phil dropped back into his seat, pulled his seatbelt tight, and again put his head between his legs. "...Oh shit..."

Ian didn't move but instead kept staring at the place where his fortune used to be. Arnie lurched to a window just in time to see the clouds part to reveal the small island looming just ahead.

With a happy whoop, Lauren nearly shot out of her seat. "There it is!"

Even Colin offered an uncharacteristic smile. "Yeah, I see it."

"Have you ever seen anything so beautiful...?"

"Not lately," he answered, then motioned at the console. "Landing gear."

She briefly looked confused. "What? Oh! Yeah." She threw the appropriate switch and spoke into the mic. "Belle Island, this is C-49er. We are coming in. Over."

Over the headset came the surprisingly clear voice. "Roger that, C-49er. Let's do this nice and easy."

Lauren pulled the headset away from her left ear and said to Colin, "He said let's do this nice and easy."

Colin offered the same look to Lauren that he had when she had first proposed this drug run. A look that would shrivel a career marine. He knew it was a bad idea then, but he needed the cash, so he went along with it—having no idea how bad it would really turn out to be. "I kind of figured on doing that without being told, but tell him thanks for the advice."

Lauren sneered, replaced the headset, and when he heard the landing gear hum and clamp into place, he called back. "You guys better hold on, 'cause I don't think this is going to be pretty."

Ian leapt into the seat beside Phil and belted himself in. Arnie chose to neglect the suggestion and instead braced both hands tight against the back of two of the seats. "Oh shit..."

The tarmac was coming up surprisingly fast, and Lauren's eyes widened. "Colin!"

"Shut up!" was his response.

The wheels hit the oddly-potted runway surface, and the plane actually bounced, knocking Arnie flat on his ass. Colin prematurely hit the brakes and grimaced when he could actually feel the rubber come loose from the tires.

Phil raised his head and asked in a surprised voice, "We're down...?"

He looked out the window as if to affirm what he had asked, then grinned and soundly slapped Ian on the shoulder. "We're down!"

Colin shook his head and said, "Yeah, we're down, but we're not stopping..."

Phil's smile faltered. "What?"

Colin slammed his feet down as hard as he could on the brakes, so hard that he thought he might push them straight through the bottom of the plane. The wheels screamed, but he wouldn't.

Lauren glanced up through the cockpit window but didn't scream. "Colin!"

Even though he saw the same thing she did, he gripped the wheel. "I see it."

"Colin!" she repeated, louder this time.

"I see it! What do you expect me to do?"

Ahead of them, directly in their path, a man in a naval uniform lay face down on the runway. As they sped toward him, out of control, Colin briefly thought that he might have been a signalman, planning to wave them in. But in the end, it didn't matter. There was no way to avoid him.

They were going to run him over.

As if reading his mind, her eyes widened. "Colin, don't do it."

He kept his hands on the wheel, refusing to look away. Horrified, she screamed louder, "Don't do it!"

The body was coming up fast.

The tires smoked against the tarmac.

Colin gritted his teeth. "Shit."

Lauren couldn't look away. She didn't even remember lunging forward, grabbing the wheel, and jerking it hard to the right. Still, the plane rolled over the body with a sickening crunch, then bounced briefly, like a basketball, before skidding off the runway and through a length of cyclone fence. The propeller immediately caught, ripping three steel posts from their foundations. A fourth post broke free and somersaulted like an errant baton before crashing through the window beside Ian, neatly snapping his wrist. He screamed.

Colin shook his head. "I can't hold it!"

Lauren gripped the armrests as the fence closed around them like a metal squid, intent on dragging them down into the ocean, now just yards away. "No! Don't let go!"

Another post came up fast. They both ducked as it shattered the windscreen. Glass rained down on them, and Phil covered his head as it seemed to fall exclusively on him. "Shit!"

Like the tailhook on an aircraft carrier, the fence abruptly brought them to a stop just shy of the beach. Colin collapsed over the wheel. As he caught his breath, he thought they'd gotten lucky. He was sure the rest of the piece-of-shit plane that Arnie had called a plane couldn't swim any more than it could fly.

Phil carefully brushed the glass off himself, glanced back, and urgently called out, "Ian's hurt! Ian's hurt!"

Even though he couldn't care less, Colin thought he should say something. "How bad?"

Phil looked over his shoulder to see Ian clutching his arm, sobbing. "I don't know. I think he might have busted his wrist or something."

Colin cut the non-existent engines out of habit and sighed. "Well, ain't that a fucking shame…"

Lauren was still catching her breath when she cocked her ear. Her eyes narrowed. "Do you hear that?"

Colin finally straightened in his seat and listened, but all he could hear were Ian's sobs. "Hear what?"

Lauren looked at him as if the answer should be obvious. "We just crashed on a naval base."

Colin unstrapped himself and rubbed his chest. "Yeah, I noticed."

"No, no, you're not getting it!"

He sighed again. This was getting tiresome. "Not getting what?"

She looked through the shattered windshield, at the tangled cyclone fence, then said, "Do you hear any sirens? I mean, where the hell are the emergency vehicles?"

For the first time, Colin realized what she was talking about. He looked out through the windshield himself, and she was right. There were no alarms. The field was clear. There wasn't anybody there—no speeding MPs, no fire trucks, no ambulances.

Nobody.

How is that possible?

No, this didn't make any fucking sense, and he puzzled over it so long that he didn't even realize Lauren had disappeared. When he did, he looked from right to left, then behind him, but she was gone. Finally, he saw that the right rear door was open. She had obviously opened it and jumped out without bothering to lower the steps.

He shook his head. "Oh, now what in the fuck?"

He untangled himself from the seat and was heading to the door when Phil called out from the back of the plane. "Hey, Colin?" He sighed again and looked over to find Phil and Arnie crouched over the still-sobbing Ian. "I'm serious, man, I think he might be hurt pretty bad."

Colin waved him off. "So?" Then hopped out the open door.

His feet thudded hollowly against the runway, and even though he managed to pull free of the fencing, the sound seemed to echo throughout the empty airfield.

Why empty?

He gave a cursory look around before spotting Lauren, now standing over the airman's corpse just a hundred feet away. Her shoulders rocked with silent sobs, and she had a hand over her eyes.

Women...

He slumped and started over, anticipating whatever you had to say to women to put a stop to this kind of bullshit. "Lauren, there wasn't anything we could do. The engines cut out on us." He stopped behind her, and because it seemed like the thing to do, he placed a hand on her shoulder. "For whatever fucking reason, he was in the middle of the runway—"

Colin looked down and froze.

He'd seen some serious shit before. In fact, he had been involved in serious shit in the past, which was why he'd been hired for this gig in the first place. But what he was looking at now didn't make any fucking sense. Not one fucking bit.

The officer lying on the runway was, without question, dead. But the plane hadn't done it. No, this man had been dead for a long time—maybe a week, maybe two. Hell, it could've been longer. The dry, gray skin was taut over his skeleton, and maggots filled his open mouth. Colin wasn't a coroner, but even he knew that this kind of shit didn't happen overnight. This took time. So, that was the question: how did this guy end up lying here, on an open runway, for all that time, and nobody did a thing about it?

No fucking sense.

Colin wasn't sure if he heard Lauren whisper, or maybe it was just what he was thinking. "What's going on here…?"

He didn't look away from the corpse but shook his head. "I don't know…"

Behind him, Phil leaned from the back compartment and called out, "Colin! We're going to need a doctor, or a medic, or whatever they call them on these bases, 'cause I think Ian's hurt pretty bad!"

Colin paused and blinked several times, as if he were finally realizing what was going on. Then, as if speaking to no one in particular, he said, "Get the Jack Dancers…"

Phil leaned out further and squinted, as if trying to hear him better. "What? What did you say?"

Colin spun around and shouted, "Get me the fucking Jack Dancers!"

Phil's eyes widened. He knew damn well that you didn't argue with Colin, and you sure as hell didn't fuck with him. He raised his hands. "Okay! I'll get 'em. I'm on my way." He ducked back into the plane.

J.D.s was their code word for .357 Magnums. For some reason, these assholes who hired him thought that deep-south drug dealers were the best of polite society and didn't believe they'd need any firepower. But Colin knew better. To use a tired cliché, this wasn't his first rodeo, so he made sure those horse-killers were clamped under the cockpit's back seats for easy access in case things went south. And things had gone south two hours ago. Still, these suburban pussies didn't have the balls or brains to use them when they had to, which was exactly why they were where they were now. Everybody—particularly in this business—should know that "better safe than sorry" is a good fucking philosophy. Right about now, looking at this corpse and thinking about the motherfuckers who did this, the rest of these dumbfucks should be starting to understand that it's a damn good motto.

Arnie carefully helped Ian slump down against the plane's shredded wheel, then turned to Colin. His voice was shrill and disbelieving. "The J.D.s? Are you nuts?!" He raised his hands and spun in a circle, "We're on a fucking naval base!" He looked down at the corpse and froze. For a moment, a long moment, it seemed he couldn't catch his breath. "What in the hell is that…?"

Colin didn't look at him but continued to survey the seemingly empty base. "I'm no expert, but it looks to me like this guy's been dead about a month."

They all looked at him, each with the same question in their eyes, but it was Arnie who actually voiced it. "What the hell are you talking about?"

Colin's eyes continued to dart. "I'm saying this may have been a naval base at one time, but I think someone else is running it now."

Arnie was uncomprehending and shook his head. "What're you talking about?"

Phil arrived, canvas bag in hand. "Got 'em, Colin." He began to pass it over, saw the corpse at his feet, and promptly vomited.

Colin dropped beside the fallen bag and pulled one of the guns free, making sure it was loaded and the safety off.

Arnie did his best to ignore Phil's powerful retching sounds and even the smell of the corpse crawling with flies as he crouched beside Colin. "What do you mean this was a naval base?"

Phil looked up, gray drool spilling down his chin. He asked in a faraway voice, "What…?"

Lauren glanced down at Colin but hesitated before taking the pistol he offered from over his right shoulder. "Who…?"

Colin shook his head. "I don't know. Smugglers. Pirates." He shrugged.

Lauren straightened, gripping the gun tightly as she scanned the deserted airfield. There was no one in sight. She turned back to Colin. "How can you be so sure?"

Colin took the last pistol from the bag, chambered it, and said, his tone blunt, "I've never been in the service, but even I know the Navy doesn't leave a corpse on the tarmac for months, just waiting to be run over by would-be drug dealers." He held out the last pistol to Phil. "Wipe your mouth, keep your eyes open, and give this to Ian."

Phil coughed, pointing toward the plane. "Ian's got a busted arm."

Colin shook his head and slapped the pistol into Phil's hand. "I don't give a fuck if he broke his back. In case you haven't figured this out yet, we're in some serious shit here. He's still got one good hand. Put this in it."

Phil nodded, his legs wobbling as he started away. "Okay..."

Lauren looked at the gun in her hands, trying to get accustomed to its weight. She asked Colin, "Are you sure about this?"

Colin slumped, as if trying to explain quantum physics to a first-grade class. He pointed at the corpse. "Somebody killed this guy, somebody took over this base, and it's the same fucking people who talked us down."

Arnie looked confused. "You said this guy's been dead for a month. Why would they still be here?"

Colin tucked the gun into his belt. His eyes kept darting around. "Maybe their ship went down. I don't know."

Lauren pointed at the plane, as if the remark were absurd. "But we told them our engines were gone!"

Colin spun to her and shouted, "Hello!" She jumped back, and he took a step closer. "We're on a Naval Base! Did you think they might not have the know-how to fix it up and fly it out of here?"

Lauren ran a hand through her hair. "...oh shit..."

Colin nodded. "Shit, indeed."

Arnie's voice cracked, revealing more of his nerves than he would have liked. "So what do we do now?"

Colin chambered the pistol and said, "Find them before they find us."

He stepped away, and Lauren took one last look at the corpse, which had not only begun to decay but appeared to have melted. Now it was just a lump of flesh wriggling with insects hungry to feed. It was then that she realized: this wasn't the grand adventure she thought it would be, or some old 'Miami Vice' episode. No, at this point, she just wanted to be back home. Back at Daddy's house. It was safe there. It wasn't like the real world, where people end up dead and rotting on some forgotten airfield.

For the first time that day, she whispered the unspoken truth. "...we're fucked..." The gun suddenly felt twice as heavy as it had a moment ago, and she let out a resigned sigh before following Colin.

After explaining their predicament to Ian, Colin told Phil to check out the beach, Arnie to check the Mess Hall, and said that he and Lauren would check out the barracks. At this, Lauren blanched. If there were indeed pirates here, that's where the majority would certainly be housed, just waiting for them.

Colin checked to make sure his pistol was loaded and, without looking at Ian, said, "Ian, you stay here with the plane." He walked toward the base.

Ian stared hopelessly at the chain-link fence before turning back. "Why?"

Colin didn't even glance back. "Because if there's going to be trouble, you'll be as useless as the plane. Just stay here."

The others continued behind him, but Ian waited until they were out of sight before muttering, "Fuck you too…"

****

While the others split up and headed toward their designated destinations, Colin moved forward as quietly as he could. He dropped outside the barracks, gently ushering Lauren to the opposite side of the entrance. As she ran, sweat beading on her forehead, Colin silently counted. Then he swung out and kicked open the door, his gun raised in both hands.

Immediately, his eyes narrowed. He straightened, scanning the room with a puzzled expression. "Where the hell is everybody?"

Lauren, curious, carefully leaned inside and saw what Colin had.

The barracks were deserted. There were several cots, some overturned—none of them had sheets. (Where were the sheets?) Half-empty cups of coffee and moldering plates of food, swarming with flies, lay scattered around. But there was no one. Not a single soul.

"Where the hell is everybody?" Colin repeated.

One overhead light fluttered and died.

* * * *

Phil kept his pistol close to his chest as he rounded the corner of the supply office. When he saw the open beach ahead, he squinted and whispered, "What in the hell is that...?"

* * * *

Unlike Colin, Arnie didn't kick in the door to the Mess Hall. Instead, he quietly opened it and leaned inside. The lights were off, except for one that seemed to come from the kitchen. Like the barracks, the room was deserted, with some overturned chairs. Other than that, it appeared to be an empty, harmless room.

"Oh man, I don't like this at all..."

He cocked the hammer.

* * * *

Ian paced alongside the plane, his own pistol tucked in his belt as he massaged his throbbing wrist. It was one white-hot knot of pain but he still stared at the buildings some one hundred yards away. His friends were now out of sight.

He was alone and he didn't like it.

* * * *

The sign over the door read simply, *Radio Room.*

Colin leaned against the side of the door, but this time, he didn't have to motion for Lauren to do the same. He looked at her, not realizing that he was sweating as much as she was. "You up for this?"

Instead of answering, she asked, "If the guy who talked us down is in here, do you think he might be the only survivor?"

Colin shook his head. The question didn't make sense. "What?"

She seemed desperate to prove her point. "You know, maybe when whatever happened went down, he hid or something until they left, and now he just wants out of here as much as we do."

Off Colin's dubious look, she added, "It's possible, isn't it?"

Colin didn't believe that explanation, but instead readied himself. "Let's find out."

He kicked open the door. Upon seeing the man seated at the console, his back to them, Colin aimed and gritted his teeth. "Don't you fucking move!"

\* \* \* \*

Arnie carefully stepped inside the dark Mess Hall, glancing quickly behind the door as he did. He'd never been a soldier—never wanted to be—but today, he had been recruited, however reluctantly. Like every soldier before him, he told himself he was going home today.

(At least, I hope so.)

He raised the gun, the barrel trembling.

"If anybody's in here," he dryly swallowed and said, "You better show yourself."

\* \* \* \*

Phil slowly stumbled forward, unable to take his eyes off the half-mile track burned into the beach sand—the one that led to the pulsating blue orb planted at its end.

His hands fell to his sides, and he shook his head. "What is going on here...?"

* * * *

Colin slowly approached the man at the console. He had never actually shot a human being before, but there's a first time for everything. He put the gun within a foot of the man's head and said, "Turn around."

He cocked the hammer. "And like you said earlier, nice and easy."

The man didn't turn.

* * * *

Arnie actually screamed when he heard the voice from the kitchen. "Who's there?"

* * * *

The blue orb seemed to pulsate, almost as if it were breathing. Phil noticed that, despite the sun being high, it was still encased in a sheen of ice. That didn't make any sense. He carefully crept closer, completely forgetting about the danger that had driven him there, and slowly reached out. "What are you...?"

* * * *

Colin inched forward. "Apparently you didn't hear me, pal. I told you to turn the fuck around."

* * * *

A shadowy figure stepped from the kitchen and, Arnie raised the gun with both hands. The barrel trembled wildly. "Don't you move!"

The man, silhouetted by the kitchen light, didn't move. Instead, he asked in a calm voice, "Are you with the rescue team?"

* * * *

Phil's fingers hovered over the orb. Despite the ice, he could feel the heat emanating from it. He considered it for a moment before placing his palm down on its surface.

He screamed.

* * * *

Colin put the gun to the man's head and hissed, "I guess you don't hear too good."

He spun the chair around.

Lauren gasped.

Together, they stared at the long-dead corpse that gaped back at them through empty eye sockets.

* * * *

The question didn't make sense and Arnie shook his head, "Rescue team?"

The silhoutted man raised his hands in a complacent manner and took a step closer, "Don't shoot. My name is Crewman First Class William Mason o"Rielly. Where have you guys been? We sent out a distress signal almost a month ago."

* * * *

Ian was shaking. He thought he heard a scream. It sounded like Phil.

* * * *

Colin crouched, stared at the corpse, and shook his head, "I don't get this. I don't get this at all."

Lauren couldn't blink. She couldn't look away.

"Colin?" she pointed with her pistol at the body, "It's wearing the headset..."

* * * *

Phil clutched at his wrist, writhing in pain. He noticed with considerable horror that his fingers were actually melting.

"...what the hell...?"

* * * *

Arnie kept the gun on him as the man slowly approached.

"Stop moving," Arnie warned.

The man ignored him and kept advancing. "You're not the only one who landed on this base."

"What're you—" Arnie backed into the table behind him, briefly startling himself. He turned back quickly, raising the gun even higher. "—What're you talking about?"

The man continued toward him at an easy pace. "You see, this is a tracking base." He offered a small shrug and kept going. "Not really very important these days. Not since the collapse of the Soviets. But they were still on the job."

Arnie's eyes narrowed. *"Were?"*

****

Ian shuffled from foot to foot. His arm was throbbing.

"Where are you guys?" he muttered.

****

By this time, Phil's hand had melted down to the wrist. He kicked away from the orb, leaving his forgotten pistol in the sand, and said in a certainly unheard voice, "...help me..."

**\*\*\*\***

Arnie found himself backing away as the crewman came even closer.

"See, in the early days, NASA sent up probes that weren't sterilized," the man said.

This guy was making no more sense than before. "What're you talking about?" Arnie snapped.

The crewman took another step forward. "And those probes spread diseases throughout the galaxy. Diseases that other civilizations had no immunity to."

Arnie took another step back and was surprised to find himself against the wall, so far from that door. He brandished the gun.

"I said, what're you talking about!"

The faceless man stopped advancing and spoke as if it should be obvious. "So one dying planet sent Earth a probe of their own." He chuckled. "With a virus of their own."

**\*\*\*\***

Phil's arm had melted down to the elbow when he finally screamed, "Somebody help me!!!!"

**\*\*\*\***

Colin and Lauren spun to the scream, but before they could move, the corpse sprang from its seat and was on them.

**\*\*\*\***

Ian reacted to the same scream. He pulled the gun from his belt, completely unaware that the corpse on the runway had crookedly risen and was now shambling toward him.

****

Arnie hadn't heard the scream. Even if he had, he wouldn't have taken his eyes off the man. He held the gun on him with two trembling hands.

"You just..." he swallowed hard, "keep away from that door..."

The man cocked his head to one side, as if studying something he'd never seen before, then let out a small, humorless chuckle.

"You see, their planet is now uninhabitable."

Arnie wasn't interested in this guy's ramblings anymore. He just wanted to get to that door and out of here. He raised the gun even higher, believing it to now be aimed between the man's eyes.

"I'm telling you for the last fucking time. Let me out of that fucking door."

The man took a step closer and shook his head.

"You really don't get it. The probe that was sent here was designed to kill and then re-animate the dead to spread the virus." He chuckled again. "And colonize."

****

Colin hit the floor hard. He'd played football in high school, but he'd never had anyone hit him with the intent to kill.

Especially a month-old corpse.

Lauren leapt back and screamed.

266

The corpse spun Colin over with remarkable ease and giggled as it clutched its skeletal fingers around his throat. As the long nails dug in, hard enough to draw blood, Colin managed to rasp out, "...get this thing off of me..."

Lauren raised the gun, closed her eyes, and fired.

****

Ian spun toward the shot, forgetting all about his broken wrist.

"What the fuck was that!" he shouted.

Of course, that was all he could say before the corpse behind him stepped up and neatly snapped his neck.

****

Arnie continued to hold his gun on the stranger in front of him, the one who said:

"Only the probe landed on this base." He chuckled. "An island base. There are no planes in the hangars, and according to the logs, a cargo ship isn't due for three more weeks." He chuckled again, an ironic sound. "And if that wasn't enough, because of the damned radiation, the radio won't broadcast more than four miles."

Sweat ran into Arnie's eyes, but he didn't dare wipe it away. He had to keep both eyes on him. Both hands on the gun.

"You come any closer and I shoot," he warned. "I can't make it any plainer than that."

The threat didn't seem to carry any weight. The faceless man continued toward him.

"That's why we talked you down."

Arnie frowned. "We?"

The stranger nodded. "To spread the virus, there has to be a way off the island." Even in the dim light, Arnie could see the man grin. There was blood on his teeth. "Like a plane."

****

Phil's arm had melted to the shoulder, now just a gooey mass of pus-white fluid clinging to his shirt. This had to be a dream, a bad dream, and as he stumbled toward the Mess Hall, he thought all he had to do was find his friends.

Then he could wake up. And everything would be back to normal.

****

Colin's face was going blue. Lauren's shot had put a foot-sized hole through the thing's head—but if it even noticed, it didn't seem to care.

Its grip tightened. More blood flowed from Colin's throat—faster than Lauren fled from the room.

****

Arnie shook his head. "Y-You're out of your mind..."

The stranger giggled. An unnerving sound.

"What's so funny?" Arnie asked. The gun barrel trembled.

The stranger waved a hand. "What you said." He couldn't seem to stop giggling.

Arnie's finger tightened on the trigger. "What did I say?" He didn't want the answer.

He got one anyway.

"No, I'm not out of my mind. My mind is out of me."

He stepped into a sliver of light, just enough to see that the left side of his head was gone.

"See, I blew my brains out three weeks ago."

\* \* \* \*

Lauren had left him. She had run off like the rich little bitch he always figured she was. And as he began to black out, he gasped, "...fuck you... you miserable cun—"

The corpse continued to giggle, until it heard the voice. Lauren's voice.

"Hold its head up."

Colin managed to glance over and saw her standing in the doorway, a fire axe gripped tight in her hands. And Colin did exactly what he was told.

\*\*\*\*

Arnie screamed, closed his eyes, and fired, blowing the rest of the stranger's head clean off.

But damned if it didn't keep standing.

\*\*\*\*

Lauren sprang forward, surprisingly fast, and swung the axe. Colin managed to roll aside, massaging at his bleeding throat, staring wide-eyed as she began to hack and hack at the corpse until there wasn't anything left to hack.

*Didn't think the chick had it in her,* he thought.

\*\*\*\*

Arnie spun and flung open the door, only to find what looked a little like Phil. Only now, he appeared to be a full-sized human melting candle. The flesh rained from his body like a summer shower, forming a purplish puddle at his remaining feet.

What used to be his friend reached out with its remaining hand and pleaded, "...help me..."

Instead, Arnie wet himself, screamed, and slammed the door, only to find the headless corpse on him.

****

Lauren dropped the axe and looked down at the still-writhing pieces at her feet. What had once been a human being now appeared to be a spilled bucket of live bait. And even as the sight repulsed her, she couldn't look away.

Almost unheard, she whispered, "We've got to get the fuck out of here..."

Colin managed to push himself to his feet, massaging his own blood back into his neck. He looked at her and said sarcastically, "Gee, do you think?"

Her eyes darted around, searching for any escape and finding none.

"What are we going to do?" she asked, panicked.

Colin looked down at the squirming mess somehow still alive at their feet, searching for an answer. "We'll go to the hangar and find us a plane. Or go to the beach and find a boat. Shit, if we have to, we'll fucking swim out of here."

Surprisingly, Colin had to damn near drag Lauren to the front door. But when he flung it open, he found the corpse from the runway standing outside. It crookedly smiled and giggled as it held up the not-so-neatly severed head of Ian and said through rotted vocal cords, "We send you greetings."

Lauren's eyes looked in very real danger of popping from their sockets as she screamed, "Ian!"

Colin gripped her hand tighter, kicked the creature out of their path, and shouted as he pulled her with him, "Come on!"

She stumbled after him, still trying to catch her breath until she looked up and screamed again.

Because what she saw was Phil in front of the Mess Hall. Or at least she thought it was Phil. Now he was just a grotesque pile of flesh that was rapidly puddling onto the pavement. Still, it held out what was once an arm, its one pleading eye saying what its lips could not, because his mouth had melted shut.

Lauren turned to Colin urgently and gasped, "Get me out of here, Colin... Please get me out of here..."

Colin held her hand tight, his eyes darting, but he didn't have one fucking clue what to do. Finally—

"We'll go in here."

He kicked the mass that was once Phil aside, nearly getting his foot caught in the goo, then opened the door to the Mess Hall and roughly shoved her inside.

"Get in!"

Lauren stumbled, looked up, and screamed again.

Colin turned and saw Arnie there. Only now his head had been completely spun around, making it appear as if he were walking backward as he advanced. Still, he grinned and asked, "Where have you guys been?"

Colin pushed Lauren forward again. "Find me a fucking back door and let's get our asses out of here!"

He then turned, raised his pistol, and fired a shot that put a clean hole through Arnie's backward head.

It was a remarkable shot, really.

Still, Arnie came closer, briefly stopping to politely help the headless corpse that killed him to its feet.

"Hey Colin, I know we've never really gotten along," he said casually, "but don't you think that was a little over the top?"

Colin backed away from the two things now shambling toward him and muttered, almost without realizing it, "...shit..."

Behind him, he heard Lauren chuckle. He glanced back, confused, and saw her stretching a wide, humorless smile.

"No kidding—shit," she said. Without looking away from him, she tugged on the back doors, which had been chained shut. "We are seriously fucked."

The two corpses moved closer—they seemed to be in no hurry.

So Colin kicked her in the ass. "Get in the fucking meat locker!"

She continued to smile.

(*She is fucking losing it.*)

"Why?" she asked.

He pushed her harder. "Because I fucking told you to!"

Lauren kept smiling, shrugged, and opened the door. "Okay."

Frost swirled out, bringing a rancid odor with it. When she didn't move, Colin shoved her inside, leapt in behind her, and slammed the door shut. On a tray to his left sat a canvas toolbag, he snatched a screwdriver, jammed it into the lock, and stepped back.

"There!"

Outside, he could hear them pawing at the door, but he didn't care. For the time being, they were safe. And for the first time that day, he smiled.

"Well, we might freeze, but at least we won't starve."

Behind him, Lauren chuckled again.

"Colin?" she said.

He didn't turn. "Yeah, what?"

She didn't stop chuckling. She couldn't. The joke was too obvious.

"We're on a naval base."

He rolled his eyes. "No fucking shit."

She kept chuckling. An unnerving sound.

"So haven't you wondered why we haven't seen any of the base personnel?"

Colin stepped back from the door and that awful scratching sound. His brow furrowed.

She was right.

Aside from the corpse on the runway, they hadn't seen anyone else. Not one uniform.

So where were they?

He wasn't sure he wanted the answer, but she seemed to know, and so he asked anyway.

"What're you saying?"

This time, Lauren laughed out loud. The kind of high-pitched laugh that truly proves you've finally lost your mind.

"I'm saying I think we found the rest of the company."

It wasn't the chill in the air that made him stiffen. It wasn't that chill that turned his blood to ice.

It was the simple knowledge that he had fucked up royally.

Again.

He turned, ignoring Lauren's mad laughter and even his own frosted breath, to see over two dozen corpses stored behind him—all draped in what most certainly were the sheets from the barracks. Brought here to literally be kept on ice.

That was all he had time to realize—before every corpse, every damn one, sat up. The sheets slipped away, revealing purple dead faces and glazed white eyes.

And the nearest one to him grinned, raised a hand in a Vulcan greeting, and repeated his earlier comrade's remark:

"We send you greetings."

Colin didn't even realize his own scream as he raised and emptied his pistol.

\* \* \* \*

Just like Arnie told him, Colin found that there were no planes in the hangar, but there were parts and tools, more than enough to fix up his own plane. Just four hours later, they were in the air.

The voice crackled over the radio: "This is Miami International. You may begin your approach."

Lauren flicked the switch overhead, her hand still sticky with her own drying blood, and said into the mic, "Copy that, tower. But you'd better have emergency gear on standby."

She glanced over her shoulder at the full company behind her, then to Colin, who sat at the wheel—his severed throat seeming to grin even wider than the mouth above it.

"We're in pretty bad shape," she said.

Colin giggled.

# A HOMELESS MAN FINDS SHELTER

It was cold, and Eddie Fimble was hungry.

For most of the past four years, Eddie Fimble had been cold and hungry. You see, good old Eddie decided that a loving wife, two wonderful children, and a good job as an insurance agent weren't enough. No, he had to have cocaine, lots of it, and so he lost all of the above.

All of it.

Now, he couldn't even afford his beloved powdered mistress—admittedly a tired, trite, yet distressingly true metaphor—and spent the better part of his days wandering the streets of New York, begging for change in the hopes of getting something as simple as a bottle of Mad Dog. It wasn't just his only form of warmth; it also helped wash down his pride, so that he could find the courage, for lack of a better wor, to lower his head and seek refuge in a shelter. Maybe even get a bowl of soup.

Only today, the shelters were full, and there wouldn't be any soup, all because of the power outage. He didn't know what caused it. He was, by now, way out of the loop when it came to news or any other kind of information, but every streetlight was out as far as the eye could see. At this moment, Eddie wasn't even sure where he was.

He couldn't see a fucking thing. Nothing. And right now, he was shivering in some unnamed alley, his stomach in spasms, looking—and not finding—for some good Samaritan who could spare him some change. Any comfort.

There was no one on these streets, and for the first time since he lost everything, he actually felt like he *lost* everything. For the first time, in this total darkness, he truly felt alone.

He crumbled against the wall and felt the usual spasms that every drunk feels, unsure if he was going to vomit or have a heart attack. He knew he had to have something, anything, in his gut.

**Anything!**

In his former life, he had never been hungry. Never. And back then—

*(So long ago)*

—he couldn't conceive of what he was going through now. All he could think of were the meals his mother used to make. The meals his wife prepared for him. The meals he shared with his family.

Turkey.

Meatloaf.

Steak so rare you didn't have to make your mouth water. It did it for you.

The list was endless.

All those meals he took for granted.

He rubbed at his unshaven face, so hard that it actually hurt, rubbing away the cold, awful-smelling sweat. Wiping away the stench of the drunk he had become. He could feel the tears roll over his fingers as he said, "I am so hungry..."

His chest heaved. He looked up at the sky overhead and screamed, *"Give me something to eat!"*

His strength gave way. He fell back against the door behind him—and it opened, spilling him to the floor.

276

And that's when it hit him.

Someone must have neglected to lock the back door to this particular restaurant, or the power outage had somehow messed with the electronic locks. Whatever the reason, he was now inside, and the delicious odors washed over him.

He wasn't sure where he was, but by the smell, it could have been Carlotto's on 3rd or even Genovilla's on 5th. But he had literally stumbled into this glorious place that had apparently been forced to close early, and by this magnificent fragrance, the crew hadn't bothered to put everything away.

As he pushed himself to his feet, he was overwhelmed not only by the unmistakable aroma of roast beef and barbecue ribs, steak and pork loin, but by the fact that his prayer had been heard.

Not only heard, but *answered.*

He was not only warm, safe, and dry. He was going to be able to eat his fill.

All his previous thoughts about deserting his family, leaving them to fend for themselves, disappeared. They no longer mattered—if they ever did—and like the blind man he had suddenly become, his arms worked wildly in the dark, drool spilling down his chin, seeking that delicious food that was certainly here.

He could smell it. So close. *So close* to real food!

It had been years since he'd had real food.

But now it was here.

It was *all* here.

If only he could find it...

His hands groped out in increasingly desperate circles, but he simply couldn't find the source of that glorious aroma. He found the serving tables, three of them anyway, but as he searched those smooth metal surfaces, he found no plates, no cutlery, and certainly no food.

"Where the hell *was* it?" he muttered, frantic.

He ran his hands over the tables again and decided this had to be a banquet hall, and that the outage had possibly interrupted a wedding or anniversary, or some other event that he used to frequent during his sober days. During his other life.

They had deserted their business before they had a chance to serve dinner.

But damn it, the food still had to be here.

It *had* to be!

And then he realized—it was so obvious.

The food was in the kitchen.

It had to be.

It *was* in the kitchen!

All he had to do was find it.

Using the tables as a guide, Eddie made his way to the east wall and, with palms flat against it, began feeling his way. The door to the kitchen had to be close—if not on this wall, then the next. Or the next.

He would find it.

He would!

And sure enough, he did.

As in most restaurants, there were two doors to the kitchen. When he pushed his way inside, he was overwhelmed with the scent, the fragrance of the room. Every glorious aroma from his previous life came rushing back to him—Thanksgivings, Christmas gatherings, just sitting around the dinner table, or something as mundane as a business lunch.

It was all here.

Just inches away.

Inches.

He could smell it.

He could taste it.

He felt himself drooling again.

And then....his fingers tapped the metal storage compartments.

They were here!

They were *right* here!

The caretakers had had time to lock all that delicious food away, and now it was just waiting for him.

All of it.

Just for him.

He eagerly flung open the first compartment, inhaled deeply, and thought that, for the first time in years, he was going to eat his fill.

\*\*\*\*

It took two full days before the power was restored.

When two beat cops found the back door to the building open, they entered, and both immediately fainted. They were now on paid sick leave.

The detectives currently on the scene, namely Hopper and Cooke, had to step outside to catch their breath.

"I've been on the job for twenty years now, and I thought I'd seen everything," Hopper said. He crouched down, put his head between his legs, and let out a heavy sigh. "I really did…"

Cooke tried and failed to light a cigarette. His hand was trembling too badly.

"Did you know he was still in there eating, right up until the time they put the straightjacket on him?" he said.

Hopper shook his head. He didn't want to think about it anymore. "I know. I saw."

Cooke paused, then crumpled up the cigarette and dropped it at his feet. "We're gonna have to go back in," he said, his voice low and resigned.

Hopper nodded but didn't straighten. "I know…"

Cooke patted him on the shoulder. "You gonna be okay?"

Hopper let out a loud sigh. "No." He pushed himself to his feet and shook his head. "I don't think I'm ever going to be okay again…"

And with that, they walked back into the building, closing the door behind them.

The door that read: **CITY MORGUE.**

# THE MAN WITH THE BOX

I remember the first time I saw the man with the box.

In fact, I remember it with crystal clarity. I have to. It's my penance. Not being a religious man, I never really understood that word before. But it seems everyone really does have a cross to bear.

Or a box to carry.

Well, anyway, I first saw the man when I was taking the Ell to see my probation officer. See, I used to be—well, let's call a spade a spade—a heavy nightclubbing, drug-using thief. And so, I figure that's why they always arranged these meetings in the morning. Just another way to keep an eye on me, to make sure I'd had no mother-fucking fun whatsoever the night before.

Like I say, there I was on the early morning train when this guy walks into the subway car.

He was a weird-looking little man, dressed in an old black trench coat and fedora, who chose to sit alone and silent, clutching an old wooden box to his chest. The box itself didn't appear to have any value. In fact, it looked handmade, as if it were crafted from old driftwood. But still, he grasped it with the desperation of a man guarding his only grandchild.

It had to be worth something.

That's what intrigued me.

That's why I followed him.

Shit, I even missed my appointment—a parole violation. But I couldn't help myself. I had to know what he so coveted in that strange little box. Something so potentially valuable, so precious, that he didn't even dare release his grip on it.

Still, what puzzled me was this: if what was inside that box was so valuable, why was he going into *these* neighborhoods?

These were the Dead Zones. No one came in here without packing, and they sure as hell didn't come in here alone. And if anyone in the history of this planet was a walking victim, it was him.

Seriously, it was as if he were begging to be mugged.

Or worse.

And as I followed, with a lifetime of stealth-like ability, I saw a number of predators move toward him. He was a bunny among wolves, and though it looked as if he knew it, the man walked on, seemingly unconcerned.

It didn't make sense.

But what really struck me as odd….No, more than that, *unbelievable*—was that none of them, *none*, took advantage of him like I would have done. Like I was planning to do.

Instead, when each approached him with a knife—and even at one point, a gun—he merely held up the box, and for some inexplicable reason, they simply backed away.

I mean, can you beat that?

Some of these guys would've scared the piss out of even me. But the old man simply looked at them—a look that seemed to, I don't know… shrivel them. That actually stole the potential malice from their souls.

I know. That sounds like crap. But there it was.

Everywhere he went—punks, druggies—they all parted like the Red Sea at seeing his look, their expressions revealing something like profound confusion. Their eyes seemed to ask the same simple question:

*Why didn't I do it?*

Me? I didn't have that question. It never even crossed my mind as I chased him down that alley and threw him against the wall.

A second later, my knife was positioned tight against his throat.

His eyes met mine. I leaned close to his face and hissed, "I want the box."

He clutched it tighter. "You don't want this box," he said calmly.

I pressed the knife even tighter against his rubbery throat. "If I didn't want it, would I be here?" I growled.

He offered a small, sad smile and said, "Unfortunately, you would be. You're supposed to be."

I dug the knife in just a little. Just enough to draw a drop of blood, to make my point.

"Why is that?" I asked.

He shook his head, but his eyes never left mine. "Because I was like you," he said. Then he chuckled softly. "I *was* you."

I was ready to cut his throat. I really was. I wanted to see what was in that box. I wanted to see what it possessed.

"What the hell does that mean?" I snapped.

He didn't release the box but instead said, "I was a punk." He shrugged. "In my day, we called ourselves gangsters."

"Look, I don't want to hear any more shit from you," I snapped again. I didn't lower the knife but wagged my free hand. "Just give me the fucking box."

He offered another small smile, but at the same time looked close to crying. At the time, I thought it was out of fear.

Boy, was I wrong.

I was later to find that it was relief.

He passed me the box and said, "Thank you."

It was a heartfelt remark. One I didn't appreciate until long after I killed him and ran away.

I guess I'm still running.

But I keep the box close to me. Being the idiot that I am, I opened it. And like every idiot before me, I discovered its contents.

I don't know how many owners…. protectors, had come before me, but now I'm one.

Hopefully the last in a long line of idiots.

The one that started with Pandora.

And so now I ride the subways and cruise the bad neighborhoods, collecting the sins of others, hoping against hope that I can get them all.

But there's only so much a box can hold.

So watch yourself.

I've found that this box can be very, very heavy.

# GO AWAY

If shit were luck, Bob Castelloto would have died of terminal constipation years ago.

First, he sets up his picture at Paramount, and not one damn week later, there's some bullshit shake-up at the studio and he's back pounding the bricks. UA wanted nothing to do with it, Universal wouldn't even take his calls anymore, and MGM—don't get him started.

He was forced to sell his condo. A substantial loss. And then had to take on a low-budget shlockfest called *Biker Whores From Hell* just to cover his alimony bills. They had wrapped this morning, and since he couldn't even get a flight out of Dirtwater—or whatever the hell this town was actually called—he was forced to rent a car so old he believed it was the one Archduke Ferdinand had been assassinated in.

The car that now sat two miles behind him, dead in the middle of butt-fucking nowhere.

So here he was, walking down a road that couldn't possibly have a name. No fucking cell service, of course, and he couldn't even find a house—not that any sane person would live out here.

He stepped into a puddle, sighed, leaned against a wooden post that he assumed was some half-assed attempt at a guardrail, and looked up at the full moon looming overhead.

"Good one. Are you happy?" he muttered to the sky.

Now, Bob didn't believe in God. Never had. But any bitching storm in a port suited him.

"I mean, what else can you do to me? Tell me that," he said.

He shook his head, leaned harder against the post, and it snapped under his weight, dropping him unceremoniously into the puddle.

For a moment, he just sat there, then nodded. "Okay. Okay, I'll give you that one."

He slapped his hands on his pants—the three-hundred-buck pair he had made in Milan back when he was on top—and pushed himself up.

"Look," he said to the deity he didn't believe in, "all I want is a break. Just one fucking break. Is that too much to ask? A house. Any house. Or is that too much to ask for? If it is, let me fucking know."

He looked down at his feet and asked the same question in a different direction. "Either one of you."

He certainly didn't expect an answer, but got one, nonetheless.

To his left, he saw a brief flash of light and heard the sound of a door being soundly closed.

He leaned forward and squinted. That fuck of a doctor Fishburn hadn't fitted him with the correct contact lenses, but even so, he could see the house some hundred yards away. Another flash of light—heat lightning, he supposed—lit up the sky, just long enough to get a good look.

And damned if it didn't look just like the one from *Psycho*.

Fucking great.

He sighed. "Yeah, like you've got options..." he muttered, then trudged toward it.

When he reached the property, he found the entire area surrounded by a rusted but magnificent ornate metal fence. Certainly fanciful, but to him, it seemed an unnecessary luxury, especially in the middle of nowhere. But then again, he was in the old South. Up the rebels.

Still, he figured it wasn't much different from the homes in Beverly Hills he used to frequent. Just another way of saying, *I've got more money than you, so go fuck yourself.*

But when another flash of lightning came, he realized he'd made another miscalculation in a long string of them.

The fence wasn't an ornament or a pompous display of wealth.

It surrounded a graveyard.

At one time, the house itself might have been a Tara of sorts, but now it was condemned to be merely a caretaker's shack for this forgotten boneyard. The windows had been boarded up, and if it hadn't been for the flickering lights inside—kerosene lamps, he presumed—he would've thought it deserted. Just a hospice for derelicts.

Still, someone had to be inside. He tucked his wallet into his sock, pushed open the outrageously loud squealing gate, and mounted the steps to the front door.

There was a bell. Naturally, it didn't work. So he used the oversized knocker. While he waited, he glanced over his shoulder and, with no small amount of curiosity, noticed that all of the graves had been dug up. The coffins were opened and propped up against their various tombstones.

Someone had exhumed them all.

For the briefest of moments, Bob thought about the film *Deliverance* and figured maybe they were moving the bodies to make some kind of bullshit reservoir.

(But he was up in the mountains.)

A small voice from behind him asked, "What do you want?"

Bob damn near jumped a foot in the air and clutched at his chest—the one thumping like Tommy Lee at an '80s Mötley Crüe concert.

Even while catching his breath, he saw the old man peering through the crack in the door, the latch partially obscuring his pale blue eyes.

The man repeated, "What do you want?"

Bob inched closer, causing the old man to close the door just a touch.

He pointed over his shoulder. "Excuse me, but my car gave out on me about two miles down the road—"

The old man snapped, "What do you want!"

Bob slumped, hands in his pockets. "I just told you."

"Why are you here!" the old man barked.

Bob was rapidly losing patience. "Because my damn car broke down and I need to use a phone! Can I use your friggin' phone?"

The old man sadly shook his head. "I can't let you in..."

Bob let out a heavy sigh, louder than necessary. "Okay, so you can't let me in. Could you maybe at least call me a tow truck or something?" He fished in his back pocket for his wallet. "I'll be happy to pay you."

"No," was all the old man said.

Bob looked puzzled. "No?"

"No. Go away," the man repeated, barely visible behind the door.

As the door began to close, Bob slipped his foot inside like some door-to-door salesman from a '50s black-and-white sitcom. He snapped out a bill. "Fifty bucks."

The old man blinked. "What?"

Bob sighed. "Fifty bucks for a phone call. What's the problem?"

The old man shook his head, baffled. "Don't you know what day this is?"

Bob glanced at his $400 watch. "It's March twelfth."

"Yes!" the man nodded fervently.

"So it's March twelfth. What's that got to do with me using your phone?"

The old man's eyes widened in horror and sudden comprehension. "You don't know...?"

Bob sighed again. "Don't know what, Clem?"

The man paused, glanced over his shoulder, then leaned in closer and whispered, as if afraid someone, or something, might hear, "It's Zombie Night."

Bob leaned in out of courtesy, then immediately leaned back. He must've misheard. "Zombie Night?"

The old man offered a grim nod. "That's right."

"Zombie Night?" Bob repeated, baffled.

"The one night of the year when the dead are allowed to crawl out of their graves to feast on the living."

This time, Bob nodded, because now he understood.

Too much inbreeding.

"Yeah, I saw that—" he started, glancing back at the open graves behind him, "—movie." He turned back. "Did some serious box office. But what's that got to do with me?"

The old man looked anguished. "Don't you understand? That's why I can't let you in!"

Bob pointed at his chest. "What? You think I'm a zombie?" He chuckled. "You really believe I'm a zombie? One of the living dead?" He raised his hands and wiggled his fingers. "Oooo, wooo."

He dropped his arms and sighed. "My movies may have been death, but that doesn't make me a zombie."

The old man eyed him. "I know exactly what you are."

He started to push the door closed again, but Bob's foot stopped it short.

"Look," Bob snapped, "I don't give a flying fuck how crazy you are or what you think I am. All I know is I'm tired, I'm dirty, and I need to use a phone."

The old man's eyes filled with tears. "You don't understand! It's Zombie Night! I can't let you in! I can't!"

Bob had had enough. He kicked the door hard, sending the old man sprawling to the floor. He strode in, unsympathetic, eyes locked on the old man cradling his clearly broken wrist.

"Your ears don't work so well. I'm using the phone, and then I'm getting the hell out of here."

He walked past him, and then heard the door close behind him.

When he turned back, he felt his heart stop.

Because now he was staring into the moldering face of a corpse, which offered an ingratiating smile even as its voice rasped, "Come in."

It turned the deadbolt with a loud *clunk* in the sudden silence. "Be welcome."

Bob staggered backward, bumping into an end table. The rotary phone tumbled to the floor.

"What in the hell...?" he whispered.

The old man clutched his wrist, tears now spilling freely. "Why didn't you listen to me?"

Bob stumbled further back—then caught the smell.

A sickly, rancid odor that made him gag.

And then he saw the dining room.

The one filled with the dead.

Though unaware, his eyes widened as over two dozen corpses rose from their seats, nodding politely and offering playful waves. At the center of the table lay a nude woman, neatly sliced like a Thanksgiving turkey.

The old man dragged himself upright, tears streaking his face. "Why don't people like you ever listen? I told you it was Zombie Night."

He gestured at the room full of corpses, one of whom was now grinding two butcher knives together.

"One day out of the year they crawl out of their graves for their annual feast. The rest of the year, I care for them. That's why they leave me in peace."

He raised his hands. "I wasn't trying to keep you out. I was trying to keep *them* in. Do you get it now?"

Bob shook his head. "N-No, this isn't right..." He turned left, then right, but every direction held another grinning corpse. "This can't be happening! Zombies aren't real!"

As if to prove him wrong, the nearest corpse tapped him on the shoulder and grinned.

Bob screamed.

The old man sadly lowered his head and removed a pistol from his coat.

"I keep this for people like you..." he said.

Bob stared, uncomprehending. "What...?"

"For people who don't go away when I tell them to."

"What are you talking about...?" Bob asked.

"It's a choice. One last courtesy." The man held it out. "You can have it."

Bob looked at the many corpses circling him. "One gun for all of them?"

The old man shook his head. "It's for you. There's only one bullet inside."

Bob stared at the pistol, his voice breathless. "You expect me to...?"

The old man shrugged. "I told you—it's a choice. I'm afraid it's your only one. You can be dinner... or a dinner guest a year from now."

Bob looked infinitely confused as the old man gently pressed the gun into his hand. "It's your decision," he said, and turned to climb the stairs.

"I'm going to bed..."

Bob clutched the gun in his clammy hands and took a desperate step after him, but a corpse's claw pressed against his chest, holding him back.

"You can't just leave me here!" he cried out.

The old man stopped at the landing and looked back with a sad gaze.

"Later you'll have to tell me your name. I'm also the stonecutter."

And with that, he was gone.

Bob screamed.

A single shot rang out.

And a year later, another place was set for dinner.

# THE CLINGING VINE

It was President's Day. Rah-Rah.

Dave Edmunds had spent the better part of his morning pasting up posters to commemorate the non-event on the last remaining DVD store in Jersey. The posters advertised: **"Rent one DVD and get one for a penny!"** Each one featured a poorly drawn picture of Washington and Lincoln, done by the boss's daughter, Mamie, who had the artistic ability of a cabbage. Dave hung them up for every unimpressed passerby who rarely entered the store anyway.

In fact, there was only one customer in the whole damn place. A weird-looking chick with black, greasy hair stood unmoving in front of the counter. The one with the dull, glassy eyes that didn't appear to blink.

Since she didn't seem to hear him the first time, he repeated himself, "Can I help you, miss?"

She didn't answer for a moment. A long moment. Then, in a soft, halting voice, she said, "I've been watching you..."

Dave sighed. "Well, I appreciate that, but it's not really necessary," he said, turning to gesture at the camera mounted on the wall. "I'm on video."

It was a small joke that elicited no smile from her. Instead, she continued to stare at him with those blank, doll eyes.

"I've been watching you for a long time. A long time."

Now, Dave had a bad hangover. He'd been drinking all night with his roommate John until three in the morning, and he still had five more friggin' hours before he could even dream of getting out of this DVD graveyard. In short, he had no time, and even less patience, for this bullshit.

"Look, miss, if I can help you find something—"

"My name is Kim," she interrupted.

His head throbbed. "What?"

She repeated, "My name is Kim."

He shrugged. He didn't care. "Well, that's a mighty fine name, but I'm really busy right now—"

(He wasn't, of course, but any port in a storm...)

"—and so, if I can't help you, you'll have to exit the store."

She didn't appear to hear him. Didn't blink.

"I have a present for you," she said.

Dave sighed again. "A present? For me?" She nodded, and he added, "Why?"

With some effort, she lifted a large package and set it on the counter. It rattled.

"It's President's Day," she said, as if that should explain everything.

And with that, she suddenly ran from the store and disappeared into the crowd outside.

Dave shrugged. Sure, that made perfect sense.

"Of course. It's President's Day."

He looked at the lovingly wrapped package and rolled it to the other side of the counter. It weighed a ton. He couldn't figure out what it could be until he opened it and found that it was a jar filled with Lincoln pennies, Jefferson nickels, and Washington quarters.

"What the fu—?" He spun around the counter and shouted, "Yo, miss!"

But she was long gone. When he turned back, he found a card that had fallen from the wrapping paper. It read:

*I Will See You Again On Our Next Holiday*

— Kim

Dave lowered the card, shook his head, and muttered, "What a freakin' nut..."

****

John was stirring spaghetti when he turned and shrugged. "So what's the big deal?"

Dave finally finished counting the money on the coffee table and slumped back on the sofa. "What's the big deal? Some weird chick comes into the store, gives me two hundred and thirty-seven bucks, and you don't think that's odd?"

John shrugged again. "So it's odd." He picked up the steaming pot and carried it to the dining room table, setting it beside the two salad bowls. "You got a couple hundred bucks. What are you complaining about?"

Dave pensively ran a thumb over his lip. "She said she's been watching me..."

John pulled out a chair, sat, and said with more than a touch of sarcasm, "Oh, and who wouldn't? You're cute."

"Fuck you."

John smiled and ladled out a heaping portion of spaghetti. "Not today, boss." He waved a hand. "Come on, come and get it."

Dave looked again at the money spread across the table. She was a weird chick, no doubt about it, but this...

"Yeah... come and get it..."

****

The days came and went with no sign of Kim—until Groundhog Day, of all days—when he again found her standing in front of the counter. She was dressed in the same clothes, and by the smell of her, she hadn't washed them since their last meeting.

She still didn't blink.

"How are you, Dave Edmunds?" she asked.

He sighed. "Can I help you?"

"I told you I'd be back."

He wearily leaned his head against a fist. "Why?"

The question seemed to genuinely confuse her. "Why?"

He nodded. "Yeah. Why? Tell me why."

She looked briefly puzzled, then smiled, as if the answer was obvious. "Because I love you."

Dave wasn't aware of it, but his eyes widened, the way some people react when they realize they're talking to someone who's retarded or insane. "You love me?"

She looked amused, as if his response made no sense. "Of course I do."

He shook his head. "You don't even know me."

Her expression didn't change. "But I do. I told you on our last holiday that I've been watching you."

He rubbed his forehead. "Look, lady—"

She glared and corrected him, "I told you my name is Kim!"

297

He conceded, "Alright, Kim. Look, I saved all your money. I even turned it into a cashier's check." He reached under the counter and produced it. "I got it right here."

She shook her head, clearly confused. "But that was my present to you..."

Dave sighed again. "I don't know what your problem is, Kim, but I want you to take the check and just go away." Her unblinking eyes looked close to tearing, so he added, "Use the money to get some help. You know? The psychiatric kind?"

Now her eyes actually did begin to tear. "Why are you doing this to me, Dave?"

Dave Edmunds would never be described as a modern man. In fact, most women would call him a dog, but even he responded to tears. He slumped. "Look, don't do that..."

She sobbed. "What did you think I would do...?"

He offered a frustrated, exaggerated shrug. "I don't know what you'd do!" He leaned over the counter. "I don't know you, lady!"

She wiped away the tears and said, "My name isn't 'lady'! I told you my name is Kim!" She leaned in so close that Dave actually backed away as she bared her teeth. "My name is *KIM!*"

Dave raised his hands in a calm, placating manner—the way you would if a robber had a gun in your face—and said, "Okay. Okay. Your name is Kim. My mistake. Breach of etiquette and all that."

She leaned away and even offered a small smile. "It's okay." She reached into her coat and placed another package on the counter. "I have another gift for you."

He raised his hands again. "Look, I told you... I'm not taking any more money from you."

She cocked her head slightly. "It's not money."

Dave's eyes shifted to the package. Although he couldn't explain why, this one seemed somehow more sinister. "Then what is it?"

She smiled without humor. "It's Groundhog Day."

And once again, she raced from the store.

Yet again, Dave sighed, opened the parcel, and went straight to the police.

\* \* \* \*

The desk sergeant looked into the box and said in an unimpressed voice, "So what do you want me to do with it?"

The question was ludicrous. "What do I want you to do? Arrest her!"

The desk sergeant merely smacked his hips. "For what?"

Dave found himself repeating the sergeant's question, incredulous. "For what?! The girl guts a groundhog, wraps it in a pretty pink box, gives it to me for a present, and you ask *'for what'*?"

The sergeant absently played with his pencil. "Look, even if I caught her in the act, the best I could do is give her a citation. She'd walk with a small fine. Maybe not even that."

"You're telling me someone can just hand me dead animals and there's nothing you can do about it?"

The sergeant dropped the pencil and said in a profoundly uninterested voice, "That's about it."

Dave shook his head. He couldn't believe this. "Okay, how about a restraining order? Can I get one of those?"

The desk sergeant shook his head again. "Not from me. You'd have to see a judge and prove that she's a reasonable threat."

This was outrageous, and Dave's voice climbed several octaves as he held up the box to display the slaughtered animal. "You don't consider this a reasonable threat?!"

The sergeant shrugged but didn't look up. "Might be if you were a groundhog."

Dave dropped the box on the desk. "So there's nothing I can do? That's what you're telling me?"

This gnat was beginning to annoy the sergeant. He waved a hand at him. "Just stay away from her."

There was a small tremble in Dave's voice as he responded, "She says she watches me…"

The sergeant shrugged yet again. "There's no law against that either."

"So this nutcase can just keep stalking me? She can just keep giving me dead animals?"

The sergeant sighed one last time. "The whole friggin' city's full of nuts. That's why we've got a police force."

Dave left the box on the desk, stood, and turned to leave. "Yeah? Well, you're doing a hell of a job."

The sergeant shuffled some papers and muttered under his breath, "I don't know what she sees in the little prick…"

\*\*\*\*

John tossed Dave a beer and sat in the chair across from him. "So they didn't do anything?"

Dave cracked it open and took a sip. "Not one damn thing. Nada. Shit, they didn't even take her name."

"So what're you gonna do?"

Dave shrugged. "I have no freakin' idea." The phone rang and he motioned toward it. "You want to get that?"

John pushed himself up. "It's what I live for."

Dave sipped his beer—gulped it, actually—as John called over, "It's for you."

Dave sighed wearily. "Who is it?"

John shrugged and set the phone down on the kitchen counter. "She didn't say."

Dave's eyes widened, and he barely caught the beer as it slipped from his fingers. "*She?*"

John raised his eyebrows, looked at the phone, then back at Dave. "You don't think it's her?"

Dave stared at the phone with a growing sense of dread. "I don't know..."

"How could she have gotten this number?"

"We're in the book, John."

John looked at the phone again and asked, in an uncharacteristically helpless voice, "So what do you want me to do? Hang up? What?"

Dave hesitated. He honestly didn't know what to do. Then finally, he set the beer down, stood, and crossed the room.

"No. I'll take it. I'm gonna take care of this once and for all."

John offered a sideways nod and handed over the phone. "It's your call, chief." He stepped away, then added with a smirk, "No pun intended."

Dave reluctantly put the phone to his ear and tentatively said, "Hello…"

There was a pause on the other end. Then Kim whispered, "Why did you go to the police?"

Dave cupped a hand over the receiver and turned to John. "It's her."

John ran a hand through his hair. "Shit…"

Dave uncovered the receiver. "This is you, isn't it, Kim?"

"Who else would it be?" There was a desperation in her voice. "Are you seeing someone else?"

He rolled his eyes. "What the hell are you talking about?"

He could hear her sobbing as she said, "I thought we had something special…"

Dave reeled. "Something special? We didn't have anything! Did you hear that? We had *nothing!*"

He could barely understand her through her heaving sobs, but this time he was determined not to be swayed.

"But I love you! *I LOVE YOU!*"

Dave rubbed at his throbbing temples. "Look, I *don't* love you! I don't know you! *You* don't know *me!*" He shook his head, growing louder. "I don't want to see you again! I don't want to hear from you again! Stay the hell away from me! Am I clear on this?"

He heard her sniffling. "…I can't live without you…"

Dave rolled his eyes again. "Oh for cryin' out loud! You *can* live without me, you *have* lived without me, and you *will* continue to live without me!"

"...no, I won't..." she whispered weakly.

He still wasn't moved. "Don't call here again." He hung up the phone and turned to John. "I mean really, can you believe this shit?"

John shrugged and drank his beer. He'd already lost interest.

Besides, *Bugs Bunny* was on.

* * * *

Dave quit the store and found another job over at Manny's Market on 42nd Street. After his first day, he awoke with a voracious hangover, finally managing to stumble into the kitchen, where John had prepared an unappetizing breakfast of scrambled eggs and bacon.

He pointed at the plate and muttered, "You really don't expect me to eat that, do you...?"

John didn't look up but continued to gobble his portion. Dave felt a tug of envy for the cast-iron stomach he must possess.

"Suit yourself," John said, mopping up his eggs with a piece of toast. "I'm not your mother."

Dave massaged his face. "Oh, trust me, you're a mother all right..."

John briefly motioned with his fork. "There's a package for you."

Dave peered through his fingers. "What?"

John pointed again with his fork at the coffee table. "Over there. Came this morning."

Dave turned and looked at the beautifully wrapped box, then back at John. "Who delivered it?"

John kept eating. "What do you mean?"

Dave sighed, his head throbbing. "I mean was it her? Was it Kim?"

John didn't bother to look up but dismissed him with a wave from his decidedly overused fork. "Naw. It was some weird-looking guy."

"What do you mean 'weird-looking'?" Dave asked, frowning.

John finally stopped eating and mused on that a moment. "Dark, slicked-back hair. Sunglasses. He didn't look like a happy camper, I can tell you that." He rolled his hand and added, "And it looked like he was wearing surgical garb."

The remark didn't make sense.

"Surgical garb?" Dave echoed.

"You know? Like a doctor wears," John said, returning to his plate. "Even wore gloves."

Dave snorted. "It's February."

John shook his head and wiped his mouth on his sleeve. "Not those kinds of gloves. I mean rubber gloves."

*Rubber gloves?*

It didn't make sense. Dave looked over his shoulder at the package. That beautifully wrapped package.

His eyes narrowed. "What's today...?"

"Monday," John answered through a mouthful of eggs.

Dave shook his head. That's not what he meant.

"The date. What's the date?"

John looked amused. He fell back in his seat and wiped his mouth. "It's no wonder you can't keep a babe."

Dave didn't look away from the box. "Why...?"

As if it were obvious, John said, "It's February 14th. Valentine's Day, you unromantic bastard."

Dave paused. Then, summoning all of his courage, he walked to the table and unwrapped the package.

John was right.

It was Valentine's Day.

And Kim had given him her heart.

# LISTEN UP

It had been two years since Vincent Capiletti had seen his one-time partner, Gabriel Kosh—and if he'd had his druthers, he would've gone another two, or five, or ten. To put it kindly, old Gabe was a loser. Had been all his life. And so Vinnie was glad—no, make that relieved—when Gabe allowed himself to be bought out to pursue his lifelong dream of becoming an inventor.

Edison, Ford, and the Wright Brothers had been Gabe's heroes, while Vinnie leaned toward Getty and Rockefeller. Of course, of the two of them, Vinnie had achieved his goal through shrewd business dealings and a little insider trading. Shit, it didn't even make sense why he bothered to stay in touch with the old fool.

As already stated, Gabe was a complete loser who had sold his fifty-thousand shares of Steam-Com for next to nothing just so he could finance this—well, I guess you could call it a lab—putting together worthless "inventions" that would never be sold. (His favorite was the electric potato peeler that, when he showed it to a potential investor, damn near cut the poor bastard's thumb off.)

Anyway, Gabe had left the message on his phone, but Vinnie knew damn well that calling him back would be pointless. You see, old Gabe was as deaf as a post.

As it was, when he reluctantly came over, all four knocks went unanswered. So he let himself in with the key Gabe ridiculously left under the mat. He found the old fool seated at his oak desk with his back to the door and shook his head.

This guy was just a victim in waiting.

"What is it now, Gabe?" Vinnie called.

Gabe didn't turn.

Vinnie sighed. *(Deaf mother-fucker...)*

He raised his voice. "Gabe!"

Still nothing.

He crossed the small room and soundly patted him on the shoulder. "Gabe!"

Gabe spun with a start, his bifocals flying free, clutching at his heart. "Vinnie?" he squinted. "Is that you?"

Vinnie shook his head. What an ass. "Who the hell else would it be?"

Gabe chuckled. "I didn't hear you come in."

"There's a shock," Vinnie muttered. As a simple courtesy, he bent down and picked up the glasses. "Here."

Gabe cocked his head to one side. "What's that?"

Vinnie didn't have time for this. He roughly pushed the bifocals into Gabe's hand. "Your glasses! These are your glasses!"

"What?" Gabe looked at them. "Oh. Thank you." He slipped them back on and, upon seeing Vinnie clearly, stretched a wide smile. "Vinnie! It's good to see you again!"

"Yeah, right," Vinnie said, shrugging. "What do you want?"

"I'm sorry," Gabe said, leaning closer. "I can't hear you."

Vinnie deflated and leaned in. "I said it's good to see you too."

Gabe smiled, stood, and vigorously shook the hand that hadn't been offered. "It's been too long!"

"No, it hasn't. What do you want now?"

"I'm sorry. I can't hear you—"

Still gripping Gabe's hand, Vinnie pulled him closer and damn near yelled in his ear. "You said you had something to show me! What is it? Unlike you, I'm a busy man!"

"I didn't get that," Gabe said, shaking his head. "Could you say it again?"

Vinnie violently tossed down his old friend's hand, nearly knocking him off balance. "WHAT DO YOU WANT!"

At that moment, Gabe looked every bit the absent-minded professor he dreamed of being. "Oh. I wanted to show you this." He turned back to his desk, disoriented. "Where did I put it?"

Vinnie rubbed at his forehead. This was a bigger fool than he remembered…if that was possible. "Shit…"

"I was right here…" Gabe muttered, looking left and right.

"I've got a lunch in twenty minutes," Vinnie said, glancing at his watch. "With people that actually matter."

"I was just looking at it…" Gabe scratched his head.

"Gabe!" Vinnie growled, gritting his teeth.

Gabe patted the sides of his oversized trench coat, spun toward Vinnie, and beamed. "Here it is! I knew I had it!"

He held it up triumphantly.

An earplug. Just some cheesed-up earplug. That was it.

Vinnie looked unimpressed. "What is that?"

"I can't hear you," Gabe said, cocking his head again.

"WHAT IS IT?!" Vinnie yelled.

Gabe smiled, revealing dentures that should've been replaced years ago. "It's a hearing aid!"

Vinnie blinked. That didn't make a fucking bit of sense. He shook his head. "It's a what?"

"What did you say?" Gabe leaned in.

Vinnie slumped. He had come clear across town to this toilet hole for *this*.

"If it's a hearing aid, then why don't you turn it on?" he asked, exasperated.

Gabe stopped smiling and leaned closer. "What was that? I can't hear you."

Vinnie roughly snatched the device from his hand and screamed into it, "*THEN TURN THE FUCKING THING ON!*"

Gabe raised his hands defensively. "Oh. Oh, no, no, you don't understand."

Vinnie tossed the device back onto the desk and even had his hand on the doorknob when Gabe grabbed his arm.

"Wait!" Gabe said quickly.

Vinnie turned back, his teeth bared like an angry dog. "Wait for what?!"

Not surprisingly, Gabe didn't hear him. Instead, he turned and lovingly picked up the device.

"No, see this here is special," Gabe said, cradling it.

With all the patience he could still muster, Vinnie asked, "What's special about it?"

Gabe continued to stare at the device—this seemingly simple device. "It can hear anything."

"Like what?" Vinnie muttered, narrowing his eyes.

Unaware that Vinnie had spoken, Gabe held it out. "Anything you can *see,* it can hear!"

The statement didn't make sense. "What're you talking about?" Vinnie asked.

Even though Gabe obviously hadn't heard him, he again offered the device.

"Try it. Just plug it in your ear and turn it on," he said with a wide smile. "I think you're going to like this."

Gabe passed it to him.

Vinnie hesitated, then took it and did as he was told. Just like he expected, he didn't hear a fucking thing. Not one fucking thing. Again he shook his head.

"I don't hear dick," he said flatly. He began to unplug it and sarcastically added, "Yet another great job, Gabe."

Gabe held up a finger—wait just one second—and scribbled something on a pad of paper.

Vinnie's eyes narrowed. He could actually *hear* him writing. In fact, it was explosively loud, and he winced until Gabe held up the page.

It read simply: **Look At The Cockroach At The Baseboard.**

Vinnie looked confused, then turned to where Gabe was pointing. Sure enough, there was a cockroach scurrying along the baseboard. And damned if he couldn't hear the tiny, almost invisible legs scrambling against the floor.

His eyes widened, and he spun to face Gabe, who continued to grin. Gabe motioned for him to remove the device, which he did.

"That's not all," Gabe said.

Vinnie looked at the device with an unbelieving expression. "What's not all?"

Gabe sat down, clearly pleased by the reaction. He grinned even wider.

"You can hear anything you can see. No matter how far away it is," he said.

Vinnie snorted. The idea was absurd. "Oh, come on."

Gabe motioned eagerly. "Put it back in. Put it back in!"

Vinnie shook his head. "What you're saying is not possible."

Gabe cupped a hand to his ear. "What's that? I can't hear you."

Instead of pointlessly repeating himself, Vinnie grabbed a pad of paper, scribbled a message, and held it in front of Gabe's face. It read: **That's NOT possible.**

Gabe squinted at it, then giggled and slapped a hand against his knee. "You don't think so!"

In lieu of a verbal response, Vinnie shook his head. Gabe stood and stepped over to the window.

"Then I'll prove it to you," he said. When Vinnie didn't follow, Gabe waved him over. "Come on over here."

Vinnie sighed loudly, as was often the case in Gabe's presence, and joined him at the window, looking puzzled as Gabe scanned the skies and pointed.

"There! Look up there."

Vinnie followed his gaze. "It's a plane. So what?"

Gabe leaned closer, grinning, and held up the device. "Put it back in."

Yet again, Vinnie sighed, inserted it back into his ear, looked up, and screamed. Loud enough for even Gabe to hear.

He quickly, desperately pulled it free and spun toward his one-time friend, grasping Gabe by the shoulders as if to stay on his feet.

Gabe briefly looked panicked. "I'm sorry. Are you okay?" he asked, concerned.

Vinnie clutched his ears. The sound of the plane's engines had nearly shattered his eardrums. His eyes even throbbed, and he suddenly found himself as deaf as this idiot—

(*Genius*)

—standing in front of him. He couldn't even hear his own voice as he answered, "I think so..."

Gabe looked apologetic and took the device, twisting what Vinnie assumed was a volume control. "I'm sorry. I wasn't thinking. Excited, I guess. I should have adjusted it for you." When the level was now marked at '1,' he passed it back. "Go ahead. Try it again."

Vinnie shook his head. The throbbing was fading and his hearing had returned, but he sure as hell didn't want that thing back in his ear. "Are you crazy? You damn near had my ears bleeding!"

"Just one more time." Gabe held it out again. "Try it just one more time."

Vinnie hesitated, then reluctantly took the device, cautiously placing it in his ear. Gabe put a finger to his lips— *shhh*—and pointed at the plane again. Vinnie waited, then looked up, and his eyes widened almost instantly.

Because he could actually hear the pilot of that plane requesting landing instructions for Flight 501 out of Cincinnati.

And then Vinnie grinned.

Not like Gabe's gleeful grin, but one of pure greed and malice.

Still unaware, Gabe motioned for him to remove the device. "So what do you think?"

Vinnie blinked. "What do I think?"

*I think it's a fucking miracle.*

This crazy old fuck had actually invented something worth millions. Possibly billions! Not just for the private sector. Think of what the military would pay for this! There was no ceiling for something like this. None.

Of course, he didn't voice any of that. Instead, he said, "Pretty impressive."

Gabe's smile fell. He had anticipated excitement. Hell, jubilation. A lifetime of dreams and work had finally been realized, and this certainly wasn't the reaction he'd expected. His whole body seemed to deflate. "That's all...?"

Vinnie pulled the device free and gripped it tightly in one sweating hand. He was holding the Hope Diamond, and he wasn't going to let it go. He had to stall, come up with a reason, until he could think of his next move. His eyes darted.

"We'll need some development money before we can go forward."

"What was that? I didn't hear you," Gabe said, disappointed.

Vinnie turned back and leaned close. The wheels were turning, and even though he feared someone might overhear him, even in this roach-house, he loudly asked, "Do you have the blueprints for this?"

Gabe smiled, pointing at his head. "No. It's all up here."

Vinnie could feel the excitement rising inside him as he held the device in front of Gabe. "So this is the prototype? The only one?"

"The only one in the world," Gabe said, proud as ever.

Vinnie grinned.

He knew all kinds of young tech-know rats. They would dismantle this thing, reverse engineer the details, and in no time it would be on the production line.

It was worth billions, buddy. Billions.

Seeing Vinnie's expression, Gabe offered a triumphant smile. He had finally managed to impress his long-time buddy.

At least, that's what he thought, right before Vinnie picked him up and threw him out the office window.

* * * *

Good ol' Gabe landed headfirst on the sidewalk, splitting his skull like a fragile walnut.

Reconstruction was impossible—the top of his head was just gone—and so it was a closed-casket ceremony. Still, there was a surprisingly large turnout at the cemetery. Vinnie had no idea the old coot had so many friends and took a ghoulish delight in listening to their hushed whispers at the gravesite with the aid—

(*Aid. Get it?*)

—of his new acquisition.

To his left, a woman—maybe his daughter, he didn't know or care—said through flowing tears, "He didn't even leave a note explaining why—"

He cocked his head to the right. Another man, some friend he supposed, whispered into his clasped hands, "...You could have talked to me..."

Vinnie looked at the Rabbi, and even from this distance, with the volume turned down to virtually zero, he could hear him let out a sigh of profound grief.

(*This is great! Nobody suspects a thing! I am golden!*)

As the service ended and the mourners went about their lives (forgive the terminology), the gravediggers began their task—filling in said grave, careful to avert their eyes from Vinnie, whom they believed to be a grieving family member. As they shoveled in the dirt they had removed just the night before, it was a good thing too. That way, they didn't see the smile as Vinnie gleefully watched the coffin slowly disappear beneath the moist soil.

He whispered to himself, "Thanks, Gabe. You set me up for life."

He smiled even wider as he turned away. Then, he heard a small, muffled voice rasp, "...or death..."

Vinnie looked puzzled and turned to the gravediggers. "How's that?"

The elder digger stopped, looked puzzled, and respectfully removed his hat. "What's that, sir?"

Vinnie glanced at the disappearing casket, then back to him. "Did you just say something?"

The elder digger looked at his partner, possibly his son, then back again. "No sir."

Vinnie frowned. "But I heard..." He froze and looked into the grave.

There was a soft scratching coming from inside. Like a dog pawing at a door, demanding to be let in.

Or out.

He took a step back, confused.

And then, from inside, came the whisper: "That's right, Vincent. It's me. Your old friend, Gabe."

Vinnie's eyes widened. That was Gabe's voice. But how?

The whispering continued, "It's kind of funny, isn't it?"

He could barely catch his breath. "...What is...?"

The elderly digger looked at him curiously. "What is what, sir?"

The coffin-muffled voice kept on. "Now that you're actually listening to me... you don't want to hear what I have to say?"

At this, Vinnie turned and ran. A move so sudden, so startling, that the elder digger scratched his head and looked at his partner. "That guy is one strange duck."

****

Vinnie retreated back home, locked all the doors, and turned on every light. There was a handgun in his night table—fully loaded, of course—and he cradled it to his chest while rocking back and forth on his bed.

It wasn't just his imagination. He had heard Gabe's voice. He knew that voice as well as he knew his own. Talking to him straight from the grave.

(*This is straight-up bullshit. It's your conscience, you idiot. Gabe is dead. He's fucking dead!*)

He paused, chuckled, tossed the pistol on the pillow beside him, and laughed out loud as he wiped sweat from his forehead.

"The motherfucker is dead! You saw him planted today, for cryin' out loud! He's worm food!"

And then he stiffened when he heard a window break somewhere downstairs.

If it hadn't been for the aid, he never would've heard it through the oak door.

No, someone had broken in.

He could even hear the halting footfalls on the carpeted staircase.

Someone was coming up the stairs.

Someone was coming to his room.

(*It was Gabe. Somehow, he had clawed his way out of the grave and was coming for him.*)

He grappled for the gun—

(*This was bullshit! Gabe is dead! He is fucking dead!*)

—and aimed it at the door.

"I don't know who the fuck you are, but I've got a gun here!" he shouted, cocking the hammer. "And I'm not afraid to blow your fucking head off!"

Unfortunately, his trembling hands belied that claim.

There was nothing for a moment. Vinnie dared to take one hand off the pistol to turn up the device.

And downstairs, he could actually hear a hand grip the banister. He could even hear the mud under the stranger's shoes on the carpeted stairs as they rounded the landing.

The gun barrel trembled. "I'm not kidding! I'll kill you! I will, I swear!"

There was a brief silence.

Then the bedroom door came off its hinges, see-sawing twice before it hit the floor.

Vinnie's eyes widened even further—nearly burst from their sockets.

Because Gabe was standing in the doorway.

Or what was left of him.

The reason for the closed casket was obvious now. Although the morticians had put Gabe in what was presumably his best suit, everything above his upper lip was gone. The entire top of his head had been sheared off.

Still, he raised a hand in a playful wave and croaked out through rotted vocal cords, "Hi, Vinnie."

Vinnie screamed, "YOU'RE DEAD!" and fired the gun.

It left a bloodless hole in that suit. Gabe started toward him—his fractured legs wobbling, his dirt-covered fingers— the ones that no longer had fingernails since he clawed his way out of the grave—leading the way to a chokehold.

"I'm sorry, Vinnie," he rasped. "But since I've lost my ears... I *really* can't hear you."

# "TURNABOUT"

Jackson Rollins ground out his cigarette—his third in less than half an hour. He immediately lit another and shook his head with frustration.

"You're not listening to me!"

In the calmest voice he could manage—the voice he'd been trained to use during his internship at the clinic—Dr. Douglas Everett replied,

"I *am* listening—"

Jackson exploded.

"No, you're not!"

Douglas sighed as his lifelong friend jumped to his feet, vigorously wiping the sweat pouring down the back of his neck.

"You hear the words, but you're not *listening*!"

"It's my job to listen—"

Jackson spun around and pointed with his cigarette.

"—*Not that voice!*"

Douglas gave a brief shake of his head.

"What voice are you talking about?"

Jackson stepped closer.

"*That* voice. That one, right there."

"I'm not sure I understand what you're—"

"I'm not crazy," Jackson said, running a hand through his already matted hair.

"I never said you were."

"Then stop talking to me like I am!"

Douglas offered a small nod.

"Alright."

From Jackson's expression, it was clear the conversation wasn't helping. He seemed to deflate as he collapsed back into one of Douglas's three chairs.

"I'm telling you the truth..."

Douglas leaned forward, clasped his hands together, and said as evenly as he could,

"I'm sure you *believe* what you're telling me is the truth—but that doesn't necessarily make it true. You might be experiencing—"

"I *know* what I'm experiencing!" Jackson shouted. "I *know* what I'm experiencing! You just don't want to hear it! You *won't* hear it!"

Douglas sighed. He'd had plenty of patients with delusions before—but none quite this vivid. And none of them had been his best friend.

"Okay, Jackson. Tell me one more time."

Jackson ground out the cigarette and lit another.

"Alright. One more time—and then I'm out of here."

Douglas nodded.

"Fine. Go ahead."

Jackson exhaled a stream of smoke.

"Like I said, it started about a week ago. I had a cold—a bad one—so I went to the drugstore. I tried everything on the shelf, but nothing worked. So I asked the pharmacist if he had anything else. You know, behind the counter?"

Douglas nodded.

"I understand."

Jackson snorted.

"Yeah, right." He tapped off his ashes. "Anyway, he said he had something called *Xymaxidreil*."

"Xymaxidreil?" Douglas jotted the name down on his legal pad. "I've never heard of it."

Jackson nodded and waved a hand.

"It's some new shit. So I took it home, tossed back a shot or two, and passed clean out. Slept like a baby. Only the next morning..."—he inhaled half the cigarette in one drag—"...everything was different."

"Different how?"

"Well, first there was Angel."

Douglas looked confused.

"Angel?"

Jackson waved a hand.

"That's not her real name. I don't even know her real name. It's just what I call her. She works over at Dan's Donuts on Fifth Street. You know it?"

"No, I'm afraid I don't."

Jackson sighed out smoke.

"I guess it doesn't matter..." His eyes seemed to deepen. "...maybe it does. I don't know..."

Douglas leaned in.

"Tell me. How does it matter?"

Jackson took another puff—his hand visibly shaking—and said,

"Like every morning, I went in to get a jelly donut. I've got a bit of a crush on her." He rolled his hand through the air; smoke curled between his fingers. "Left over from high school, I guess."

Douglas nodded.

"Not uncommon."

But instead of the smile Douglas expected, Jackson frowned.

"I always had a thing for blue eyes."

Douglas nodded again.

"Also not uncommon."

Jackson shook his head.

"You don't get it..."

Douglas sighed.

"What don't I get?"

Jackson looked up at him, helpless.

"When she served me this morning, her eyes were brown."

Douglas shook his head.

"I'm not following."

Jackson looked utterly exasperated.

"They were blue *yesterday*—but they turned brown *overnight*!"

Douglas chuckled and leaned back in his chair.

"Well, they do have tinted contact lenses now. Maybe she just wanted a change. Women often like to change their appearance."

Jackson adamantly shook his head, cigarette ash raining onto the carpet.

"No, no, no! You don't understand!"

"Then explain it to me."

323

Jackson let out a loud sigh.

"I came back later for lunch."

Douglas leaned forward again.

"And what happened?"

Jackson took a long drag from his cigarette.

"I looked into her eyes again."

Douglas made a rolling gesture with his hand.

"And?"

Jackson looked close to tears.

"She didn't have them anymore. She didn't *have* eyes."

Douglas blinked.

"What?"

Jackson began to pace.

"I mean, they were still in her sockets, but..." He trailed off.

Douglas repeated the gesture.

"But what?"

Jackson shook his head.

"You won't believe me..."

"I'll try. Go ahead. Tell me."

Jackson looked directly at him.

"They were white."

Douglas shook his head again. None of this made any sense.

"White? What do you mean they were white?"

Jackson slumped in his seat. "I assume you've seen a corpse or two in your day."

Douglas nodded. "I have."

"Her eyes were like that. Like they'd just rolled back in her head." He ran a hand over his mouth. "But she was smiling—the way she always did." He began to cry again. "Only she didn't have any eyes!"

Douglas picked up a pencil and tapped it nervously against his desk. "Is this the only..."—he paused, searching for a phrase that wouldn't set Jackson off again—"...instance you've experienced?"

Jackson sadly shook his head. "No..."

*Tap-tap-tap.*

"What else?"

Jackson dropped into a chair as if his legs could no longer support him. "My neighbor... His name is Ed..."

"What about him?"

Jackson's voice grew faint, his expression distant, as if he were beginning to disassociate. "After I left the diner... I went home... He was watering his yard..."

Douglas leaned forward. "And?"

"He lost an arm during the war..." Jackson swallowed, the sound loud and dry. "Only today... it was back."

Douglas frowned. "Back? What do you mean 'back'?"

Jackson sighed. "It was back! Only now it was sprouting out of his chest! And he even waved to me with it, like it was just another day."

Douglas dropped the pencil and shook his head. "I see..."

Jackson screamed, "HOW?"

Douglas blinked in confusion. "What?"

"How do you see?"

Another shake of the head. "I don't understand what you're asking, Jack—"

Jackson let out an anguished cry. "You're like Angel! YOU DON'T HAVE ANY EYES!"

Curious now, Douglas leaned forward, brow furrowing over the skin that had replaced his nonexistent eyes. "What are you talking about?"

Jackson looked away, another helpless expression clouding his face. Douglas held out a hand.

"If that were true, then how can I see you? And I *can* see you."

Jackson ran a hand over his face. "I don't know… I don't know why children suddenly have their brains on the outside of their skulls. I don't know why some people have seven fingers or three legs. I don't know why others no longer have skin and I can see their internal organs. I don't know. I DON'T KNOW!"

But Douglas figured he did. In fact, it was all too clear.

Different drugs affect people in different ways, and this *Xymaxidriel* must have some kind of narcotic effect. He had been a psychiatrist for over twenty years. He'd seen many psychotic episodes before. All he needed to do was get Jackson off this drug, let it run its course, and his friend would be fine.

The real challenge was convincing Jackson.

"I think I know what we have to do."

Jackson shook his head. "No, you don't."

Douglas gave a calm nod. "Actually, I really think I do."

Jackson continued shaking his head. "No. No, you don't. You don't even know why I'm really here…"

Douglas settled back in his chair. "Then tell me."

Jackson took a long drag from his cigarette but didn't exhale. "I'm afraid to look in the mirror…"

Puzzled, Douglas asked, "Why?"

Jackson's eyes looked haunted. "Because of what I'll see…"

Douglas shook his head. "I don't—"

Jackson waved the cigarette at him. "—I know!" He stepped toward the circular mirror mounted on the wall but carefully avoided standing directly in front of it. "I'm not sure how, but I think this drug,"—he let out a muted chuckle—"this cold and flu medicine somehow takes the blinders off."

Douglas clasped his hands together. "How do you mean?"

The mirror loomed ahead, but Jackson still didn't look up. "It lets you see what you really are…"

"And?"

Jackson shook his head. "And I don't think I want to see what I really am…"

Douglas sighed again, stood, and came around the table. "Jack, the only way I can help you—"

Jackson laughed loudly and turned to him. "—When has a psychiatrist ever helped anybody?" He flicked the cigarette across the room. "Tell me something, Doug. Have you— have any of you in your so-called profession ever *cured* anybody?"

Douglas was used to these kinds of outbursts—his professors had warned him to expect them. So he said, "Jack, you're going to have to look in that mirror."

Jackson shook his head violently. "I can't! I can't! I can't!"

Douglas approached him gently and placed a hand on his shoulder. "Jack, you've got to trust me. I'm your friend."

Jackson kept shaking. Kept trembling. "I can't... I'm afraid..."

"There's nothing to be afraid of."

Jackson began to sob again. "Yes... there is..."

Using his most reassuring voice, Douglas said, "No, there isn't. Just look at yourself, and I'm sure you'll see that Jackson Rollins is the same Jackson Rollins he's always been." His friend turned toward him, and Douglas smiled beneath eyes that weren't there. "Trust me. Go ahead."

Jackson stared at his sightless friend and, summoning the last of his courage, stepped in front of the mirror.

He would have screamed at what he saw.

If he could.

But he didn't have a face.

\* \* \* \*

The police came to take their reports and claim the body. One officer, a patrolman named Owen, asked his routine questions while doodling on his notepad.

"And he never said a word, is that right?"

Douglas sniffed and wiped at his running nose. "Nothing." His tears weren't of grief; he had known Jackson had mental problems for years. Of course he was going to miss him—but deep down, he'd always known it was only a

328

matter of time before some misadventure ended his life. Still, to Douglas, it just seemed like he'd caught something from a patient. A cold, or the flu, or something.

Owen continued his monotonous writing. "So you were treating him then?"

Douglas pulled a handkerchief from his back pocket and wiped his nose. "Off and on. Informally, yeah."

"And so he just walked in here?"

Douglas sneezed again. "Like I told you—he walked in, looked in the mirror, and dropped dead on the spot." He wiped his nose again.

Owen pocketed his notepad. "I'm sorry."

Douglas looked up, his eyes watering. "What's that?"

"About your friend. I'm sorry."

Douglas moved to stifle another sneeze. "I appreciate that. Thank you."

He sneezed anyway.

Owen motioned at him. "You should take something for that."

"What's that?"

"That cold. You ought to take something for it."

Douglas waved a hand dismissively. "Oh, I will. Don't worry about it. Thanks though."

Owen began to leave, then turned back. "You know, I've heard about something. It might help."

Douglas sniffed. "Heard about what?"

"It's called *Xymaxidriel*. Over-the-counter stuff." He shrugged. "Can't hurt."

Douglas shrugged as well and picked up his pen. "How do you spell that?"

# ERIC AND ME

There was a monster loose in the streets.

Mrs. Wilconson was the first to see it. She was recently divorced from good ol' Dan over at Tires R Us and had moved into a small colonial on Jameison Street. Depending on who you asked, she ran hot-or-cold on Saturday nights at Duffy's Pub. That particular rumor notwithstanding, she had been making her son Arnie a peanut butter and baloney sandwich when she looked up through the window over the sink—just in time to see it cut across her back lawn.

According to her official statement (which, off the record, includes a somewhat lengthy psychiatric report), the monster was primarily black, somewhat stocky, and appeared to lope rather than run—favoring one of its paw-like feet. As she watched, wide-eyed and open-mouthed, the creature—admittedly an unusual sight in small-town, middle-class suburbia—groped blindly forward. It drew only a frightened whimper from Adolph, the German Shepherd she'd bought for protection, but who now cowered comfortably in the doghouse she had originally feared would be too small for such an imposing animal.

The only physical evidence the thing left behind was a long strip of red-and-green plaid fabric caught on her chain-link fence as it clumsily crawled over, finally disappearing into the Caulfield lot. While the whole incident had lasted barely ten seconds, hot-or-cold Gloria was surprised to find that along with slicing her son's sandwich in half, she had also neatly sliced off the tip of her index finger.

Two blocks down, in a house off the cul-de-sac on Squire Street, a woman named Betty Grant was apparently the second witness to the monster's impromptu sightseeing tour. She had been hanging her laundry on the clothesline she shared with Lila Hicks. When the police arrived some thirty minutes later, she was still there—sitting cross-legged in a pile of her husband's work shirts and trousers, her teeth chattering mindlessly while drool spilled down her chin.

Oh, there was a monster loose in the streets all right, and the hunt was on.

The Spikes brothers, Greg and Kyle, rumbled through town in their '67 pickup—the one with the "Forget Hell!" license plate—each cradling a shotgun across their laps while they guzzled can after can of Black Label beer. Piled in the payload were the usual layabouts from the Pig 'N' Weasel, always up for a monster hunt, no matter the season. There was even Matt Brewster, his soon-to-be best man Eddie Sheedy, and his brother Chester, who proudly proclaimed that even though he had the flu, he "just had to come out for this, yessir!"

Hell, even Murry "The Bucket"—a fixture at any bar come closing time—was out, already stewed to the gills but still clutching a loaded rifle to his chest like it was the teddy bear he slept with until he was twelve.

Yeah, it was redneck heaven. As they cruised past the early-closing shops on Main Street, they hooted and howled, making mostly failed hook shots with beer cans at the trash bins on the curb—only keeping a routine eye out for the monster.

Despite it being fish fry night over at the Federation of Eagles—usually a helluva crowd-pleaser—the old timers were out in force. Warren Campbell's dusty gray Impala was even seen weaving through the project streets, spewing thick blue smoke that was hardly a glowing tribute to his paint-and-body shop. Sitting beside him was Wine-Daddy Grass, so named for the winery he ran until the late seventies, which had shut down after some serious health code violations. Most locals had long since tired of his drunken ramblings—including Warren. But tonight, Warren gratefully accepted the company. Despite gripping the wheel tight, his hands were sweating like a nervous pig, and more than once he had to wipe his palms on his already spotted pants leg. More than once, he braked and cried out—though there was never anything truly there—and let out a little laugh, more cat-gut nerves than he would've liked to show.

Off Old Wash Road, the swamps were already filling up with men in thick, down-filled jackets and bright orange caps, shotguns gripped in both hands, pockets filled with shells. The thought being: all monsters naturally gravitated to swamps.

In town, Sheriff Bob made the routine call to order—which was routinely ignored—and the liquor stores were doing slam-bang business from guffawing would-be monster hunters buying up cheap whiskey and even cheaper beer.

Yep, a genuine monster had been seen in the streets, and the hunt was on.

Even I had gotten into the act. But instead of arming myself with a shotgun or duck-hunting rifle, all I had with me were the shackles the creature had escaped from. The rusty-brown chains now sat in the passenger seat beside me.

They were the monster's chains.

Eric's chains.

* * * *

Eric and I were born on November 2nd, 1992, not twenty minutes apart—and oddly enough, exactly three months to the day after our grandfather's death. Grandmother served as midwife, and since our family—such as it was—had long since severed ties with the townsfolk, our births went unrecorded. We were what the government might have deemed "non-people."

Oh, forgive me. Raised as I was, I sometimes forget social graciousness—if that's even the right word.

My name is Martin. My last name isn't important, as so many aren't. And aside from washing my hands, tucking my napkin in at meal times, and obeying my maternal parents, I'm not really acquainted with the social graces. There was never much point in learning them, given our lot in life. But I digress—and should I do so again further into my story, well, you'll just have to forgive me again.

As I was saying, Eric and I were raised in a stately home—you could even call it a mansion—off old Taft Road. When it was first built, it must have been something. Back in the days when homes weren't thrown together by pot-smoking construction workers sneaking beers on their frequent breaks, but by craftsmen—the kind of men who took pride in their work. Those days are long gone—along with the men—and as if in mourning, the house itself had fallen into disrepair. Not for lack of care from my mother and grandmother—no, they did what they could. It just seemed that when the builders died, the house itself began to grieve their loss.

Be that as it may, Eric and I were tutored at home. Grandma was our teacher. She read to us from the encyclopedia, made sure we learned to spell, and that we did our sums. She taught us with the diligence of a convent nun—though we'd only heard of such women, never seen one. On the few occasions we were allowed to play outside—never leaving our own land, never within sight of the road—Mother kept a close eye on us. In fact, the first real beating I ever received was when I was six years old and broke that unspoken rule.

Eric and I—syntax never being my strong suit—were playing catch in the backyard, one of the few games we were permitted. The overgrown grass on the acres surrounding us provided enough cover to keep us hidden from any passersby who might have seen us. But that day, Eric accidentally threw the ball over my head. I was the runt of the family, and the ball sailed past me, rolling down the hill toward the stream behind our home.

I foolishly ignored Eric's warning and went after it. You see, one of Mother's strictest rules was that we were never to go near the stream. Under no circumstances. I was

334

reminded of that rule when she appeared out of nowhere, snatched my wrist, and yanked me back before I could reach the ball.

I still remember her wild eyes as she clutched my arm and screamed, "Did you touch the water?!" I had never seen her so crazed. For a moment, I thought she was going to rip my arm right from the socket as she screamed again, louder, "DID YOU TOUCH THE WATER?!"

I kept shaking my head, insisting that I hadn't. Still, she took my hands and inspected them for even a trace of moisture. Then she dragged me up the hill, across the lawn, into the house—and beat me with Father's belt until I bled.

We never played catch again.

Because of our confinement, Eric and I became very close. We grew fearful and mistrusting of all strangers, even those we never met. We were prisoners in that house—but at least we had each other.

Eric and me.

We studied together. We played together. We watched TV together—until the picture tube blew. It had been our only connection to the outside world, and we begged Mother to call a repairman. She sat us down and, as patiently as she could manage, said, "But we can't let a repairman come. If he did, he'd have to come inside. And we can't have that, now can we?"

She was right, of course. We couldn't risk that. It was too dangerous. And so, from that day on, Mother and Grandmother remained our only role models—the only real adults we had ever seen.

Even though Grandfather lived with us, we had never met him. We often heard him shuffling around in the attic above our bedroom, but we never saw him.

"It's something in the blood," Mother would say. Something that affected him so badly that he had to be locked and chained in the attic—to keep him, as she put it, from "hurting himself."

He was sick. Very sick. Too sick even to attend Grandmother's funeral after she died of a massive coronary on our twelfth birthday. She lingered for several weeks, but since Mother refused to call a doctor, there was little we could do but watch her waste away. We listened as her breathing became shallow gasps, and then… nothing.

I remember standing at her bedside, staring into her lifeless eyes until Mother closed them and ushered us out of the room. Later that day, we buried her in the family plot—Mother in her favorite green chiffon dress—beneath a headstone Grandmother had prepared years ago. As Eric and I stood by that simple grave, I thought I heard Mother mutter something under her breath. Something about Grandfather.

I didn't understand what she meant until—

Grandfather died two days later. We weren't allowed to attend that funeral. During the service—if you could even call it that—we were locked in the downstairs bathroom, the one without a window. Mother didn't return for almost four hours.

For the first hour, we could hear muted digging in the backyard. After that, Eric—always the more curious of us—kept one eye at the keyhole and one ear pressed to the door, reporting everything he heard. At first, it sounded like Mother was dragging something heavy down the stairs. We heard a soft thudding with each step and the clinking of metal—chains, maybe—until the sound disappeared behind the creak of the kitchen door.

Then we heard the shovel again.

And then the sound of a wet mop being dragged across the landing. And the stairs. And the floorboards overhead. For reasons we couldn't understand, she scrubbed the entire house—attic to kitchen—with ammonia. When she finally came back to release us, she was in tears.

We were confused, of course. Even more so when she dropped to her knees and clung to both of us like she was holding on for dear life.

Looking back, I guess she was.

I remember wincing at the sharp smell of rubbing alcohol on her hands and the warm tears that spilled down my cheeks. At the time, I thought it was the sting of the ammonia making me cry.

Now I think—no, I *know*—it was fear.

Fear she couldn't mop away. Fear she couldn't wash down the stairs. Fear she couldn't bury in the shallow grave out back.

It was fear for us.

For Eric and me.

* * * *

Since birth, we were as different as brothers could possibly be. It wasn't until years later, when I studied genetics, that I realized just how unusual—how striking—those differences truly were.

As I've already said, Eric was taller, more muscular—the kind of person you'd expect to see snarling at you from behind the face-mask of a football helmet (had we ever been allowed to play football).

I, on the other hand, was short and thin—bony, really—the kind of kid you'd picture in the chess club, hunched over the board behind Coke-bottle-thick glasses. Eric's hair was dark and wavy; mine was thin and fair. As I've alluded to, he was always the healthier one—even the usual childhood ailments seemed to pass him by. Hell, he had never even had a cold, let alone a fever.

You see, Eric had only been a monster for a year.

Looking back, I can't even remember exactly when it started. August, maybe. Late fall? Anyway, it was a hot morning when Eric came down to the breakfast table, complaining of a dull ache that had settled in his joints during the night. It was the kind of ache most people—especially Eric—would shrug off and make excuses for. You know, *I must've slept wrong, maybe it was the workout, probably just a cold in my joints.* That kind of thing. He even joked that all he needed was a good oiling.

But it didn't go away. And even then, I should've seen the look in Mother's eyes.

The dread.

She had seen it coming, of course—maybe even since the day we were born. Probably the real reason she had aged before her time. I can't remember her without gray hair, not even in her late twenties. That fear had carved itself into her face—grim, black specks in her green eyes, radiating out like some terrible web she couldn't escape.

Haunted eyes. Watching. Waiting.

In the weeks that followed, Eric began to move with arthritic slowness. Gone was the eager bounce in his step. Instead, he shuffled, dragging his feet across the hardwood floor with a faint, grinding sound. Soon, even bending his fingers became a struggle. The simplest tasks were nearly impossible. His muscles, tendons—even veins—began to stand out beneath the skin, giving him a skeletal appearance, though he still outweighed me by twenty pounds.

His speech became strained, almost painful, and I suggested to Mother that maybe he had tetanus. Maybe he'd cut himself on one of the hundreds of rusting tin cans in the basement—cans that she and Grandmother refused to throw away. I told her we should call a doctor, unlike Grandmother.

But Mother just sat in Father's favorite chair, her eyes blank and staring into nothing. She shook her head and said, in a flat, hopeless voice:

"It wouldn't help… Even if we could call a doctor, it wouldn't help…"

* * * *

I think she gave up all hope when Eric started wearing Father's old black wraparound sunglasses.

I was the one who found her. The note she left behind explained it all. It was pinned to her faded wedding gown—the same gown she put on before tying the plastic bag around

339

her head. When I looked into her wide, lifeless eyes, I felt my own begin to tear.

I won't go into detail. That will come later.

But the note said Eric's condition was one she knew well—one she couldn't bear to witness again.

As I sat there on the floor, my legs splayed out, back pressed firmly against the door in case Eric came by, I started wondering what had really happened to Grandfather the day he was buried. I'm sure it was in her note, but before she took her life, she had crossed that part out.

Still, I think I know. At least, I suspect.

I believe Grandmother killed Grandfather to end his suffering. And I think Mother did the same to Father. Maybe she killed herself because she couldn't bring herself to do it to one of her sons.

I don't know.

I kept the truth of Mother's death to myself. I told Eric she'd suffered a stroke, just like Grandmother. And because he couldn't help me dig the grave, I did it alone. While Eric watched—his eyes hidden behind those sunglasses—I remember thinking that maybe Mother wouldn't have wanted to be buried beside her husband.

Still, it was Eric's wish, and I chose to honor the wishes of the living over the dead.

But now I wonder… maybe Eric only wanted to know where she was buried.

So he could find her.

And dig her up.

\* \* \* \*

In the months that followed—such long, dragging months—Eric deteriorated at an alarming pace, becoming little more than a walking corpse.

He seemed to be rotting before my eyes.

We still had dinner together—our last thread of social connection—but I found it harder and harder to bear. Even with the lights turned down (his request, not mine), I couldn't bring myself to look at him across the table, let alone make conversation.

He noticed, of course. Eric wasn't stupid.

And perhaps because of that—at least, I believe that's why—he began wearing Mother's old makeup. It only made him look more inhuman. He no longer had the dexterity I once envied, and his now-arthritic fingers couldn't apply the makeup with any precision.

If anything, it made him look even worse.

No, Eric was turning into a monster. And he knew it.

Soon, I was eating alone. Eric began locking himself in his room, so I started setting a plate outside his door every night. But as the days went on, I noticed he barely touched the food. The plate remained, but the food looked merely picked at, as if he were searching for something he never found.

And that's when I noticed something else. Something I didn't want to admit...

In a house as big as ours, rodents were inevitable. It was just a fact. As kids, we'd sometimes run into traps during games of tag or hide-and-seek. Now, it was my responsibility to check those traps.

But they were always empty.

When I turned on the cellar light, there were no scurrying shapes, no tiny feet padding away, no tails slipping into the half-rotted bag of grain that neither of us could stomach throwing away.

The traps were still there. Some were even snapped shut. A few had tiny specks of fresh blood on the wood.

But there were no mice.

There were no mice anywhere.

* * * *

Eric never left his room anymore—not for anything.

Even though he no longer touched the food I left for him—not even picking at it—I kept setting out a plate every night. Sometimes I'd crouch at the top of the stairs, hoping to catch a glimpse of him.

But I never did.

And now I know why.

He could smell me there.

* * * *

The food Eric refused to eat ended up in a dish I set out for a stray dog I named Sam.

The first time I saw him, I was washing dishes and caught sight of him through the kitchen window. He was rail-thin, digging through our overturned trash barrel for scraps.

I guess I panicked. I don't remember grabbing the steak knife or even stepping outside. But I do remember gripping it tight behind my back, crouching down, and patting the ground, coaxing him over.

I had to be careful not to scare him off. If he ran, I'd never catch him. In the softest voice I could manage, I called to him.

He only cocked his head and looked at me—curious.

Don't get me wrong—I was still ready to cut his throat. I didn't have a choice.

But that look...

Shit. I figured he was just hungry. Homeless. If I kept an eye on him, everything would be fine.

And with Eric no longer a part of my life, I desperately needed someone.

I knew we had a length of chain in the cellar. I just had to be careful. Very, very careful.

I welcomed him.

In the weeks that followed, Sam became a kind of godsend. A replacement for Eric.

We ate together, slept together, played ball. He was a good listener.

But as much as I appreciated—and needed—Sam's company, I still longed for human connection. Any kind.

That's why, when a thunderstorm knocked out our phone line, I waited for the repairman. I still didn't want to be seen, so I crouched by the window with binoculars, peering through the blinds.

I watched the lineman for over an hour, fascinated. He was the only adult male I'd ever seen in person. When his truck finally drove off, I felt a hollow kind of loss.

The same loss I felt when Sam ran away.

The next day, I found his chain empty.

And—may Heaven forgive me—I hoped he'd been hit by a car before reaching town.

Not because I was cruel.

But because the thought of him finding another human terrified me more than you can imagine.

You'll come to understand why.

* * * *

Foreseeing her untimely demise, Mother had set up a trust fund and arranged for groceries to be delivered weekly. And since Eric no longer ate the meals I left for him—

(At the time, I wondered how he was staying alive. I know now, of course.)

—I used the money to subscribe to the local paper.

At first, I searched for articles about Sam, as if there were some sort of bogus animal obituary column. Thankfully, I found none. The truth is, I found the paper just as boring as I feared: endless articles about sports teams from schools I'd never attended, upcoming weddings of people I'd never met, and recipes I couldn't hope to cook with my meager resources.

Then, one day, I came across a story so grotesque I read it three times.

A woman named Irma Dunn had been found dead by the milkman during his morning delivery. He'd taken a quick glance through her kitchen window and saw her sprawled in the middle of the floor—not only dead but partially devoured.

He called the police immediately, and when they arrived, they shot her little terrier, Napoleon, on sight.

I'll admit, the story horrified me—but I also caught myself smiling. Maybe the world hadn't just gone mad in my little corner after all. Maybe it was happening everywhere. As I set the paper aside and stared out at our overgrown lawn, I began to wonder:

In our world, who would go crazy first?

Eric, or me?

Unfortunately, I was to find out exactly one week later.

* * * *

Two months earlier, I had sent away for a correspondence course on TV repair I'd seen advertised in the paper, but it turned out to be mostly useless. I gave it an honest effort, but in the end, I was left sitting in a tangle of wires and burned-out tubes.

But as I sat there, confused and disappointed, I heard something.

At first, I thought it had to be my imagination. I cocked my head to the side and for a long moment, heard nothing. Then—again—I heard it.

My name.

The voice was weak and strained, but it was unmistakably Eric's: "...Martin...?"

As I've told you before, I was never the athlete Eric was, but I raced up the stairs with surprising speed, nearly tearing the banister from the wall. That's when I saw Eric's door—open. For the first time in months.

I remember catching my breath, my eyes wide. "Eric...?"

I stood frozen, staring at the open door until I heard, "Come in..."

I didn't move.

A foul smell was wafting from the room, thick with the sound of flies. That's what made me hesitate. He was my brother, but something in me—something primal—feared that room. It was his voice, mostly. That awful, croaking voice, muffled by the pillowcase he'd fashioned into a hood. I imagined it was for my benefit, and for that courtesy alone, I stepped inside, slowly, beginning to close the door behind me.

"Leave it open!" he snapped. I instinctively jumped back.

Of course, he noticed and slumped onto the edge of his unmade bed, turning his back to me. With a heavy sigh, he said, "But you might not want to stay..."

I remained at the threshold. "Why wouldn't I want to stay?"

He wrung his unseen hands. "I'm worse now, Martin." There was anguish in his voice. "I don't even look like a man anymore..."

I carefully stepped further inside, avoiding a pile of discarded clothes crawling with maggots. At some point, he'd smashed the mirror above the dresser.

"Eric, I'm your brother. It doesn't matter what you look like to me."

(It was a lie, but I had to say something.)

"You don't have to lock your door and hide away—"

He leapt to his feet and shouted without turning, "—I don't do it because of that!"

I stared at him, confused. "Then why?"

He paused, wringing his hands again. Eric—my only brother—couldn't even face me as he said, "I didn't... I didn't want you walking in during one of... one of my spells."

"This doesn't make sense," I said, shaking my head. "Spells?"

He began to pace, still not looking at me. "I've been having these spells." He dropped back onto the bed and, to my horror, ran what looked like a black paw over his hood. "They started a couple months ago... but they're getting worse."

I grimaced at the sight of that gangrenous hand. "What do you mean?"

He sighed, phlegm rattling in his throat. "I've been going out, Martin." He almost turned to face me but stopped. "I mean, haven't you wondered how I've stayed alive all these months?"

I had—but like so many things, I hadn't wanted to know the answer.

"...Yes."

He nodded sadly. "I've been going out at night." He motioned to his broken window, loosely covered by an old brown blanket. "I crawl out the window."

"To do what, Eric?"

I didn't want to know the answer.

But I got one anyway.

He was choking back tears. "I can't... I can't eat your food anymore..."

(My food?)

I shook my head. "What are you talking about?"

As if mimicking me, he shook his head too. "I can't eat it! I just can't! I've tried to keep it down, but I can't!"

There had to be something I could do. "What do you need, Eric?" I asked. "I'll get it for you. Just tell me."

He shook his head, his voice full of despair. "You're not listening to me." He gripped the sides of his head in frustration. "You're not hearing me!"

I threw up my hands. "What am I not hearing?"

Again, he shook his head. "I used to be able to just eat raw meat but now..."

"But now what?" I asked, still not understanding.

He spun toward me—and I actually leapt back.

I hadn't noticed it before, but he had cut a hole in the pillowcase revealing one enlarged yellow eye, wide and staring.

And then he screamed: "IT HAS TO BE ALIVE!"

I ran.

Straight to the attic—the only part of the house I had never entered—and found the rusted shackles buried in spilled straw.

I knew what I had to do.

Because I couldn't do what he wanted me to do. I couldn't. Not even for Eric.

I finally understood what had happened to the mice. And to Sam.

And maybe even to that old woman in town.

Ignoring his desperate pleas, I dragged him up to the attic and shackled him there, double-locking the door behind me.

Like Father and Grandfather before him, I realized I would have to leave Eric to rot.

I even went to the family graveyard and dug a plot for him.

It was only a matter of time.

As I dug, I fell to my knees and wept—for the first time since our mother died.

I would be alone, then.

And looking back, I still wonder: was I crying for him?

Or for myself?

What I didn't realize was that the shackles I had bound him with were as rusted as the bars on his windows.

So he escaped.

And now—

The hunt is on.

* * * *

As I drove through the unfamiliar town, I noticed a hunter on every corner, each gripping a rifle, eager to bag a monster. Only I knew something they didn't. I knew Eric. You see, when we were ten, the city council had decided that the old barn on Salem Road was a fire hazard, so, ironically, they chose to burn it down. It was a spectacular sight, visible for miles. I remember watching the blaze with Eric from our room until the last embers died away, leaving smoke swirling into the clear night sky. Although we were never allowed to visit the site, we knew it fascinated the local children. It was off-limits, dangerous, out of bounds—in short, a veritable Disneyland for the kids of a small town—something we could never be a part of.

Until now.

That's where I would find Eric. Only now I knew he wasn't searching for other children to play with.

He was searching for food.

I didn't bother closing the car door. If he was indeed here, I didn't want to alert him, so I silently crept closer to the silo that still stood against the billowing cornfield. As I moved closer, the new chains clasped in one hand, I had to step over a discarded baseball cap—one covered in blood.

I found Eric crouched about twenty yards behind the burnt-out foundation of the old barn. Even from there, I could hear him feeding on the young boy's corpse. I called out, "Eric?"

He turned to me.

And I screamed.

Because he had removed his hood.

All his hair had fallen away, exposing open sores sprouting from his scalp. His left eye had burst from its socket, yellow pus running down his face, while his right eye gaped at me—though it was clear he no longer recognized me. Instead, his black paw, stained crimson-red from the half-eaten boy, continued to funnel the meat into his open mouth.

"...Eric...?" was all I could manage before he turned back to his feast. I couldn't look anymore, couldn't witness this horror, and spun away—only to find a man standing behind me. Just like I had only moments before, this man—who I later discovered was named Stilman—had witnessed the same atrocity.

Only he had a shotgun. And even as chewing tobacco spilled like vomit from his open mouth, he raised the gun and fired before I could stop him.

* * * *

I answered questions for what seemed like hours.

As I did, good ol' boy hunters—who apparently heard about the incident through CBS, police scanners, or whatever social media they used these days—circled my brother's body, laughing, joking, and drinking beer while their friends took photos. The young boy's body had been lovingly covered and taken away, but Eric's now headless corpse was staked out like one of those old-time gunfighters, so everyone could get an up-close, personal view of the dead monster.

The sheriff—I don't even remember his name—asked me again, so I wearily answered, "Yes, he was my brother. We were twins."

"Twins?" The sheriff looked over his shoulder, shook his head, and actually chuckled as he wrote in his pad, "You don't look alike."

Several men chuckled.

I bristled. "Eric wasn't a monster."

This seemed to amuse the good ol' boys even more, and the sheriff turned back to me. "Really? So what was he then?"

"He was the victim of a disease," I said simply.

All the good ol' boys' laughter immediately stopped. Beer cans slipped through suddenly sweaty hands, and the sheriff's pen dropped. His eyes widened. "What's that you say, son?"

I didn't bother looking at him. "He had a disease."

All the men stepped away from Stilman, who coughed up a mouthful of recently installed tobacco. The sheriff himself leaned away from me and looked again at Eric's corpse. "Did you say disease?"

Suddenly, these good ol' boys weren't so interested in having their pictures taken with my dead brother. Seeing their reactions, I actually managed a small smile. "Not to worry, Sheriff. He was infected with the disease; he wasn't a carrier."

That seemed to put the whole posse's mind at ease. Smiles returned, coolers were opened, beers were passed around, and more photos were taken beside the monster's corpse. It was once again party time.

What I didn't tell them was that the disease was incredibly infectious, although it shows no signs until a male reaches puberty. That's why I never touched anything the delivery boys brought to the house until they were long gone. It was the reason we burned our trash in the backyard and never left our tract of land.

See, once you've passed puberty, the disease works fast. Very fast.

And as I watched them truss up my brother's body like so much roadkill, I caught myself smiling again.

Have you figured out why yet?

It's because all these redneck bastards suddenly looked arthritic. Some were moaning and groaning; others rubbed at their shoulders and knees, complaining that it must be the weather or they'd slept the wrong way. But it was Stilman who gave me the most trouble—fishing in his duck-hunting jacket for more tobacco even as he rubbed the newly-acquired welt on his forehead. Amused, I shook my head.

"No, Eric wasn't a carrier." I chuckled. "But I am."


lightjlight@aol.com